CHARLOTTE BARNES is an author and academic from Worcestershire, UK. She is a lecturer in Creative and Professional Writing at the University of Wolverhampton, and she has guest lectured at several universities around the West Midlands.

Charlotte has published a number of poetry collections, as Charley Barnes, and several novels. She has penned a trilogy of detective novels – the DI Watton boxset – and a selection of psychological thrillers, including *Intention* and *All I See Is You*.

When Charlotte isn't writing, she's likely reading or wandering with her pup, Benji, in tow.

T0318042

The Break Up

CHARLOTTE BARNES

ONE PLACE. MANY STORIES

HQ
An imprint of HarperCollins*Publishers* Ltd
1 London Bridge Street
London SE1 9GF

www.harpercollins.co.uk

HarperCollins*Publishers*
1st Floor, Watermarque Building, Ringsend Road
Dublin 4, Ireland

First published in Great Britain by
HQ, an imprint of HarperCollins*Publishers* Ltd 2022

ISBN: 9780008511593

For every Lily, Betty, Cora, Molly and Faith I've known –
I'm lucky there have been so many of you along this
journey.

Chapter 1

Neither of us knew where we were; we were taking the sat nav at face value and hoping Google Maps would get us home. But it didn't matter how long it all took. We had that horrible lovesickness that radiates off happy couples – and it was bloody brilliant. After the day we'd had, there was no way we could be anything but disgustingly pleased with ourselves. I could already imagine the fake groans of the girls when I told them about the day and the sites and—

Rowan reached over and squeezed my hand. I took a glance at his profile. It was dimly lit by oncoming headlights, and I could still see a smile teasing at his cheeks. He pulled over as soon as we found a pub.

'This'll do, right?' He steered onto the car park and straight into a space, where he hurried to yank the handbrake on. 'Edi Parcell …'

'Yes, Rowan Ness?'

He smiled and let out a huff of air. 'We're engaged.'

We chased each other along the car park and through the door of the pub. Our laughter grabbed everyone's attention, but we refused to apologise. I could only think, *I'm engaged!* on a loop, as though that were a response to everything in the world now.

1

Rowan leaned on the bar and waited for the woman behind it to migrate our way.

'You kids eating?' she asked.

Rowan glanced at me and I shook my head. Of all the pubs on all the country roads, we'd managed to stumble into the 'They're not from round here ...' sort. There were awkward glances flickering in our direction long after our happy laughter had died away. And I wasn't convinced I could keep my glee in check for an entire meal without alarming or outraging someone – assuming we hadn't done that already. I caught the eye of an elderly farmer who I flashed a wide smile to, only to have the expression met with a steel glare.

'Just drinks,' Rowan answered. 'A lemonade for me and ...'

'You're not even having a sneaky one?' I asked.

'Heck no, I'm driving important stuff around with you in the car, Parcell.'

I turned to the barwoman. 'I'll have a lemonade, too, please.'

'Edi, you don't have—'

'We can have a proper drink when we tell everyone.'

Rowan shrugged and turned back. 'Two lemonades then, please, and whatever you're ...' His offer died out as the woman turned away from him. 'Okay, never mind,' he faced me. 'I'll tell her when she's back.' He held his hand palm up and out towards me and I placed my hand into it. He laughed. 'I want your phone.'

I dug around in my pocket. 'Why?'

'To turn it off.' He powered down his handset and rested it on the bar. By then the woman was back, setting two half pints of pop in front of us. 'Thank you. Take one for yourself, too?' Rowan handed her a twenty-pound note and she smiled.

'You're celebrating?' she asked when she gave the change back.

Rowan nodded to me to break the news and I felt myself bounce. 'We're engaged!' I made the announcement with such enthusiasm that even the miserable sods around us murmured a congratulations. 'Yes, we're engaged,' I said again, but a little quieter.

'Congratulations,' she replied.

We waited until she was out of earshot to pick up where we'd left off.

'Why are we turning our phones off?' I asked, powering mine down, too.

Rowan eased it free of my hand and rested it on the bar with his. 'Because from tomorrow things are going to be mental and we'll hardly have a minute to ourselves for bloody ages.' He pulled me towards him. 'And I'd like a minute or two with my future wife, to myself. Is that okay?'

Future wife. I felt the phrase echo in my head. 'Christ. Wife.'

He laughed. 'That usually comes after the engagement?'

'I hadn't thought about it that way.' I quickly tried to change the tone. 'So people know?'

'Nope.'

'You didn't tell *anyone*?'

'Not true, actually, sorry. Your parents know because I asked them.'

'You asked both of them?'

He smiled. 'I asked both of them whether they thought you'd say yes. I didn't ask their permission, because you are your own woman, and no man or woman owns you. But I wanted your mum involved because, well, why wouldn't she be?'

I kissed him. 'Bloody love you.'

'Bloody love you. So, they know. And the lads know but the girls don't.'

'And Mum and Dad don't know you planned it for today?'

He shook his head. 'Not a clue. But I know the temptation will be great to get on the phone to Betty and Molly and, and, and … So, before that temptation kicks in, let's just be us for a bit?'

'Deal.' I sipped my drink.

3

'Did I hear that right?'

We both craned to find the source of the question. There was an older man perched on a barstool behind Rowan. He was wearing a thick jacket and a flat cap, as though he were ready to up and leave the pub at any second, and his cheeks had that rosy blush that comes from endless hours of outdoor work. The question was slurred, though; the words sounded lazy as they left him.

'You two are engaged?'

It was Rowan's turn to bounce on his heels. 'You heard that right, sir.'

'Jesus.' From his tone it was clear he didn't exactly share our delight. 'You can't have known each other five minutes.'

'Actually,' Rowan started, 'we've known each other since we were fresh out of school. Not secondary school either but ...' This was one of his favourite stories to tell, even though the older we got, the more tweaks he made to it. '... And then I saved her from the playground bully, essentially.' I shook my head and he noticed. 'Even though you would have definitely hit Owen on your own one day.'

'Even though you definitely didn't hit him, you mean.' I stretched up to kiss his forehead. 'Nothing cool about violence, babe, not even made-up violence.'

'So you've been together since you were knee-high?' The words knocked into each other in the same way as before. The man leaned forward slightly and then in a jerked motion he snapped back. I recognised the gesture from the boys I'd avoided at university; he was a drink away from tipping off his seat. 'Like, since you were wee?' he added.

'You heard right.' Rowan tried to sound breezy, but I knew he was forcing it. He'd always had a terrible poker face. 'Couldn't let this one get away.'

'No.' The man didn't sound convinced. He narrowed his eyes like he was physically inspecting something. That, or trying to work out the maths of an especially tricky equation. He laughed

4

and the noise was a horrible one: outdoor work mixed with too much alcohol mixed with ... *Does he smell like smoke even from here?* 'I can't get my head around kids so young trying to be so grown up.'

'Well,' I took over, 'when you know you know.' I physically turned Rowan back to face me and positioned myself so I didn't knock eyes with the man still sitting behind. 'Leave it?'

'He's being friendly.'

'No, Rowan, I don't think he is.'

He shook his head. 'Okay. So, future wife—'

'Edi is fine.' I play-punched him. 'But you can have future wife for tonight.'

'How do you want to tell people? Update our social media and call it a day?' He took a sip of his drink and it felt timed for dramatic effect. 'Or we tell our families privately and then invite friends out one evening for drinks and tell them all in a massive group.'

'Fewer messages involved.'

'Get all the responses at once.'

'Don't accidentally forget to WhatsApp someone who you should have remembered.' I was certainly leaning towards the second option. 'Okay, this weekend? I can text the group chat and suggest ...' I reached for my phone and Rowan pushed my hand away. 'Tomorrow, I can text the group chat tomorrow and suggest drinks for this weekend. Friday?'

'Perfect.'

'I'm sorry ...' The intrusion erupted from behind Rowan again and from the brash tone of it I guessed the man wasn't really all that sorry at all. 'But you're *engaged*, like, to be wed?'

'Smithy,' the barwoman cautioned, and I was glad of it. She spoke with the curt tone of a woman who handled drunk men all too often. 'Leave it alone.'

'Come on ...' *He's not leaving it*, I thought as I pulled in a big breath. 'They're engaged,' he reminded her before he turned back

5

to us. 'You're mid-twenties at a push, like, and you're engaged to be married already in your lives. By Christ.' He paused to wet his lips with beer. 'Are the pair of you sure you're thinking straight?'

'Smithy,' Rowan answered, using a tone surprisingly like the barwoman's, 'I've never thought straighter about anything in my life.' He turned around and kissed me square on the mouth. It wasn't exactly the stuff of *Notting Hill*, but it'd do ...

Chapter 2

The morning after, I woke with a dull feeling of tiredness still. The bubbles and excitement of our quiet celebration had kept me and Rowan awake until the early hours of the morning. We'd stayed at mine – to avoid his noisy, nosy housemates – and as the sunlight flooded in through wildflower-print curtains, I thought everything in the world was a bit perfect. I rolled over to face Rowan's side, though, and saw that perfect or not, I was waking up alone. The bathroom door was wide open, too, so that ruled out him disappearing for a morning wee. It crossed my mind for the flicker of a second that he might be making breakfast for us both, but I laughed the thought away.

'Not that future husband of mine,' I said quietly into the room to try the phrase on for size. It didn't taste right yet, though, and I thought that was even more reason to keep trying. 'Future husband, dear future husband …' I kept going until I broke out into a gentle hum of music, my bum moving in sync to my song as I danced flat against the bedsheets.

'It *is* bloody connected to the Wi-Fi.'

The words burst in from the living room and brought with them a horrible realisation: *He's calling his parents.* The night before we'd agreed to call his today. Out of our respective relatives, they were the trickier customers and so, bloated on bubbles and bright-eyed feelings, we'd agreed to tell them before telling mine. *And he's coming good on the promise,* I thought as I threw back the duvet and climbed out of bed. I plodded to the bathroom and considered nesting there. But I couldn't spend the entire Skype call hidden away. To start with, Rowan would think I was having an IBS flare-up; and second, Mum had raised me better than to ignore my in-laws.

I heard the ringer for the video call, so quickly pulled my hair into a ponytail – and arranged my face in a suitable smile. Rowan tapped the seat next to him when I walked into the living room.

'Come on, it'll be fine.'

'Rowan, dear.' I heard her before I could see her. 'Oh, and Edith.' My stomach turned at the thought of her being able to see me already; like she was some kind of wildlife predator, higher up the food chain. The screen flickered then, though, and both his parents came into view. Rowan's dad was smiling. Rowan's mum was the sort of woman who surely asked her facial technician to make it impossible for her to smile – or frown. 'It's so lovely to see you both.'

'You're looking well,' Gregory said – always Gregory, *never* Greg, I had learnt early on – although it wasn't clear whether he was speaking to one or both of us. 'Wonderful to be able to have a chat, too. Penny and I are delighted with the news, of course. Marvellous, just – truly, a huge congratulations to you both.'

When did he tell them? I tried to keep my face neutral. But for them to already know, he must have told them *before* he called. And if he told them before he called then he must have broken our pact from the night before and, what, texted them?

'Thanks so much, Dad.'

'Thanks, Gregory.' The excitement overrode the irritation, and I was painfully aware of the growing grin that gave me the appearance of a woman who'd slept with a hanger in her mouth. 'It was such a beautiful surprise.'

Meanwhile, Penny managed to raise something that wasn't quite a grunt, as though even being disinterested was too much cheer for the occasion. 'A surprise for us, too,' she said, although the remark went uncommented on.

Rowan tried to steer the conversation. 'You're looking well also, the pair of you. North is treating you well?' Out of view of the camera he felt around for my hand and gave it a tight squeeze. It was a sore point, that Rowan's parents had moved so far out of Birmingham. Rowan didn't mind it much. But his parents – despite him being in his final year of university, with a house for afterwards already lined up – had expected him to move with them. When he'd asked what would happen to his relationship with me, his mother had said, 'Well, if Edith really wants to be a part of this family ...'

'It is, immensely well, boy, immensely,' Gregory answered, and Penny grumbled again. They'd moved there because Gregory – the owner of four high-end car dealerships in our hometown – had decided to try to conquer a different part of the country, with a new set of partners to support the venture. He was essentially a car salesman, but the first time I'd said that he'd gave me such a fierce look that I'd thought he might never speak to me again. I was thirteen at the time. I hadn't made that mistake again. 'We're getting a lot of interest up here with hiring firms, people who aren't necessarily looking to buy, but for their companies they'd like to ...' He then went on to explain the definition of what it meant to hire a car, in case Rowan and I weren't sure. *And this is what you're marrying into.* I squeezed Rowan's hand again and tried to tune back in. '... some of the older clients from that way.'

'Your father is excited at the prospect of turning the wedding into a large-scale business meeting.'

'We'd better get a big enough venue then.' Rowan forced a laugh. 'So, Mum—'

'Actually, son,' Gregory interrupted. He put his arm around Penny and gave her a squeeze. 'I've been doing a lot of work with the Flynns.' From the look on Penny's face, an ignorant bystander might think someone had just announced she were pregnant with a litter of piglets. It was the most animated I'd seen her in years. And it was the most contact I'd seen Rowan's parents have with each other. 'You remember them, don't you? Skye's parents?'

Rowan matched the gesture to give me a hug. But it was too late; I'd already started to fall to pieces – and I imagined my expression wasn't too dissimilar to Penny's now either. 'I'm so sorry, can you excuse me for a minute?' I didn't wait for anyone's approval before standing up and scooting out of the room, though. I only hovered outside to make sure I didn't miss too much.

I took deep belly breaths while Gregory explained how helpful it might be – to *them*, of course, two-fifths of bugger all to do with *us* – if the Flynns could be invited to the wedding party. Rowan had three false starts before he answered. 'I can throw names around with Edi later. We haven't exactly started planning.'

'Of course, boy, of course. Think it through.'

'Fuck's sake, Parcell,' I whispered on my way back to the kitchen, 'get a grip of yourself.' Everything I did, I did with the brute force of a hundred women scorned by their in-laws. 'What an ugly cliché.' Bang went the fridge door as I took out the milk. 'What a horrible, boring thing to take umbrage with.' Bang it went again when I replaced the carton. I left our teabags in to stew – *don't I just know how that feels* – and fished around in the freezer to see what I could throw in the oven for breakfast. 'This will not be a bad day,' I said under my breath as I moved about the kitchen. 'Today will not be a bad day. Today will not be a bad day. Today will not be—'

'With all this talk of how well the business is doing—' Penny had taken over talking; the rise in volume significant enough to carry through to me '—what your father means to say is that we'd like to contribute to the costs, when you get to a point of needing the help.' And even though she hadn't outright said as much – and wouldn't, because it wasn't her style – the offer itself felt like a judgement on Mum and Dad. They were meant to pay, of course, if tradition had anything to do with the wedding.

'Mum.' Rowan sounded like a nervous schoolboy. 'Edi and I haven't said as much. But we've always been equal in things and, really, I think …' I felt my tummy tense. If Rowan knew me as well as I hoped, then the only possible thing he could say next was: 'Edi and I would really like to pay for the wedding ourselves, or pay for as much of it as we can. We'd like to start married life equally, financially and all, as we mean to go on.'

I dropped myself hard against the kitchen counter, exhaled and smiled – the same coat-hanger smile from earlier. *So he does know me that well.* 'Today will not be a bad day,' I said again as I flicked the kettle on. I was preheating the oven by the time they'd arrived on the topic of grandchildren, they being Penny – 'Of course, you'll be thinking of where in the country is best to raise children before you know it' – but I did a fine job of convincing myself the worst was over with. 'Today will not be a bad day.' Realistically I knew the worst – the absolute *worst* – had already happened. 'Today will not be—'

'Bloody right it won't,' Rowan interrupted from the doorway.

I froze, bum in the air and head buried in the second drawer of the freezer. 'It won't be.' He didn't say anything until I'd righted myself.

'Everything okay?'

'Of course!' I made an effort to lower the falsetto into something that didn't sound quite so utterly fake. 'Of course. I didn't hear you finish.'

He crossed the kitchen to join me, then, as though sure he'd dipped a proverbial toe in the waters. He grabbed at my hips and my mind flashed back to the night before; our first time having sex with a ring on my finger although it hadn't felt any different – and I *knew* Molly would ask. 'Parcell, are you in here making breakfast sandwiches without me?'

'I am if I can find the sausages.'

'Third drawer.' He let me go, then, and crossed to where the tea was still brewing. I imagined the brown particles that must have formed on top. Rowan hated that but I'd always quite liked them. 'How much did you hear?' he asked, stirring each drink in turn.

'I'm sorry?'

'Nice try, but you heard the question.'

I dropped six sausages onto an oven tray. 'How much do you want me to have heard?'

'Wait …' He cupped a hand around an ear. 'Would that be thin ice I can hear cracking?'

'Cute.' I dropped the sausages back in the drawer and launched a search and rescue for hash browns. 'I'm serious, though, babe. How much do you want me to have heard?'

'I'm serious, though, babe.' He matched my tone. 'Come on, Edi, you aren't that girl.'

I coughed. '"We've always been equal in things and, really, I think—"'

'I don't sound like that.' He pushed a cup along the worktop towards me. 'She's fine with it, really. Mum just likes to throw Dad's money around, doesn't she? Meanwhile, Dad is – Christ, I don't know. He's more worried about work than anything. Which gives Mum too much time to think. When she has too much time to think, she …' It felt like Rowan was getting tangled up in side issues, but I nodded along all the same from behind my mug. 'Dad is happy for us.' He hesitated before he added, 'Mum will be when she's bought something for us.'

'Jesus.' I opened the oven door and slid both trays in to cook. 'Here's hoping mine'll take it better than yours. Fried bread?'

Rowan thought for a minute. 'Sure, fuck it, we're celebrating. Chuck me the loaf?'

'Bedded and breakfast all in one morning.' I pulled ingredients from the fridge and threw them one by one across the room. 'A woman could easily get used to this.'

Chapter 3

Mum and Dad were both standing at the door ready to greet us. They'd guessed.

'What a lovely surprise this is,' Mum started, arms outstretched. I let her pull me into a hug.

'You know?' She squealed into my scarf and shook with what I thought must be the beginnings of excitement finally spilling out. 'You know?' I asked Dad over her shoulder and he nodded. 'So, you know.' I bounced with her, then, feeling a fresh wave of enthusiasm, too. After the talk I'd had with my one-day mother-in-law earlier, it felt nice to be superglued back together by a mother's touch. 'When did you guess?'

She held me at arm's length. 'When have the two of you ever stopped around for a cup of tea in the middle of the week for no reason at all? Why aren't you both at work? Why are you two hours later than you said you'd be? Why didn't you call last night?' It felt like her questions had veered off track somewhere and I laughed. 'Come in.' She stepped aside. 'Come in, come in.'

'Sweetheart ...' Dad pulled me into an even tighter hug. 'Congratulations.' Before I could thank him, he'd released me into the hallway and extended a hand to Rowan. 'But the congratulations really should go to you, young man, for tying this one down.'

'Ah, excuse me,' I started.

'It's a turn of phrase, Edith.' Dad sounded exasperated. I couldn't see his face, but I sensed the eye roll all the same. 'Congratulations, Rowan. Whisky?'

'I'm driving, Peter—'

'Nonsense. Whisky it is. We'll get you a taxi.'

Mum steered me towards the living room door while Dad pushed Rowan towards the dining room – or rather, the drinks cabinet.

'Let yourself in,' she said, still bouncing on her heels. This looked like a fresh wave of excitement on top of the first, though. When it came to subtlety, Mum typically ranked at the same level as a large bomb detonated in an enclosed space. She had a poker face worse than Rowan's – and he hardly had one at all. So it didn't come as a total surprise when I walked into the living room and straight into strings of bunting …

'Happy engagement!' Mum shouted from behind me.

The sheer extent of the bunting, though, now *that* was the surprise.

'Mum, the place is …' I frantically felt around for the right word. Bright? Loud? 'Perfect.'

She rested an arm around my shoulder and squeezed me tight to her. 'I went out and bought everything when Rowan told us he was going to ask. I've been itching, I tell you.' Another squeeze. 'Itching. Shall we get the kettle on?'

'Rowan gets whisky and I get tea?' I joked.

'Oh, my sweetheart.' She moved in front of me and set a hand on each cheek. 'It's an expression. There's white wine stacked to the roof of that fridge.'

'What a way to celebrate.'

'You lovely girl.' She stepped around me and made for the door. 'That's just weekday stock.'

*

14

Dad was showing Rowan baby pictures two rooms away. It definitely wasn't the first time he'd subjected me to such an embarrassment, though. So much so, it no longer felt embarrassing, really, but more like part of the experience of visiting my parents. Rowan being shown the sight of my bare backside poking out from a flowerbed while my front end was hurriedly searching around for lost snails was, I hoped, something he found endearing. His parents hadn't ever shown the same enthusiasm for making him feel uncomfortable. Well, not through the means of flaunting baby pictures at least. But given the choice between bare arse cheeks and loud, aggressive accusations, I thought I'd stick with my own wild-haired, overtly proud relations rather than instigate a swap with Rowan's. His folks were (I thought, not for the first time), the one real drawback of agreeing to marry him.

Dad and Rowan let out a burst of laughter loud enough to make Mum wince and she picked up the bottle of wine from the kitchen table. She topped up her own glass and then moved towards mine. But I placed my hand flat over the top.

'I'm okay, Mum.'

'Nonsense! We're …' She petered out and her eyes stretched as though someone had delivered a surprise. 'You're not?'

I narrowed my eyes, but then matched her shocked expression when realisation dawned on me. 'No, I'm bloody not. Christ, we're only just engaged.'

She laughed. 'Well, your father and I only waited that long.'

'Oh, good, sex antics. On second thoughts—' I reached across the table to take the bottle '—maybe another sip won't hurt.'

'Edi, don't be such a prude.' She took a generous mouthful. 'Now, wedding plans.'

'Rowan and I haven't talked yet, Mum—'

'Don't try to tell me you haven't thought ahead already.'

'I've had a few thoughts,' I lied. I'd had all the thoughts at one time or another in the years and months we'd been together. But I thought I'd burst with joy if I shared too much of that quiet planning yet. 'It's the wrong time of year for it really, though, isn't it?' I nodded towards the window, stained with rain that hadn't let up for most of the day. 'It'd be better to wait until summer.'

'How quick do you think wedding plans come together?'

'I don't know. A few months?'

'Pah. Years!'

'Mum, you're exaggerating.'

'Well, certainly longer than a few months.' Another sip. She lowered her voice and said, 'Long enough time for someone to change their mind. And that's the last I'll say on that matter.'

I sank back in my chair. 'You think he'll change his mind?'

'Silly girl.' She squeezed my knee and laughed. 'You might. You could go all *Runaway Bride*.'

'I don't have the hair for it. And I can't run in heels.'

'You're inventive enough to make your own romantic comedy.'

'Well …' I pushed back from the table. 'Hopefully no one will be jilted at the altar in mine.'

She grabbed at my hand. 'Sit down a second, will you?' I followed her instructions while she leaned across to the seat next to her and grabbed at something out of sight. When she lifted her hand, she was holding a neat square box.

'Present?'

'Sort of.' She handed it over, the lid still in place. 'Something old, and borrowed, but you can keep it if you want. It might be something you pass down one day.' She shook her head softly as though remembering something. 'If you decide to have children, which you may not but … Oh, never mind that anyway, let a mother have a moment with her only daughter, would you?'

I lifted the covering slowly, as though something might escape. But when I fought my way past the tissue paper, my fingers soon hit upon lace. I handled the garment with care until it was free of the box, then I held it up in front of me to get a proper look. It was a garter. Lace, and greyed from years in a box, I guessed.

When I looked past the fabric to Mum, I saw what looked like the beginnings of tears.

'Oh, Mum.' I dropped the garter back on the tissue. 'It's yours?'

She shook her head. 'Not now, no. It's yours.' She wiped her eyes and forced a smile. 'God, whatever is the matter with the pair of us, Edith.' There was a time when the sound of my full name being used would have sent a shiver down my back. But there was something warm in the way she said it that day. 'It was mine, from mine and Dad's wedding. Purely decorative, of course. Otherwise, that would be a bit odd. But your nan bought it for me. It was my something new.'

On second inspection, I found a trail of blue ribbon stitched into part of the lacing. Mum laughed and wiped her eyes again. 'Your nan stitched that in. She was always trying to be so efficient with these things.' She stood up and gave my shoulder a squeeze. 'Of course, your dad said she was being tight. But he meant efficient.'

I set my hand over hers before she could pull it away. 'Thank you, Mum.'

'Nonsense. My pleasure.' She stood and leaned over awkwardly to kiss my forehead. 'I'd give you the world if I could, Edith Parcell, with a big yellow bow on and all.' She grabbed at the wine bottle that sat had between us, which I saw, then, was empty. 'Top-up?'

'God, please.' In a twenty-four-hour period I'd gone from on top of the world to underneath it and back again, between the reactions of Rowan's parents and now my own – and let's not forget are-you-thinking-straight Smithy! 'All the top-ups, all the happy feelings.'

'I should say that's the least you deserve, sweet Edi. I'm sorry for getting us both upset. Well …' She ran a fingertip under each eye to remove the final traces of tears. 'You didn't cry but there we are.' With a half-laugh she made her way back to the fridge. 'Come on, let's go and snatch those baby pictures off your father and pour some more whisky down his neck. I might get a quiet night out of him at the end of this.'

Chapter 4

I was standing with my front door gaping wide as a not-so-subtle signpost to Rowan. We were getting ready at mine – to avoid his housemates, again – and he was the only bloke I'd ever heard of who managed to turn getting ready for a night out into *this* much work. As I waited, I could hear the wind lapping at the outside of the building, and I began to worry about my bare calves that came with my show-stopping dress: a wraparound in white linen, dotted with blue and red flowers and the occasional dandelion wish. It struck me as a dress that would photograph well, so at least I could put that worry to bed when the Instagram and Facebook notifications started flooding in the next morning. But if I'd put a little strategic thought into my outfit, then Rowan was putting third-year-university-exam-level thought into getting ready. I'd stayed in the bedroom long enough to watch him try on his third shirt before I migrated into the living room, where I'd finished spraying my curls in place. By then he still wasn't ready, though, and I'd resorted to standing with the front door open to let him know I was good to go. Not that it looked to have made a blind bit of difference.

'Rowan, come on, we told people half seven.'

'All right, Edi, Christ.' He was still adjusting his hair, pulling pieces between thumb and fingertip on his walk towards me. 'How do I look?'

'Like someone who watches too many boy-band videos. Can we?' I stepped aside.

'I'm bloody wasted on you sometimes,' he snapped. Oddly, he sounded a little too serious.

On the walk from home into town his mood softened, though, and I soon felt him tightening his grip around my left hand. The engagement ring pressed hard between my fingers and I bit back on readjusting his grasp. *Don't ruin the moment*, I thought as I hurried along with him. He was moving at a pace – to compensate for being late and all …

When I set my hand flat against the door to push into the bar, he pulled me away from the entryway so that I was facing him instead. 'Hey, gimme a sec?'

'Of course. What's happening? Are you okay?'

He looked at me hard and narrowed his eyes. My kneejerk reaction was to assume my mascara hadn't dried properly, and the power walk here had sent splashes of it flying onto my eyelids like some kind of Insta-Pollock painting. But before I could open the lips of my bag and search for a mirror, Rowan grabbed my face. With a hand cupped around each ear, he brought me closer to him and kissed me – a soft kiss, like he really meant it.

'Edi Parcell.' I still felt a swell of happiness when he said my name. 'Bloody love you.'

I kissed his nose. 'Bloody love you.'

'Come on, then, let's be having them.'

Rowan led the way into the crowded bar. A Friday night in the centre of town, it took some looking to find the friends we were after. There was an overlap in our friendship circles – some who had dated once, some who had slept together, some who still were dating – and we eventually found them huddled in small clusters near the back of the room. Beatrice – who everyone had known as Betty since midway through primary school, much to her mother's dismay – was the first to spot our arrival. She was talking to Ian – one of Rowan's housemates – but she immediately paused him, holding a finger up to halt him mid-sentence, and she coughed loudly to catch the attention of others. I felt Rowan squeeze my hand then – the left hand, still, carefully concealing the ring – before he leaned in to kiss my cheek.

'Right, folks, thanks for giving up your Friday night—'

'For a piss-up in town? What a travesty,' Hamish shouted from the back of the group. He nudged the lads either side of him, George and Leonard, who laughed like they didn't mean it. To their credit, they were nice guys. Unlike Hamish who was, from what I knew of him, a total arsehole.

'Nice one, Hamish,' Rowan replied in a half-hearted way. 'Anyway, thanks again for coming along tonight because Edi and I have got some news that we'd really like to share with everyone. We thought getting you all together like this would be the best way …'

And suddenly I erupted. 'We're engaged!' Rowan shot me a look while the rest of the guests roared in applause and excitement. 'You were taking too long.' I was about to apologise but I was soon swept away on a sea of squeals as people flocked around me.

'Edi, congratulations!'

'Let's see the ring, then.'

'You *must* tell us how he proposed.'

Their excitement was soon matched by a second chorus.

'Finally putting a ring on it, lad.'

'Congratulations, Row, she's a star.'

'Yeah, fair play, mate, you bagged a good one,' Hamish added, and he didn't sound entirely insincere in the well wishes. 'Shame about all the women you didn't sleep with yet, eh?'

My mistake, still a tosser. I tried to let the comment go and give myself over to the excitement of my friends instead. Betty, Cora, Molly and Faith were all there – carried through from primary school, including the highlights and extended editions of mine and Rowan's relationship saga. There hadn't been many tears to get me through, but what there had been they'd been there for.

'I'm genuinely chuffed for you both.' Faith pulled me into a hug. 'Sad for myself though.'

'I hear that,' Lily said as she joined the huddle. 'Imagine knowing your best mate is becoming a slave to the patriarchy with a bloke who ...' When she saw my expression, she petered out and softened her tone. 'Ah, fuck it, I'm obviously delighted for you, babes. Come here and let me at you.' Lily was my loudest and angriest friend. We'd met at university where we'd both been a part of the same feminist book club, recommended by our module tutor at the time. Lily had shouted from one side of the room to the other that, despite what another woman had argued, *Twilight* was absolutely not a feminist novel. And I'd loved her from that moment on.

'Thanks, Lil.'

'Hey.' She pushed me back to get a look at my face. 'Don't turn into one of those stuck-up married cows who doesn't see her single friends, will you?'

'Christ. Absolutely not.'

'Then we'll all get along just fine.' She set her glass down. 'I'll go and infiltrate the men to congratulate your worse half, then I'll get the drinks in. Bubbles?'

'Lil, you don't need—'

'Good, bubbles,' she said, already walking away.

'Let her fuss over you.' It was Betty's turn to pull me towards her. 'God, let us all fuss.' She rested the back of her hand against my forehead as though gauging my temperature. 'Don't seem to be signs of a fever.' She felt each cheek. 'Have you taken any hallucinogenic substances? More importantly, did he give you any?'

Cora pushed her aside. 'Betty, don't ruin the moment.'

'Oh, she knows I'm just bitter.' Betty spread her arms and wrapped one around me, the other around Cora. 'Bitter, wrapped up with a bow of excitement, and only too ready for you to be Bridezilla for months on end.'

I kissed her cheek. 'You're in it for the hen night.'

'And I'm in it for the hen ni— *night?* Not weekend?'

We created a close huddle of laughter and running mascara. The girls took it in turns to hug me – deep-feeling hugs that went all the way through my body. One by one they pulled away and wiped their eyes, apart from Molly, who didn't go to the trouble of hiding her tears. She let them tumble – bulbous and glistening black as they stripped away her eye make-up – and she moved straight from hugging me to hugging Betty (who muttered under her breath but held Molly together all the same). We laughed more, and wiped away more tears in the minutes that followed while I told them about the proposal – a cupcake, topped with my engagement ring during a day out in Stratford – and how Mum and Dad had taken the news.

'What about his parents?' Cora asked, as she inspected my ring for the third time. I was about ready for her to whip out a jeweller's loupe for a full appraisal.

I groaned. 'Don't get me started.'

'Let me guess, they're not happy.' Faith pushed another glass of bubbly my way. 'Fuck 'em. As long as the two of you are happy …' She faded out as Rowan filtered into the space between her and Betty. 'Row, massive congratulations. Dead chuffed for you both.'

'Thank you, thank you. Are we okay for drinks over here, ladies?'

'We will literally never turn down offers for drinks, if that's where this is going,' Lily answered.

'My card is behind the bar.' Rowan winked at me. 'Get my girl good and drunk, won't you?'

'Rowan …' I tried to sound light-hearted. I'd drunk more since being engaged than I ever had as a single woman. 'You're making this an expensive night.'

He leaned across the circle and kissed me in a sloppy, half-sloshed sort of way. 'We're only going to do all of this once, Edi.'

Betty snorted. 'Fingers crossed.' In unison, heads snapped around and eyes widened. Betty shifted back from us all. 'I'm sorry, I don't know why I said that.'

'Ignore her, she's pissed.' Lily leapt in to try to save the moment. 'You're right, you'll only do this once, and if you need someone to get Edi drunk, not that it'd take much—' she nudged me '—then we'll get right on that, won't we, ladies?' She looked to the others for support and everyone, Betty included, gave a murmur of agreement. 'Congratulations, again.'

The others fell over themselves to flash their smiles and thank-yous at Rowan, and asked, 'Tell us how you did it,' even though they damn well knew. But I was glad they were making an effort. Everyone apart from Betty, that is, who'd moved to stand next to me. She pressed her shoulder against mine to grab my attention and I turned.

'I didn't mean anything by it.'

I put an arm around her and squeezed – even though I wasn't sure how much I believed her. Still, I said, 'I know that, you silly arse. Sarcasm is second nature.'

She smiled and swigged her drink. 'It's won me a fiver, tonight has. I love a good bet.'

'You bet I was engaged?'

'I did.' She nodded towards Faith. 'She bet you were pregnant.' I turned in time to catch Faith doing a shot with George and Rowan. I was glad the groups were mingling; it would make wedding parties easier.

'I'd actually bet that you'd broken up,' Cora added, sounding far chirpier than I thought she should have done.

'You genuinely thought we were getting the lot of you together for that?'

'Nah, not really.' She stopped to chug from a beer bottle; Cora loved a dramatic pause for effect. 'But the girls were giving me really good odds on it and I'm a sucker for an outside bet.'

'You're an arse.' I laughed with her.

'Hey, I've lost money on you, Edi!'

Betty pointed to Rowan, George and Faith who were throwing back another round of shots already. My stomach turned at the thought of how tomorrow morning would look for them all. 'Faith will drink them under the table if they try to keep up with her. Do you know who's on the wedding party shortlist for Rowan?'

'I doubt he's even thought about groomsmen.' *Oh.* Something clicked as I answered. 'I haven't thought about the bridesmaid situation, Betty, but you'll—'

'Relax, relax,' she cut across me. 'I know I'll be involved somewhere.' She nodded towards the chaps who were drifting towards us. 'I was more wondering which one of them I'd be taking home …'

Chapter 5

The morning after the night before was the worst part of any night out. I slapped one hand to my aching forehead and felt around the bed with the other. Rowan wasn't there. *Ah.* The memories filtered back in. He and the boys had carried on drinking well into the evening and I'd said I was done – 'Babe, babe, I need to go home' – so a few of us had trickled out early. Betty and Lily had … What had Betty and Lily done? I had a half-memory forming of them saying they were going to stay on – 'We'll kick about with the lads a bit longer' – while Cora called a taxi for the rest of us to share. *Christ.* Another groan tumbled out as the pain started to shift around my head. I needed water and a shower and a follow-up lie-down, maybe even followed by … My stomach rumbled. *Breakfast. A massive breakfast.*

I grabbed my phone from the bedside table and took it with me into the bathroom. I was filling a tumbler with water when I spotted the message – *Went home with George. Not best man material. Average man. Is that a thing? Love Bx* – and it wasn't until the water started to spill over my hand that I snapped back into the room. I hit the dial button and rested my phone on the cabinet while I dropped onto the toilet. Betty answered on the third ring.

'You utter, utter tart.'

'Oh, Edi, don't. It seemed like a good idea.'

'Famous last words.'

She laughed. 'He was a really good dancer, though.'

'I'm sorry.' I wiped, flushed, and grabbed the phone. 'What does that have to do …'

'Come on, you know they say if a man is a good dancer then he's a good … you know.'

'Who, Betty, *who* says that?'

'Well, whoever they are.' She groaned, and I imagined her struggling to sit upright. 'They're a bloody liar. Christ on a bastard bicycle.' She exhaled hard into the phone and I held my quiet. I'd known Betty long enough to know that sound as the prelude to … 'No, no, I'm fine. I don't think I'm going to chunder. I'm hungry, if anything.'

'Me too. Shall I group-chat people, see who's about for breakfast?'

'Oh, but the girls are so loud,' she moaned.

'Think of it as penance.'

'For what?'

'George. I'll text you.'

I disconnected the call before she could grumble further.

*

Lily was the last to order – 'Can I get the fruit pancakes but, like, I don't know, maybe with a side of bacon? But *on* the pancakes? Is that doable?' – and then we fell over ourselves reaching for tea, coffee, more coffee. 'Hold the sugar.' Lily put her hand up to create a physical barrier between her mug and the dish. 'The last thing I need is something to make me *more* jittery today.' When everyone was settled with a drink in front of them, we took it in turns to relay our memories of the evening. The general consensus by the end of the catch-up was that it was a)

26

a cracking night out and b) definitely not something we wanted to repeat for the hen night.

'Didn't someone say something about a weekend?'

'Oh, Lily, don't.' I took a greedy mouthful of black coffee. 'I can't do a whole weekend.'

'No,' Betty agreed. 'Probably best to stick to a night.'

'In a city where Betty doesn't know anyone,' Cora added, 'ergo, the walk of shame—'

'Ah, stride of pride,' Betty interrupted. 'I feel no shame.'

'Isn't that your superpower?' Faith rested a head on Betty's shoulder and batted her eyelashes, as though that might soften the sting of her comment. 'That and being able to sniff out a single man from a five-hundred-yard distance.'

'Although …' I checked my watch. 'Given that Molly hasn't turned up yet, maybe Bet wasn't the only one who grabbed a coat last night?'

In the second summer at home from university, we'd all reunited for semi-drunken antics and a catch-up on life outside of our small and humble hometown. Betty, true to form, had managed to bag herself a man on the first night we were all back together. In a drunken stupor she'd whispered, 'I've grabbed a coat, Edi, I've grabbed a coat,' before disappearing into the night with an unknown bloke. The phrase had sort of stuck since then.

'She won't admit to it—' Cora leaned in and lowered her voice '—but her and Paddy have been messing about for a bit.'

Paddy? 'You mean Patrick Hiller?' I couldn't hold in my shock. Patrick was the quietest of Rowan's friends. The discreet smooth-talker, he always managed to wine, dine, and take a girl home without making a show-and-tell of it, unlike some of the other lads. But he'd also never been seen twice with the same woman on his arm. 'What do you mean, messing about?'

'I mean shagging, Edi, Christ.' Cora dropped back in her seat. 'I was trying to be subtle.'

'Fuck me, you don't usually go to the trouble, Cor. Just say what you mean.' Betty leaned out of the way of a waiter who was trying to deliver food to the table. She took on a sweeter tone and said, 'Thank you,' and she waited until he was out of earshot before she asked, 'So are they a thing?'

'I don't think so? Not properly, anyway – they're not status official or anything.' Cora reached over and stole a blueberry from Betty's plate. 'Whatever they are, you didn't hear about it from me.'

'Out of idle curiosity,' Lily asked, 'who did we hear it from?'

'Who did you hear what from?'

'Molly!' Cora leapt up like a small shock had run through her seat.

'That you're sleeping with Patrick.'

'Faith!'

'Oh, Cora,' Molly groaned and sank into the empty seat at the head of the table. 'You told them?' The girls giggled and whooped like a modern-day Greek chorus, while Molly set her elbows on the table and cradled her forehead.

Cora opened her mouth once, twice, as though considering a lie. But then she said, 'Yes.' She slapped Faith's outer arm with the back of her hand. 'What did I say about not hearing it from me?'

'Oh, *not* hearing it from you?' Faith's attention was pulled away by the buzz of her phone.

'Faith, you're not even sorry.'

'Nope.'

'Shouldn't we be talking about Edi, anyway?' Molly snapped. There were two pink blooms of embarrassment spreading across each cheek and I wanted to hug her, but I sensed it might make things worse. 'Edi, please? Say something about the engagement? Anything.'

'Molly, you worry too much.' Betty reached over to squeeze her hand. 'No one gives a hoot. It's your right to sleep with whoever you want.'

'Feminist right,' Lily added.

'God.' Molly made another uncomfortable noise. 'Edi, please, matrimonial bliss?'

There came a crunch of crisped bacon before Lily said, 'She's not married yet.'

I laughed. 'Are you just here for angry asides today?'

Lily shook her head. 'Not just today.'

'Molly,' I spoke softly in case what I was about to say would be a surprise for her. 'We got engaged five minutes ago. What is there to say?'

'Will it be a long engagement?' she pushed.

'I mean, we're not running down the road of a shotgun wedding. Row's away for work soon, and he's seeing his folks on his travels. But we said we might try to see a few venues before he goes, you know, just in case the waiting lists are horrific.'

'Which they will be,' Molly said with certainty.

Faith took a break from texting to ask, 'Why do you even know that?'

'Educated guess.'

'Educated my arse, Molly, don't be that girl.' Betty pointed at her with her fork. 'We've no space at this table for desperate-to-be-married girl.'

Lily's level of outrage on Molly's behalf was such that she dropped her glass too soon and sent orange juice swilling across what was left of her extra bacon. 'I tell you what we've no space for, Beatrice.' I expected her to flip the table, but she held the gesture in; I could see it was there, though, fizzing away. 'Exclusive feminism! You think that bell hooks would go ahead and—'

'I'm sorry,' the waiter interrupted while Lily took a breath. He looked terrified. 'I saw the …' He pointed. 'The orange juice?'

Lily looked down, then, and stared hard at the plate as though she couldn't quite understand what had happened. 'You're a peach.' She glanced back at the waiter who stood still, stunned by the sheer force of Lily's smash-the-patriarchy vibes. Molly spluttered a laugh from the end of the table and like a precariously balanced structure – which is exactly what we were – we all one by one followed. 'Ignore them.' Lily reached over to take the cloth that was offered and dabbed around the table. The waiter began to move away, then, but she called him back. 'Do me a solid, would you, and bring out another side of bacon? Please and thanks.'

'Work up an appetite there, did you?' I leaned over to move condiments out of her way.

'Well, come on …' Lily kept dabbing at the carnage. 'Bacon never made anything worse.'

Chapter 6

Rowan had been away for nearly a week. Between work, and life, and wedding venues, the trip had crept up on us both without warning. But it was the first time I'd seen him excited about work in as long as I could remember, so I'd practically pushed him out the door to encourage him. Anything to bolster the excitement, I thought. Still, it was the longest we'd been away from each other in years.

'Are you pining for him like a dog with a dead owner?' Betty asked, her voice heavy with judgement. There must have been an accompanying eye roll, too, so I was grateful it wasn't a face-to-face interrogation.

'Betty ...'

'I know, I'm wasted in retail. But *are* you?'

No, I thought, although I wouldn't give her the satisfaction of admitting to it. 'Of course I'm missing him.' But the regular dances around the kitchen, and the eating at whatever time I wanted, and the being able to go home straight from work, rather than home via Rowan's, well, they'd only been a few of the silver linings. 'I'll be glad when he's back in the same city as me. It's weird being so far apart.'

'Need company for the night?' *Also no*, I thought again, and

Betty read the silence. 'Say no more. Early dinner, bubble bath, Netflix binge?'

'Hard yes.'

'Treat yourself, sweets. PS: Did we say something about dinner? I told Faith I'd ask.'

'Oh, I've sorted that. I'll text you.' I laughed. 'All of you.'

We disconnected the call and I flopped back onto the sofa, my legs hooked over the armrest. It was and always had been one of my favourite things about my friendship with Betty, that I could say anything to her – including, 'Leave me alone for a bit.' – without her getting offended or sad or mad. It was like that with all the girls, though, I realised. I felt a warmth in my belly at the thought. There's a certain honesty you can only have with friends.

*

The water was so hot that my skin turned pink when I got in. The bubbles crackled around me and bit by bit I lowered myself down, until I was up to my shoulders in Radox. I'd got my laptop propped on the toilet seat, the screen angled so I could watch the latest episode of *Drag Race* while my muscles unknotted. My belly was just the right amount of full – from garlic-stuffed chicken that I could never eat around Rowan, because he hated the smell – and a long soak was my final act of self-care. I'd even messaged the group chat to tell them about the promised dinner reservation, then silenced notifications immediately after. If anything terrible happened, they'd call, and just like that ...

The episode cut out and my Skype screen kicked in.

'Bollocks.' I shifted upright and moved closer to the screen. My contact lenses were lying limp on a shelf somewhere so I could barely make out the caller without craning closer. 'Why, oh why, didn't I log out after work so ... Oh. So, Rowan couldn't call.' I tried to filter down my annoyance as I hit the green button to answer. 'Hey, handsome.' I forced a smile and leaned back in the bath.

'Are you naked?'

'Well, I'm in the bath.' I laughed. 'So, a bit naked?'

'God, what perfect timing.' He moved out of view and off-camera, and I heard a door close. 'I was just calling to check in with you, see that everything is okay.'

'Nothing to worry about here. The office computers were being given some reboot or another so we all got packed off home to work remotely, which was nice. I'm just, you know, winding down.' It occurred to me that if this were a call with Molly or Lily or … they would already have apologised and offered to call back. 'How's your day been?'

'Good, yeah, good.' He took an audible swallow. 'I can't believe you're in the bath.'

'Well, you've seen me naked, Row. Are you – I mean, is it weird? Should I call back …'

'No, no, I called you.' He rubbed at the back of his neck. 'Are you missing me terribly?'

'More than I can say. How about you?'

He huffed. 'Of course. All I've done is talk, talk, talk about you to Dad.'

Not your mum, though. 'That's really sweet.'

'I told him all about the first venue that we saw, the one that—'

'Was way too expensive? Tilbury Manor?'

He laughed. 'I was going to say the one with the moat but sure, we can use your words.'

'I bet he bloody loves the idea of a moat.'

'Please …' Rowan glanced off-screen somewhere. 'He's lord of the manor anywhere.'

'Oh boy, that bad?' I pulled bubbles closer, to protect what little modesty was left.

'Eh, yes and no. He's walked me down memory lane a lot, about when we were kids, how I always said I'd marry you.' Even through the medium of screens I could see that Rowan looked soft, loved up. He was giving me the sort of look he used to give me on a date night. 'We've spent our whole lives together, Edi. Isn't that mad?'

'Like, mad in a good way or …'

He made a noise that I thought was a laugh. But it didn't sound right. 'Yes, in a good way. It was when I was talking to Dad, that's all, it just occurred to me how mad it is that we've only ever known each other. It's special, isn't it? Not many people can say they've got something like that. Something that – I don't know, something that survives.'

Like a muscle spasm, the memory came to me: the night he told me. I tried to brush the thoughts away with a fake smile and a shrug. 'I don't know, look at me and the girls.'

He huffed. 'I like to think we're a little different to what you've got with the girls.'

Different is probably just the word, I thought but didn't say. 'You know what I mean.'

'Planning on running off into the sunset with one of them?' Even though I knew in my belly that he must be joking, there was something in his tone that made me uncomfortable. And I couldn't work out what reaction he wanted. 'Anyway, Dad just commented on how he didn't expect us to settle down and all the rest of it. He gave me the same "*Are you thinking straight?*" speech that everyone else has given us.'

I frowned. Not everyone had given *us* that speech. But the comment made me wonder who he'd been talking to. I shook my head and tried to find what felt like the right response. 'Thinking straight or not, when you know, you know. Right?'

'Right.' He fidgeted, then smiled, a wide smile that looked clumsy on him. 'So, I'm driving home Sunday morning. It should take a couple of hours, if I leave early enough, and I was wondering if I could swing by? Probably around lunchtime.'

'I can make us something?'

'No, no, that's not what I meant. I just thought – you know, on my way back, it'd be good to see you. Catch up, talk.' He gave a tight smile. 'I haven't made plans with the lads or anything. I didn't know whether you were seeing the girls?'

'Oh, no, I'm seeing them Friday night for the—'

'Ah, the master plan?'

I laughed. 'The master plan. I've got everything ready. They think it's just dinner. I don't know that they've guessed there's anything more to it.'

'Good.' He nodded and then looked around the room. 'That's really good.' He sounded like he wanted to say more but didn't.

Something's off, I decided, then. 'Babe, is everything okay? You look like there's something stuck in your throat.'

'It's just been weird, being away from you like this. I've thought too much.' He laughed, and it at least sounded more genuine than the last attempt he'd made. 'I've spent too much time with Mum, too much time talking to Dad. You know what it's like with them.'

'Parents and their crazy ways.' I tried to sound like I was talking generally. But yes, I knew all about Rowan's parents and how wearing it was to be around them for more than five minutes – let alone half a week. 'Well, you'll be home soon.'

And then he made the same noise as before, the nervous laugh that wasn't a laugh, even though he wanted me to believe it was. 'It'll be good, yeah. Be good to see you properly, and I really do want us to talk.' He took an audible pull of air. 'Christ, everything *is* fine. I'm worried I'm making it sound like it isn't now, but it is. I just want to see you.' Then he rushed to add, 'Bloody love you.'

I had the same nervous feeling in my stomach that I got before a smear test. Like someone was about to do something unthinkable but utterly necessary. I couldn't marry that feeling with talking to Rowan, though. 'Bloody love you,' I said back, like nothing was the matter. But the feeling didn't go away over the evening. Instead, I carried it to bed with me and I lay down next to it. That night, I slept with the same trepidation that I'd come to associate with speculums, lubricants and other grim but necessary things.

Chapter 7

In the days since Rowan and I had video-chatted, everything really had been normal. Apart from the Save My Soul that Cora had sent me late on Friday afternoon, asking me to meet her and Molly in The Circus Ring – personally dubbed, 'The string of stores I'll never be able to afford to shop in' – a little earlier than planned. Out of my friends, they'd always been the two to have more money than sense. On the walk there, I entertained myself by making guesses at what extravagant purchases they were looking to buy. I assumed I'd be taking the role of: 'Of course you deserve to spend that much money on a hat ...' When I eventually tracked them down, though, they weren't huddled outside of a hat shop at all. Instead, they were outside Bliss – with its brilliant white shop front visible from the moon, if not further afield than that. I rolled my eyes at Cora when she spotted me, and she held her hands up in a defensive gesture.

'I would like the record to show,' she said when I came to a stop alongside them both, 'this was absolutely not my idea and I'm simply here in a supporting role.'

'Who are you supporting?' I hugged her. 'Me, or this crazy one?'

Molly hadn't even turned to greet me. Her hand was pressed

palm flat to the window while she peered into the shop like a street urchin stripped from a Dickens novel.

'They're so beautiful, Edi, I just …' Molly sighed, and turned away from the mannequins.

'I'm not dress shopping until—'

'Oh my God, are you *actually* about to tell me you haven't put thought into a date?' she interrupted me. Her eyes were narrowed in such a way that she had a predatory look, and I didn't know whether to laugh or cower. Molly had never been the stern one in the group, but the wedding malarkey was bringing out some interesting shades …

'What I was actually going to say is that I'm not dress shopping without everyone being here.'

'Rowan can't be here,' she snapped.

Cora huffed and tapped Molly on the side of the forehead, as though checking for signs of life. 'Earth to Molly, she means our other friends. The girls who we talk to every day, the ones we're literally about to meet for a romantic dinner for six?'

'Oh. Oh, them.' She took another look at the window. 'Fine, whatever. Betty needs new boots. She told me they'd head to Wear 'Em Out and we should look for them around there.'

I linked arms with Molly. 'Then that's where we'll go, and we'll come to look at the pretty dresses in the pretty shop window on a day when we're all together.'

'But we are all—'

'God in heaven, Molly.' Cora looped her other arm. 'Leave it.'

Molly talked about different styles, cuts and colour options for my wedding dress on the way to meet the others. But she promptly stopped when they were within hearing distance. Hugs were exchanged and Betty – who by then had already bought a new set of knee-highs that she seemed especially happy with – suggested we head towards the high street. Out of the boutiques and into the daily-wear shops, we soon scattered in our separate directions: Primark; New Look; H&M. We met up for half-hourly check-ins, though, partly to get each other's opinions on clothes but mostly to assess each other's hunger levels.

'Can we just eat already?' Lily eventually said, in a whine that we all recognised as a sign of her growing hanger. 'Lucky Dragon is—'

'Where I've booked the table, yes,' I interrupted her.

'Did I tell you lately that I love you?' she answered in a sing-song voice.

I cupped her cheek and gave her a dramatic, loving look. 'But you tell me every day. Onto the main business though, beauts, it's right at the start of serving time, so if we head there now we can really make the most of the buffet.'

'Gets my vote,' Betty added.

'Mine too,' Faith said from behind her phone screen. She'd been on and off it for most of the afternoon and I wondered who'd got her attention – whether it was a safe dinner topic to bring up. Since her last relationship had gone south – 'Of the equator kind,' she'd said, with eyes that looked like infant pufferfish – Faith had been hesitant to get into anything serious. But she'd definitely been giving online dating apps a college try.

'That's settled, then,' I tried to finish the debate before Molly could find something to object to. She hadn't exactly been agree-able since we'd left behind talk of bridal gear. And I feared that if she brought up my waistline in the same mouthful as a comment about wedding dresses – *well, if she brings up my waistline at all,* I fact-checked myself – then I might disown her. On the tread to the restaurant, though, while we all chatted in our couples, Molly caught up with me and Cora.

'Edi,' she started, in a tone that was suspiciously sweet, 'you know I only want the best for you.'

'Where is this going?'

'Nowhere. That's literally all I came to say.' She rubbed elbows with me. 'Like, in life, I mean, too. I don't just mean for the wedding.'

I pulled her close but kept walking. 'I know, you dope.'

'Edi will blatantly go for all of the chow mein in the world,' I heard Lily say from behind us. 'Valid life choice, of course. Faith, you'll be on spring rolls, am I right?'

'You're not wrong.'

I wouldn't have voiced it, but my heart felt fit to burst. To be surrounded by a bunch of people who knew me so completely was at once beautiful and weirdly overwhelming, and I couldn't say where exactly the feeling had come from. But it was definitely there, fluttering about inside my ribcage like a confused sparrow. I decided to sit on it, though, and save it for the drunk speeches on the evening of the hen party. *Molly probably already has hers drafted in the Notes app of her phone.* I half-laughed and gave her arm another squeeze, and I made sure we sat next to each other at the restaurant, too. Although I still kept a watch on Faith and her influx of messages. I narrowed my eyes from across the table and she mouthed back, 'Nothing,' and stashed the handset away. She didn't check it again throughout our three trips to the all-you-can-eat food carts.

Everyone was soon settled with their piles of ice cream, half-heartedly nabbed from the dessert cart before it became clogged with teenagers from a birthday party happening on the opposite side of the room. I waited until spoons were clattering and appreciative noises were being made – 'I didn't even want this, you know, but it's *so* good, like, how can you not?' Betty said around a mouthful of salted caramel – to call their quiet attention my way.

'I've got something I'd like to talk to you all about, while we're together.'

'You and Rowan are splitting up?' Lily dropped her spoon.

'Oh my goodness.' Molly clasped her hands over her mouth. She'd gone from a Dickens urchin to an Austen side character. 'Are you, Edi, are you splitting up?'

I looked over at Lily. 'What is the matter with you?'

'Naturally pessimistic personality type?' she suggested.

'Christ, only when it comes to monogamy, Lil.' I turned to Molly. 'No, no we are not splitting up, and I absolutely promise that if we ever are, you'll all be the first to hear about it. You'll hear my wails the whole city over, in fact.'

'You would not wail,' Betty scoffed.

I made a show of thinking it over. 'No, no, I think I really would.'

'Ah shush, could be the best thing that ever happened to you.'

My head snapped around to Cora. It was so unlike her to pile on. 'Did everyone take their man-bashing pills too early today or something?'

'Ha!' The noise erupted from Lily from across the table. 'Every morning with breakfast.'

Molly's expression was one of deep concern, as though she were the one hypothetically being left at the altar. 'Molly!' I reached over to give her hand a squeeze. 'They're being cow-bags. Rowan and I are fine. We're going to have a horrendously beautiful wedding, and a horrendously beautiful marriage and—'

'Horrendously beautiful babies?' she cut me off and I winced.

'Weeeell, maybe we can swing back around to that one later? Wedding aside, though, there was ... is something I wanted to talk to you all about, before we start planning my divorce or anything ...' I ferreted about in my backpack as I spoke to them. There was a smaller bag in there that I pulled out, and then I pushed myself away from the table. I walked around my friends, reaching over and popping an off-white ring box in front of each of them. 'No, what I wanted to talk to you about was this. It's just ... I don't know, it's a silly something, I suppose. But you're all just so important, and this is a kind of token. A *really* silly token.' During my lengthy exposition I realised how silly they might think the gesture was. But I was committed now. 'Anyway, open your boxes and we'll go from there.' They all reached forward and set about unveiling the contents of the box. Molly gasped, again, as though she were actually being proposed to, and I squeezed her knee under the table. Inside every box, there was a jelly sweet ring. I pulled in a deep breath. 'Will you be my maids of honour?'

Lily threw the ring into her mouth and started chewing. She reached over the table, then, slammed the box down and said, 'No.'

Everyone stared. No longer accompanied by the sparrow, instead my heart was a tiny wounded creature using the rungs of my ribcage to make its way to my throat. *I can't believe she said no.*

'Oh fuck, Edi.' Lily pushed back from the table and rushed around. 'I will, I really will.' She wrapped herself around my shoulders and held on to me from behind. 'I've just always wanted to turn down a proposal and this might be the closest I'll come.'

I burst out laughing, but there were small tears forming, too. 'You silly cow.' The laughter moved around the table, accompanied by gleeful acceptances, and soon everyone piled into the hug. I was weighed down by their joy and it crossed my mind that it was better than my own acceptance had been. But maybe better wasn't the right word, I decided. Maybe it was just a different kind of lovely.

'I can't believe you would have ovaries big enough to turn down someone as good as Edith Parcell,' Faith said across the table to Lily as they all dropped back into their seats. 'Jesus, do you know how good you would have it with her?'

'Obviously.' Lily grabbed her wine glass. 'But what if no one ever proposes to me again, ever?'

'Oh, Lily.' Molly tried to wrap an arm around her shoulders, but Lily rebuffed the offer.

'Moll, it wouldn't be a bad thing.'

'See,' Cora spoke to Molly, 'and this is why you need to read an audience.'

'Wait,' Betty said, around yet more salted caramel. 'You're going to have us *all* as maids?'

I nodded. 'I can't choose a favourite out of you.' Lily was sitting down again, then, so I flashed her a quick wink and said, 'That's just the sort of shit the patriarchy wants.'

Chapter 8

The doorbell played its sing-song at bang on one, Sunday lunch-time. It was the first time I'd known Rowan to stick to a time schedule, which perhaps should have been my first clue that something wasn't quite right. When I answered, he stood with his face hidden behind a suspiciously large bunch of white roses. It wasn't our anniversary or my birthday, and we were well past the 'just because' phase of our relationship. Rowan had stopped with spontaneous romantic gestures in our second year of university. The fact that he looked to be making one now should have been my second clue. He waltzed in without a word and kissed me like he did when we were teenagers. I laughed as he pulled away.

'What's going on with you?' I asked, backing away to let him further into the hall.

'Can't a man miss his woman?' He winced. 'Not that you're mine, but … God, you know what I mean, right?' He carried the flowers into the kitchen and rested them on the worksurface. I was already looking for a vase. He nodded to the bouquet. 'There's a card buried in there somewhere.'

I filled a square jug with water. 'I mean, I'm pretty sure I know who they're from.'

'Well, maybe it isn't the name of the sender.' He nudged me softly. 'Find the card?'

I pushed my way through soft petals and hard leaves until I found a small white rectangle. Rowan was shuffling in the background, the way he did when he was nervous, and it was taking the edge off whatever surprise this was. His anxiety had always been contagious. I lifted the lip and pulled out the note at a speed, more to halt his obvious worries than anything else. But as I eyed the card, I noticed my share of Rowan's anxiety soon died down against the growing flames of my own. I scanned the message twice over before the realisation of its meaning fully landed on me: Save The Date. When I looked up at him, he was grinning like a schoolboy with good exam results.

'I booked Tilbury Manor.' He pulled me into another kiss before I could say anything, which was likely a good thing. He kissed away my nerves and protests and mild irritation. *He'd* decided the date; *he'd* decided the venue; *he'd*—

'Rowan, what about the budget?' I tried to force a laugh to take the edge out of my voice. 'How did you rig this?'

He rubbed at the back of his neck. 'Look, Mum and Dad really wanted to help out. They've promised they won't do anything else, at all, for the wedding. But Dad kept pushing me to talk about the wedding and the plans, and then I found out because of the date it's actually partially refundable, too ...' He noticed something in my face. 'You're annoyed.'

Yes. We hadn't made grand plans for the wedding. But of the plans we had made, the first thing we'd agreed was that we'd pay for it ourselves. 'I thought we'd already talked about the money situation, though.'

'Did we?' He sounded genuinely perplexed. *Yes,* I thought, *and your bloody mother knew about our agreement, too.* 'I mean, I know we talked a little about venues and stuff before I went away. I didn't think we'd ... I mean, maybe *I'm* wrong, but I really didn't think we'd decided on anything.'

I could remember the conversation. We'd been sitting across from each other in this same room with a laptop open between us and a castle on the screen. In the space of an hour we'd moved from howling with laughter at the prices, all the way through to a grown-up talk about finances and … *How do you not remember this happening?*

'Okay,' he started again, plugging the silence, and I waited for the memory of it all to fall out of him. 'Babes, I really can't place that conversation ever happening, I'm sorry. I can call the venue tomorrow, tell them we don't want it booked? Mum and Dad were only trying to—'

'There's no need for that, honestly.' I flashed a tight smile. It wasn't worth the trouble it would cause. 'It's a surprise, that's all.' I kissed his cheek and then picked up the flowers. 'How did you even decide on a date?'

'Easy. I picked the date when you conquered gender inequality in the playground.'

My whole body softened. The day Rowan and I first met was when I'd nearly thumped a boy in the face for not letting Molly play tag. Unless you ask Rowan about it, in which case *he* saved *me* with a punch that never happened. I hadn't even wanted to play the game myself; I only wanted the right to. In the end, Rowan and I had been huddled out of sight at the top of the field because neither of us could be arsed with running about in the heat. And that was when it all started. *God, oh God, how can I be annoyed about this?* I was facing away from him, trimming the toes of the roses. 'Rowan, that's unbelievably sweet. I – Christ, you're a good egg, you really are. Two years away, too …' Snip, snip. 'That's a really good amount of planning time.'

'Yeah, there was kind of a motive to that, too.'

Snip. 'Oh?' I couldn't keep track of my feelings. The nervous through to the delight through to – whatever was happening next. 'Go on, then, let's be having it.'

'So, I was talking to Dad a lot over the week. Mum wasn't

around that much, which was nice. But Dad was asking whether I'd had any doubts or whether I thought you had any doubts, about the wedding.' He forced a laugh. 'What he actually said was, "Are the pair of you sure that you're both thinking straight on this?" I told him I hadn't had doubts but that other people maybe did. You know, how people are always asking how we can be so sure, whether we *are* so sure. Even the conversation with Dad felt like a rerun of that in loads of ways.'

Snip. 'Right ...'

'Dad asked if we'd thought of a break at any point. Not like, not being together anymore, as such, but a break from being engaged or being – I don't know, shit. I can't remember the word he used. He might have said exclusive.'

I'd run out of flowers to cut. But I couldn't look at him. I had a horrible feeling that whoever was sitting at my kitchen table wasn't the person I would expect to see if I turned round. 'I think you mean monogamous.'

There was a long pause before he said, 'Yeah, that might have been the word. But it got me thinking about how we've never really known anyone else, have we, either of us?' The thought made my stomach roll and I clung to the counter to steady myself. 'And look, we've booked somewhere, we're settled, we know we're doing the right thing. But what if there are things we want to get out of our system?' I assumed the question was rhetorical until I felt Rowan close in behind me; he set a hand on my back and craned round to see my face. 'Edi?'

What is happening here? 'I'm sorry, I don't think I understand.'

'Come on, let's sit? I'll explain better.' He guided me through the flat to the sofa, and I let myself be led like a woman in shock. *No, wait,* I fact-checked, *I am a woman in shock.* He encouraged me onto the settee, then he perched on the edge of my coffee table so he could be opposite me. *I hate it when he does that and he knows it.* But I shook the thought away; it didn't seem like the time. 'We would still be together. And life would absolutely carry on as normal in lots of ways. But imagine, okay, imagine you're on a night out with the girls and a man comes up to you and says, hey, can I get you a drink? If you wanted to say yes, you could! It wouldn't matter, and I – well, I might be a *bit* jealous, but you'd still be coming home to me at the end of the night and—'

'Oh,' I interrupted, 'as much as *a bit*?'

He sighed. 'It's a terrible idea.'

'Besides—' I ignored his comment and ploughed ahead '—I'd only be coming home to you if I weren't going home with him.'

His eyebrows pulled together. 'I don't follow you.'

'If we're together but we're not, I can go home with someone else. Is that what you're saying?' It looked like the thought had thrown him, and I wondered how well he'd thought this suggestion through. 'And I guess, in that same scenario, or sort of the same anyway, if you were out with the guys and you saw a girl you liked and you wanted to buy her a drink, you'd just go right ahead and offer?' He nodded instantly, as though that were a much easier question to answer. 'Right. I – right.'

He lowered himself into my eyeline, forcing me to look at him. 'Are you with me?'

'Like, in the room, or with this idea?'

'It's a terrible idea?' he said again.

Yes. But I'd become so accustomed to my role as the reassuring one that even this, even with this bloody terrible idea elbowing between us, I still said, 'No, no it's not that.' I pulled in a greedy breath and steeled myself for his answer. 'Do you think you're missing out on something, Rowan? By being with me, I mean?'

'Baby, not even.' He dropped to his knees. The last time I'd seen him from that angle had been when he'd proposed, and the association stung. 'I am so, so happy with you, Edi. But I guess Dad's point was, what if we get to their age and wonder whether there was more? Do you know?'

No. No, I don't know. 'So, you don't think you're missing out on anything, but you just want to be sure you're not?'

He took my hand. 'I want us both to be sure.'

In those seconds while I looked at him, though, he was a stranger – and for the first time ever, I felt unsure. The man walked and talked like my boyfriend. But he bought flowers and made suggestions like the kind of men I told the girls to avoid. *I'll have to throw the roses out,* I thought, but that would come later. In the lengthy silence that rolled out, I guessed he was likely waiting for enthusiasm or disgust. And I would have to be the one who made the final decision; I would have to be the person out of the two of us who made this an okay thing to do – or not. Because that was my role: The Reassurer. I sighed, realising that I sounded like the world's shittest superhero.

I don't know how much time had ticked by when Rowan excused himself to make tea. In truth, I thought he couldn't hack the silence any longer and needed to be somewhere other than looking back at my catatonic stare. *Does this count as an emergency?* I wondered, while I tried to tally up how many months it had been since I'd last seen my counsellor. It would be short notice, but she'd always been good at fitting me in during a crisis. I was shaking my head again. *And if this doesn't count as an emergency, crisis, imminent existential dread, what does?* I thought of asking Rowan what *he* wanted, then; whether this suggestion ignored what might be good for both of us, and instead only came down to him being able to buy a girl a drink and tell me about it, without me flipping a table. But I couldn't get the question out and into the room. My counsellor had coached me: *We're not meant to ask things, if we're not ready for the answers …*

Chapter 9

Before

Every now and then, I'd see Rowan fidget. I thought I'd heard his mouth open once, too – the sound of dry lips breaking away from each other. But he didn't say anything. There was nothing to say, really, once he'd told me. The explanation had rolled into more information than I was ready for until eventually I'd stopped him – 'You need to shut up for a minute. Longer than a minute.' – and we'd held a silence since. It was a séance, almost, while we both tried to search for the relationship that had most definitely been lost. I heard the neighbouring flats thrown open with life; another party or another study night or another—

'Will the girls be back soon?' he asked.

My head shook; my eyes fluttered. The question – or the sound of his voice, maybe – stunned me. But the realities of it soon landed and I said, 'No, no, Betty and Lily are going to a feminist meet that's happening on campus tonight. They won't be back until later.'

'My place is empty if …'

If what? I thought. *If this takes longer than a few hours to fix?*

I huffed a near laugh and then went back to staring at my single spot on the floor. I must have looked catatonic to him. And then I laughed again; not at the catatonia, but at the thought of how he must see me. *Do you have the same worry, of how I see you now?* I glanced up at him and let the thought roll around.

'What?' he asked, spotting my eyes shift.

'Who was she?' I finally asked. In his rehashing of the whole thing, I'd told him I didn't want to know. But I reserved the right to change my mind in any situation, especially this one. Rowan was bright – normally – so he must have known the question would come.

'You don't know her.'

'Did you?'

He shook his head. 'I don't understand?'

'Did you know her, or did you just, you know?'

He pulled in a big breath. 'She's the daughter of someone Dad knows. I don't really …' His sentence trailed off. It looked as though he was struggling to breathe and in that bitter moment I couldn't even worry about him. I could only think: *Imagine how I must feel.* 'I don't really know her. She visits the house sometimes, with her parents, and we're always thrown together as the kids. You know how Mum and Dad are, getting me out of sight and all.'

'You can pop that violin away,' I snapped.

'I didn't mean – I didn't – I'm sorry. It's not an excuse or anything. I just meant, that's how we came to be alone. That's how we've come to be alone before.'

'And this time?'

Another big breath. 'She came over with her parents. They all suggested going for food and I didn't want to go, really, so I said I was going to stay home for the night. She said she'd call a taxi from our house, and skip dinner as well.'

'Smooth.'

'Edi, please—'

'Oh, I'm sorry,' I cut across him, 'does my spite hurt you? Do you

49

not want me to speak ill of the woman who fucked my boyfriend the second my back was turned?' The expletive hung heavy in the air between us. It was the first time either of us had used the word quite so viciously. He hadn't admitted yet that they'd gone all the way. But I could tell from his reaction, then, that he'd seen her naked; touched her body. A shudder ran through me.

'Are you okay?' he asked, spotting the judder. I shot him a blank look. 'Sorry. I don't know why I asked that.'

'So what, she was meant to call a taxi, it ran late and you thought you'd kill time?'

'No, we ...' he started, then stopped and tried to steady himself. I already knew that whatever was coming next would hurt. 'We just started talking. Her parents are in a similar situation to mine. They – they're not happy; they shouldn't be together. We talked and we complained and we drank—'

'Not so much you couldn't perform, though, so you must have drunk just the right amount.'

He looked ashamed, then, and swallowed so hard that I could track the muscles moving in his jaw. 'No, not that much. As soon as it happened – when it was over, I felt ...'

'Tell me, Rowan. What did you feel?'

'Disgusting.'

'Good.' I stood and walked to the living room window. The world outside was grey and I wondered whether it was observable pathetic fallacy. Lily would probably say it was. I watched rain make mismatched patterns on the pane and, for the first time in these two most hideous hours of my adult life, I let myself cry. 'Who knows?' I asked, my breath jagged and my face still fixed on the window.

'No one.'

'Actually no one, or no one apart from Hamish and the rest of them?'

There was a long pause. 'Actually no one. Skye left before my parents came home.'

Skye. I looked up. She'd even ruined the view.

'I'd appreciate it if you didn't tell anyone.' I turned to face him. 'Will she?'

He shrugged. 'I don't see why she would. I could talk to—'

'I think it's in your best interests not to finish that sentence.'

'Yep. I heard it.' A long pause stretched out between us. I couldn't look at him, but again I felt him looking at me. 'You're not going to tell anyone?'

'My friends would never forgive you.'

'I'm not exactly worried about them.'

I huffed. 'You should be. Lily is vicious and Betty's always thought you'd let me down.' It was true, too. The nearer we'd got to university, the more Betty thought that adulthood would crack Rowan somehow. She'd never said cheat – but she wouldn't have been wrong. 'What's happened stays between us.'

'Does that mean—'

'It means that what happened stays between us.' I pushed my hair back from my face and let my fingers lock together behind my neck. I could feel the tense and twitch of muscles as my body clenched and unclenched. 'I want a bath.'

'I can run you a bath?' He shot up from his seat.

'You can leave.'

'Edi—'

'Did I stutter?'

He apologised three times. There had been countless apologies before that and it crossed my mind that I should have kept a tally. Cora and Betty, on a boozy night in, had made a boyfriend-bingo that listed various fuck-ups in all their forms – and the apologies that came after them. Rowan must have been quite high-ranking in a game like that, I thought, and it nearly made me laugh. But what a terrible game to win at.

'Will we get through this?' He looked at the floor as he asked the question.

I crossed the room in quiet and unhooked the lock on the front door. 'I don't know.'

Chapter 10

Now

Instead of using my work hours for actual work, I used it for painful introspection. I created a document on my desktop with an innocuous title but contained within there was ...

Pros	Cons
??????	Rowan sleeping with other people
	Rowan leaving me
	I'll always know that Rowan *wanted* to sleep with other people AGAIN and I'll have to carry that around forever and how do I live with that knowledge?

It took me three days to build that table. During which time I ignored calls from the girls, and told Rowan five times that I needed to think. But after days of thinking, what I needed was time to talk. On my way out of work I sent an SOS message to the group chat. By the time I arrived home, Molly was already outside my building. She was leaning back against the wall with her phone pressed to her ear. Her other hand was flat against her forehead. I didn't catch any of the conversation, apart from the hurried goodbye – 'No, Edi's here now ... See you soon, yep ...' – but she looked panicked. I felt dreadful, because it crossed my mind she might be having a crisis bigger than the crisis I'd called her over here for. Then we could ignore my problem entirely and focus on whatever had made Molly look like her last slab of cheddar had gone off in the fridge.

'Edi, what's happening?' She held me by the shoulders. 'Are your parents okay?'

Shit. She's panicked about my panic. I forced a smile. 'They're fine, Molly, why?'

'Okay. Okay.' She took a deep breath. 'Then it's Rowan.'

Back then, in the weeks and months after Skye, I'd wanted this conversation so many times. I'd wanted to sit down with my friends and talk about how I didn't understand, how I didn't know what to do – talk about what an utter shit Rowan had been. While Molly waited for a response, I flashed through all the imagined versions of this very conversation and in every single one I'd mentioned Skye by name. Now, though, I was ready to cry over the girls Rowan hadn't even slept with – yet. I felt my eyes fill up and I tried to think of a way to phrase things that might sum everything up, so I wouldn't have to explain it all to Molly the same number of times Rowan had had to explain it to me. But I couldn't find anything descriptive enough ...

'I think he might be behaving like a bastard, Moll.'

Her eyes stretched. 'Okay, inside, let's get you inside, inside.' She yanked my keys out of my hand and ushered me through the entryway to the building as the first tears tumbled free.

*

I was in the bathroom when the rest of them arrived. Before that, Molly had sat me down on the sofa and asked for everything and I'd told her, in between making ugly crying faces and gulping in air like a semi-strangled fish. *Christ, no wonder he wants to sleep with other people,* I thought as I stared myself down in the vanity mirror. When the doorbell had sounded, Molly rushed me out of sight and told me to get my face back on. She'd deal with the girls, whatever that meant. I wondered whether, when I emerged from the en suite, they might all know already. My mouth formed a *petit* O as I reapplied mascara and then I blotted my cheeks with pale compact powder, to try to compensate for the pink glow of post-cry. I huffed.

'This is as good as it's going to get, Parcell.'

I opened the door slowly to try to delay the creak of it. There was a conversation happening still, but I couldn't make out the gist – nor could I hear any shouted expletives, though, which felt like a sign that they didn't yet know the reason for the impromptu gathering. When the whine of the door finally sounded, their talking stopped. I took my time walking along the hall, but when I arrived at the doorway to the living room they already had their stares fixed on me, as though they'd only been sat there waiting. Either that, or they'd sensed my gloom shifting along the corridor like a scorned woman from a B-Movie. I flashed them all a tight smile and Cora, as though spring-loaded, leapt from the bucket seat in the corner and rushed over to me.

I spoke to Molly over Cora's shoulder. 'You've told them?'

'She's told us.' Cora held me by the waist at arm's length. 'What reaction do you need?'

I shrugged. 'I really can't—'

'Can't believe what a colossal bastard he is, Edi, if I'm honest.' Betty was sitting on the windowsill. She'd got one hand dangling out of the window to keep a hold of her cigarette. I couldn't remember the last time I'd seen her smoke. 'I know you don't know what reaction you need but that's the reaction you're getting.' She moved her head out to take a drag and then came back in. When she spoke again, smoke billowed out of her and she reminded me of a dragon; a fierce, feminist, sweary dragon. 'This is exactly the sort of shit I'd expect a man of his standing to pull. Middle-class, self-important, entitled twa—'

'Betty.' Faith raised an eyebrow. 'Cora asked what reaction Edi needs.'

'And Edi said she didn't know,' Betty answered.

'Actually—' Cora squeezed in between them both '—Edi didn't answer yet.' But the comment went ignored. Still, I squeezed her arm softly in thanks.

Meanwhile, Faith only kept her cautionary eyebrow raised in Betty's direction. 'Surely that means we should check our feelings at the door and let Edi speak, which is probably what she called us here for.' She turned to me. 'Right?' Faith was the human in shining armour at the best of times. That evening, though, she was the wild-haired friend straight from the pages of a magazine, in her white T-shirt and black braces. And her level tone was a great comfort. She was trying hard to give nothing away. 'Walk us through it. What are you feeling?'

I sat between Molly and Cora on the sofa. 'I don't know. Shock? I'm confused about … everything. He doesn't want to break up. Like, he must have said that ten times over. But he also thinks it would be good for us, to have this space and this time and … I don't know.'

'So, you're both free to sleep with other people?' Cora asked, and I nodded. 'With no comeback, at all, at a later date?'

'Providing there aren't pregnancies or STDs involved, I assume?' Betty chimed in.

'Pregnancy is an STD to some of us.' Cora shuddered and Molly backhanded her thigh for the comment. 'Whatever, yeah, what Betty said.'

'We didn't talk about that stuff explicitly. I don't think he has a hit list or anything like that,' I replied, and Betty snorted from her perch. We all pretended not to hear. 'I think he just wants us to be able to explore ourselves and other people, but also not lose sight of what's important. Which is each other, and the wedding, and everything that comes after the wedding.'

'So, it isn't a permanent thing?' Faith asked.

I shook my head. 'Three months.'

'Three months?' Cora's eyes widened. She made an effort to sound less surprised on her second repetition. 'Three months. Okay, well, that's not … I mean, three months isn't that long, really. How much can possibly happen in three months?' Betty cleared her throat as though she might answer, and Cora held up a finger to pause her. 'It was rhetorical.'

Betty sparked up another cigarette. 'Edi, aren't you livid?'

No, I thought. *Only a bit sad*. I shrugged. 'I'm just … confused.' And I was. Rowan had been so remorseful after Skye – not that I could say as much to the girls – that it had never crossed my mind something like this would cross his. I thought we were fine – better than fine!

Molly put an arm around my shoulders and pulled me to her for a hug. 'Chinese?'

I laughed. 'Please.' I hadn't eaten properly since the conversation with Rowan. It wasn't a strike, only the consequence of my brain being so full of other thoughts. I'd been pacing back and forth on what to do, how to handle things, and the minutes had slipped into hours that meant self-care had become an afterthought. I'd only remembered food when I was lying in bed already, or when I was halfway to work and out of my way from getting breakfast anywhere. As Molly pulled up the menu on her iPhone, I realised just how hungry I was.

Talk turned to what everyone wanted to order, and I let them decide for me. Molly would know what was best for heartache. She'd apply chicken and rice and noodles; Cora would bring curtness while Betty brought sarcastic comments and Lily … I looked around the room for her and found her leaning on the window next to Betty. She was stealing a cigarette from Betty's pouch. I got to the window as she lit up.

'You've been suspiciously quiet.'

She smiled. 'I think Betty here has shared opinions aplenty on the matter.'

'Come on,' Betty joined, 'you're telling me you don't have an opinion on this? Or is the reason you've kept quiet because you've got exactly the same opinion that I do?'

Lily exhaled smoke through her nose. 'Maybe I've kept quiet because I've got a different one?'

'Bollocks.'

'Lil, are you serious?' I pushed.

She nodded. 'Babes, real talk for a second here. It's radical thinking and I do, as it happens, agree that he's a total shit for suggesting it.' She paused to take a pull on her smoke. 'But, while it's obviously a huge benefit to Rowan, or so he thinks, I mean, really, he isn't all that and it's going to be hard out there for him but whatever, that's his bad shout. That aside, while it's going to be hard for him, it's actually going to be pretty easy for you. You've got the world at your feet with this deal.' She pulled me into a hug.

'She's not wrong, you know,' Faith added from behind me.

'About?'

'Well, any of it.' She eased me away from Lily. 'But specifically, the part about you having the world your feet. You've literally never had a clue about how beautiful you are, Edi. It's a shit trick of Rowan, but Lily is right, you won't do badly out of this.'

'Finally, something we all agree on.' Betty winked at me.

'It's a bit outdated, isn't it? To assume that open relationships can only be good for the man,' Lily started and Faith shot her a warning look; that seemed to be what she was bringing to the evening. Lily held her hands up in a defensive gesture. 'I'm not hopping on men's rights. I'm only saying, for a lot of women in long-term relationships, if there was an opportunity to sleep with men *other* than the one they share a bed with, there's a good chance they'd take the offer.' She inhaled greedily on her cigarette again. 'They might not admit as much. But that's only because they're not supposed to.' She rolled her eyes as she spoke, and Betty rumbled her throat in agreement.

'So, you're saying I should do it?' I looked between the three of them, desperate for their guidance; better still, desperate for them to make the decision for me.

Faith gave me a kiss on the forehead. 'I think what we're actually saying is—'

'You should think about the benefits you might get out of this and make the decision you want to make. Right, Bett?' Lily looked to Betty for support, but she couldn't muster it.

'That—' she dabbed her cigarette on the outside wall of the building '—or you chuck him.'

Chapter 11

After seeing the girls, I found myself drawn into a web of sexual possibility. Every attractive man set me thinking: *Could I approach you? Could I let you take me home?* And worse thoughts: *Would Rowan care?* I hadn't mustered the courage to talk to him, beyond sending a text about our arranged dinner with my parents at the weekend – *I'd like to go alone, if that's okay? xx* – and he'd replied with a pleading message, the end of which was yes, it was fine for me to go alone. But after every read receipt on WhatsApp, he messaged me again: *Babe, look, maybe this has been a terrible mistake? Maybe we should talk more? Could we?* I typed back: *Maybe I can't live my life knowing you wanted this. Maybe we have to do this now,* then backspaced to delete the message. It already felt like a burden, a messy rockery in my belly that I'd been carrying around since I'd seen him. But I didn't have answers to his questions yet. One thing I did know was that I wasn't ready to try and find the answers either. Instead, I let the question marks hang unfulfilled and went back to thinking. *Could I approach you, man on the train platform? Would my partner even care if I did?*

Gwen – my counsellor – had appointments packed to the rafters, which gave me a sad sort of comfort. At least I wasn't the only person in the city with a relationship in tatters. The receptionist could offer me an appointment weeks away, although she did promise to call if a cancellation came up. *Unlikely*, I thought, *if anyone else's partner happens to be half as horny and stupid as my own!* I shook the thought away and agreed to the time and date she'd offered. I'd started to have these bursts – flurries of intrusive anger where I thought of Rowan not as my partner, but as the partner of a friend – but they never lasted long enough for me to stick with a decision. So I booked in – 'Actually, is there any chance I could get like, a double appointment? A two-hour slot?' – and went to the next best thing: dinner with Mum and Dad.

I didn't think to forewarn them that Rowan wouldn't be coming. When I arrived at the restaurant – 'I think my party might already be here. Parcell?' – a beautiful woman guided me through the packed dining area to drop me off at my parents' table. My arse had hardly touched the seat when Mum asked, 'No Rowan?'

I half-laughed. 'Hi, Mum.'

'Hi, Edi, sweetheart.' Dad stood and leaned over the table to kiss my cheek. 'Everything okay? You look a little flustered.'

'Long day,' I brushed the question off and looked at Mum. 'No Rowan.'

'Long day for him, too?' she asked.

I murmured behind my menu, 'Something came up.' I saw them swap a look but neither of them was brave enough to push. 'What are you both having?'

'We're having one of the sharing platters, I think,' Dad answered. 'The chicken one.'

My stomach turned over. *There's no one for me to share food with. If Rowan leaves me, there won't ever be anyone for me to share food with.* I jerked as my phone vibrated in the front pocket of my jeans. I wondered whether this was something that developed after years of friendship, or whether it was a unique skill Faith had honed. But, as though sensing my sadness from ten streets away, she messaged: *I know they're a lot. Remember you don't have to tell them. But you don't have to protect him either.* While I scanned that message, another came through: *If you need an emergency then I came on my period today and I'm more than happy to call and cry down the phone. Send any emoji.* In the seconds after, she sent through a sequence of smiling faces, flowers and food items. When the string of vibrations had stopped, I stashed my phone away and apologised.

'Don't ever apologise for that smile. I remember the days of your father making me smile like that.' She squeezed his hand on the table. 'Rowan?'

I cleared my throat. 'Faith, actually.'

'Oh.' She set the menu flat and leaned on the table, arms folded. 'How's she doing?'

'She's really well, thanks, Mum. Enjoying work and—'

'Still single?'

I frowned. 'I have literally no idea. Maybe? She hasn't mentioned anyone so …'

'Are you ready to order?' the same waitress from before asked and I snapped, 'Yes,' at such a speed that she looked taken aback. 'Okay, then. What'll it be?' Dad ordered for him and Mum; a sharer with a side of tomato and herb flatbread. *Rowan's favourite flatbread. Never anything with garlic.* There was a pull in my stomach. 'What can I get for you?'

I hadn't decided. But it needed to be something I wouldn't have been able to have if Rowan had come with us. I scanned the listings again. 'Can I get the garlic and tofu bake?' I shut the menu and handed it back to her. 'Garlic bread would be great, too, thanks. With cheese.'

'You got it.'

In the minutes after, Mum and Dad tiptoed around asking whether something had happened. Neither of them said anything outright – it wasn't their style – but there were questioning into-nations and presuppositions scattered in every other comment. I thought back to what Faith had said, about not needing to protect Rowan, and, while in many ways I agreed with her, there was also the nagging fear that if this storm somehow passed with us both intact, I didn't want other people to carry a judgement – on either of us. Plus, they were my parents. They'd always been the pillar of romance and honesty; the only couple I'd ever known to make it work. *Unless there have been times when they haven't made it work …* The intrusive thought appeared while I watched them hold hands on the table still.

'We're allowed to touch in public, you know,' Mum joked, which pulled my eyes up.

'God, I'm sorry.' I forced a laugh. 'I was staring?' She nodded. 'Sorry, I – can I talk to you both about something?'

Mum yanked her hand free of Dad's and stretched across the table to reach for mine. 'Rowan?'

I felt a prickle of feeling behind my nose and I realised then how close I was to tears. 'Nothing has happened, like, really nothing. I actually asked him not to come tonight.' Mum looked surprised, but at least I could tell myself I'd been sort of honest. 'I'm just having a lot of big worries, and I don't know how normal they are, and, I don't know, it might really help to talk to people who have also had the big worries and still somehow made it work.' I felt myself running out of breath as I spoke, but if I stopped I knew the tears would come. 'I think I'm just worried that we're not really thinking straight in getting married so young.' Dad pushed back from the table and came to sit in the spot next to me; he tucked an arm around my shoulder. 'What if there are all these things we haven't done yet that we might like to?'

Mum lowered her voice. 'Is there someone else, sweetheart?'

I actually laughed. 'No, Mum, and I don't know that there ever could be.'

Dad's face was out of my eyeline. But from Mum's expression I guessed there was a quizzical look being thrown to her. 'Edi,' he spoke over me, 'I'm a bit lost, love. You're saying you can't imagine being with anyone else, but you're worried that, in getting married so young, what happens if you meet someone in the future?' He was making it sound ridiculous – which it was in many ways. But I nodded. 'Edi, you can meet someone else at any age, regardless of how long you've been married, or how old you were when you got married. Sometimes people just meet along the way and fall together, no matter how they feel about their spouses. Your age, your experiences – I don't know they've got anything to do with that.'

I sucked in a big mouthful of air to rush through the next question. 'Mum,' I knew I could ask her easier than him, 'was there anyone else, before Dad?'

She looked at Dad, then back at me, before she shrugged and said, 'Yes.'

'But there wasn't for me.'

I pulled away to stare hard at him. 'Serious?'

He laughed. 'Seriously, yes.'

'Do you feel that you've missed out?'

And he laughed again. 'No, love. I don't. Your mother worries about that more than I do. Not that she's missed out, I don't mean that, but that I might have done. But I've had a fulfilling relationship with someone who loves me and whom I love.' He kept his arm around me but reached across to touch the inside of Mum's forearm; there was something unexpectedly intimate in it. 'Not many people are lucky enough to say that, especially not these days. Oh, bugger.' He snapped out of his stupor. 'That was insensitive, Edi, I'm sorry.'

'Don't be.' I leaned into him. 'It's nice for a girl to hear her parents love each other.'

'And have good sex,' Mum added. She winked at Dad then apologised to me. It didn't sound sincere, but at least it made me smile. 'But it sounds to me like you're worried you're missing out on some big bad world out there, Edi, is that about right?'

No, I don't think that; he does. 'Yes, yes, I suppose that's what I think.' It occurred to me that they'd judge me less than they'd judge Rowan, though, so I took the hit. 'I worry we're not giving ourselves the chance to explore things properly, you know, ourselves, our likes, our – I don't really know what else. Just ... things. I worry for Rowan, too, that he might want to be with other women and end up feeling trapped. You hear about it all the time, don't you? Especially, like Dad said, our generation and all.'

Before Mum could answer, Dad shifted position so he could set a hand on each shoulder. He looked at me dead on and stared like he was searching for something. 'Edith Parcell, you're a beautiful and intelligent woman. You're giving and loving and brave and hilarious, especially when you don't mean to be. And don't let the fact that I'm your old dad undercut any of that, do you hear? Rowan is mighty lucky to have you, and I'm sure if you told him these worries, about not experiencing enough and what have you, I bet he'd tell you exactly the same as I have. Then he'd kiss you, and tell you you're being daft.' There was a single tear track running from each duct, en route to my chin, by the time Dad had finished. He pulled me to him, kissed my forehead and said, 'Now, you're being daft.'

'Talk to him, why don't you?' Mum added. 'Rowan that is, not your dad. He'll be bawling his eyes out when we're home later; there'll be no talking to him after this. But talk to Rowan? I'm sure if you told him this business about other people, experiencing more ... whatever it is you think you both need to be experiencing, he'll tell you things are just fine as they are.' Every strike of reassurance felt like a blow to my belly. He could tell me no such thing, I wanted to say, because this was his bloody suggestion! 'Oh.' Something behind me caught her attention. 'Thank you.'

Mum leaned away from the table to make room for the waitress, who was balancing ridiculous amounts of food on each forearm. When everything was down in front of the right place setting, she turned to me and pulled a napkin out of the small apron that was fixed around her waist.

'I saw you across the room.' She handed it to me. 'Don't think me rude, honey, but in my line of work I see a lot of girls crying and let me tell you, whoever he is, he's probably not worth it …'

Chapter 12

Rowan met me from work and we walked back to mine together. It had always been the scene for our biggest discussions, for the sake of privacy, I guessed. But I wondered whether his friends knew about this suggestion of his. *Christ,* it occurred to me as we rounded the corner to my street, *did they encourage him?* He went in two distinct and different directions with the apologies – implying remorse – and the justifications – implying nothing like remorse or regret. By the time I was putting the key in the door, I had no idea whether Rowan was taking back his suggestion or trying to add further support to it. I listened to the next round of speeches, though, while I filled the kettle and set it to boil. Then I leaned back against the work surface and watched him yammer until he came up for breath. Which he eventually did when the kettle clicked off.

'It would have to be something we were both comfortable with,' he said. Which seemed to me one of the daftest comments for anyone to have made during a discussion where the other person – me in this scenario – was so blatantly not comfortable with it. I bit back on speaking, still, while I added water to teabags. When Rowan came to stand behind me, though, and he wrapped his arms around my waist, I jumped so much that boiling water leapt over the side of his mug. 'I'm sorry.' He pulled back and reached for a towel. 'I'm so sorry, Edi, are you okay?'

No. No, I don't think I am. I nodded all the same and quietly cleaned up his mess, before I slid the mug across the counter to him. See, it didn't matter whether he wanted it *now*; he'd wanted it *then*, when he'd suggested it, and that was enough to cause a clump of something sordid and hard-edged in the pit of my stomach. I pulled in a big breath like I was about to launch into a speech but then swigged my tea instead.

'Edi, have I totally fucked this?'

The question shocked me. But so did my answer. 'I hope not.' When I looked up at him, then, I realised he was about to cry, and I couldn't remember a time before when I'd seen him moved to actual tears. This was the man who, when his own grandmother died, had said what a good innings she'd had anyway! Meanwhile, I'd sobbed along with his cow-bag mother. 'The thing is,' I started to explain, without fully knowing yet what explanation it was I was about to fling at him, 'even if we don't do this, like, even if I say, actually Rowan, the thought of you fucking around with other women makes me wildly uncomfortable …' And that was it, it was out there. I'd thrown the words into the air between us and, as though breaking a charm that came from hearing it from other people, hearing it from myself hurt a fraction more.

He opened his mouth to speak and I held a finger up to pause him. 'Even if I tell you it makes me uncomfortable, I'm always going to know that a little bit of you wanted this. Maybe not even a massive bit of you. But … I don't know, a chunk of the I-Love-Edi in you must have broken away, at least, to wonder what other women are like.' He looked deeply ashamed and I wanted to comfort him. I hated that. 'Now, if I say, sure, let's do it, I have to deal with you sleeping with other women. And if I say, hell no, are you crazy, I just have to deal with knowing you *wanted* to sleep with other women. *And!*' I felt as though something had been uncorked. 'The other variable, I say no, and you do it, anyway.'

'Edi, I wouldn't do th—'

'What, again?' The colour slipped from his face. I opened my mouth, as though I could suck the words back in, but I swiftly realised I didn't even want to. Instead, I added, 'You have to go into this with eyes open, Rowan, you know that?'

His shame shifted to worry. 'What do you mean?'

'If you're fucking around, then I'm fucking around too.' I managed to muster a tone that implied much more confidence than I felt. 'And if one of us meets someone else, the other is just going to have to accept that it's happened, and that it's a risk we took.'

'Edi, we won't meet someone else.'

'You're sure of that?'

He nodded. 'One hundred per cent sure.'

Then why are we doing this? 'Well, I hope you're right. But the venue deposit is refundable?'

'I mean …' There was a long beat of silence. 'I guess, sure, partly refundable.'

'Christ.' I rubbed at my forehead. 'Why did you even book it?' Before he tried to explain, I started again, 'Whatever, it's part-refundable, so it'll all work out. I'd say we need some ground rules, though, before we start.' I pulled a notepad out of the junk drawer in the kitchen and then searched through my handbag to find a pen. 'Right.' I sat down at the table and clicked the biro to life. 'First of all, are we having sex or are things limited to sexual contact …'

*

Rowan tried to act normal in the days after, but it was hard. I couldn't stop thinking I'd made a massive mistake. 'He's the one who's made the fucking mistake, Edi,' Betty snapped, when I shared the worry with her – but I was dangerously close to telling Rowan that I took back any permissions I'd given him during our talk. Still, it felt like going back on a spit-shake after the deal was in motion, and I remembered enough of the playground politics to know that was bad form. So, I kept a healthy distance from him – which was a strange thing to do while I was still wearing the engagement ring, which had somehow lost its shine already.

On the Saturday of our first weekend together but not, Rowan asked whether I wanted to have dinner. He called, rather than texting, which made me think he must be nervous of asking. He'd always hated waiting for a response to things he was nervous about; phone calls were much more immediate. Still, I'd lied and told him I had plans with the girls for the afternoon and it would probably spill into the evening.

'Are you going out?' he asked, and I couldn't decide whether he had a right to know. Despite having drawn up a sexually explicit guidebook, the simple feelings of the matter were turning out to be more complicated.

'No, we're having a night in. I think I mentioned it a couple of weeks ago?' I lied, knowing he wouldn't remember either way, so he'd likely just agree. I hurried him off the call after that, knocked my phone into airplane mode and headed for the door. I wasn't seeing the girls; I wasn't seeing anyone, and I had designs on keeping it that way.

Instead, I navigated my way through the city and enjoyed the sensation of being lost in the bustle of people. The place was loud enough to forget your problems, but they caught up to me soon enough when I bumped into none other than Hamish – 'Hey Edi, look at you! Glowing. Engagement suits you' – and I needed something to counteract the blunt force of his throwaway comment. The nearest sanctuary I came to was the city centre's museum and I ducked in, reasoning it would at least be quiet. I had to walk past the café to get to the main entrance of the portrait gallery – but I didn't quite make it that far. The stench of sweet cinnamon and steamed coffee caught me by surprise and, led by my stomach, I decided that the four-hundred-year-old paintings were probably okay to leave for an hour longer.

'What'll it be?' the young lad behind the counter asked. He was spotty and toothy and altogether geeky, and I thought back to a time when one of the popular girls would have probably described Rowan in exactly the same way.

'Flat white and a toasted cinnamon ...' I pointed. 'Whatever that is.'

He laughed. 'Sure thing. Someone will bring that over.'

I found the quietest corner by a window, so there were distractions close by. But in a bid to be brave, I pulled my notebook out of my backpack. I skipped past the first three pages, to avoid the bulk of rules that Rowan and I had come up with. I knew them by heart now; I hardly needed a copy. So, I flicked to a clean page halfway through the pad instead. At the top of the page I wrote 'Ways to meet people' and then I wrote the number one and then I put the pen down, and looked around the busy space. It had never crossed my mind that people who didn't find their soulmates at an early age might have to actively look for them. *The poor bastards.* I looked out of the window, then. *How many of you haven't found them yet?* Alongside the first bullet point I wrote 'through friends', then followed that with a second: 'through work'. The bullet points after were populated by 'blind date', 'speed dating' and 'online dating', the latter of which sent a cold chill running over me. I'd watched enough *Catfish* episodes to know what a terrible idea Tinder could be. How Faith did it so often was beyond me.

'Where do people even meet each other?' I said to no one at all while I looked back through the window.

'Ah,' came the beginnings of an answer, 'your order.'

My head snapped round, and I caught sight of the waitress. She was my age, I thought, maybe a little older. Her hair was a deep brown, tied up in a stylishly messy bun that was balanced in a gravity-defying way on her head. She had a cup and saucer in one hand and a plate in the other.

'I'm so sorry.' I pulled my notebook back to make space. 'Researching something.'

She laughed as she set down the items. 'So I see. Will that be everything?'

'Yes, thank you, that looks great.' I tried to avoid eye contact but the only other place to look was down at the list, and I wasn't keen on seeing that either. 'Thanks again.'

'You're welcome.' She dropped a slip of paper onto the table. 'That's your ticket, so just take that up when you're ready to pay.' She made to walk off but then turned back to me. 'At a museum.'

'I'm sorry?' I looked up in time to catch her nod to the paper in front of me.

'Places to meet people. At a museum.'

Chapter 13

'I mean, that's definitely flirting, right? Did she flirt?'

Everyone's eyes shifted to Faith, who was too busy scrolling through the dating app, Plenty of Fish, to notice. She looked up when the silence stretched out longer than it took for her to type a message. 'What?'

'You're the resident homosexual,' Lily said, looking at Faith between applying dabs of foundation. 'This is when you translate.'

'Fucking hell, we don't have a code.'

'But was that flirting?' I pushed.

'Yes.' She went back to typing. 'I'd certainly take it as flirting.'

'That's the first time someone has flirted with me in years.'

'Edi—' Betty cosied up to me '—that's bollocks.'

'What Betty means to say is that it isn't the first time someone's flirted with you,' Cora said, taking a softer approach. She and Molly had become the bumper friends since I'd decided on this break; the ones at the sides of the aisles, keeping me on some kind of track. 'It's only the first time you've noticed someone flirting with you. Different things.'

Faith reached over to squeeze my knee. 'I actually flirt with you all the time, you just don't spot it. Now put some make-up on – you're coming out.'

The girls had spent the entire week trying to convince me to have a night out with them. But I wasn't exactly invested. Rowan and I had had dinner three times; once we went out and twice he cooked. I couldn't place the last time he'd made a meal for me before that. It had left me wondering whether he already had regrets about the break and, while I wasn't exactly sitting around waiting for the phone to ring, I didn't want to miss a call from him either.

'You don't think he's out tonight?' Lily asked.

'He isn't. I asked him.' But I caught a look between Cora and Molly and it was impossible not to ask, 'What?'

'Tell her,' Cora encouraged.

Molly rubbed at her neck, tipped her head back, and spoke to the ceiling. 'He is out.' When I didn't answer, Molly held her stare upward and carried on. 'Patrick told me that he wanted to see me tonight but they'd all promised Rowan a night out, and he was really looking forward to it, so they've made plans to go out for dinner and then they're going to hit the clubs after and—'

'Moll, you can stop now,' Betty interrupted. 'I think that's quite enough fuck-wittery for Edi to be getting along with.'

'Quid pro quo, Edi.' Lily pulled a cigarette from her packet and opened the window. 'If you're giving him permission to go out, why aren't you going out?'

'You know she means business when she breaks out Latin.' Faith dropped her phone, then, picked up her make-up bag and threw it into my lap. 'Suit up, Parcell. You're coming.'

*

The music was so loud in the club that I could feel the thrum of it moving through my whole body. Betty, Lily, Cora and Molly were dancing in perfect time to each other, and I wondered whether this was a night-out ritual that they'd patched together – whether it would somehow summon a man, or repel them all, depending on the mood the girls were in. Meanwhile, Faith was two strides away at the end of the bar talking to a woman who she seemed to know already. It wasn't like this was my first night out in years. I'd been out with the girls more times than I could remember. *In this very club,* I thought, taking another glance around the room. But somehow – minus the engagement ring that Lily had confiscated when we were on our way out the door – the entire experience felt different, and I couldn't find a way to enjoy it. For the third or fourth time – *or fifth* – I pulled my phone out to check whether there was a message from Rowan. Nothing. I clicked into WhatsApp and saw that he was online, though, and I wondered who he was even talking to at this time of night and if—

'Babes!' Lily shouted over the bassline. 'Dance with me.' She didn't wait for an answer. Instead, she snatched my phone away and stashed it in her back pocket before taking each of my hands in each of hers and guiding me to the dance floor with her.

'Lily …'

'Edi, you're beautiful and bright and brilliant. I will not let you stand there and feel bad about yourself.' She started to move me in gentle time to the music. 'Feel your way through it, Edi, because you deserve to be here and you deserve to be enjoying this.'

'What are you, a motivational speaker?' Betty shouted, bumping her hips against Lily's. As Lily bumped back, Demi Lovato's 'Sorry Not Sorry' burst through the speakers, and I doubled over with laugher.

'Now, if that isn't a fucking sign,' Lily shouted.

'All right, folks,' the drag-queen maestro came through the speakers. 'We've got a special request tonight for Edi. Edi, baby girl, don't you feel sorry in the slightest. You do you, honey.'

Betty wrapped an arm around my shoulders and gaze me a squeeze. 'From me to you, babe.' She moved away from me, then, an arm's distance away, and she offered her hand out. 'Edith Parcell, may I have this dance?'

It still didn't feel quite right. But I was getting there. Cora and Molly danced around us and we became a gaggle of laughing, twerking twenty-somethings, making noises that emulated flocks I'd seen and heard on the Discovery Channel. Midway through the song we attracted a round of unwanted attention from two men – Rowan's age, I guessed – and then, as though sensing a fellow female in distress, Faith appeared. She danced one of them to one side of the dance floor and cupped her hand around his ear to speak to him. He shrugged, then, called his friend away and disappeared.

'What did you say?' I asked as she came to jig next to me.

She winked. 'Magic.'

The rest of the song – the rest of the night – played out in peace. But once the clock had chimed for the early hours, and I'd finally wrestled my phone back into my own clutches, I decided I should maybe go home on a high note. Lily and Betty took themselves into the smoking area with the promise of bringing back someone interesting – 'I don't even want to know what that means,' Faith shouted back – and Cora and Molly teamed up for a bathroom break. Faith and I found a quiet booth to settle down in, and when we'd escaped the immediate vibrations of Little Mix's 'Salute', I told her that I thought I was done for the night.

'Okay.' She grabbed her phone from the table. 'Food?'

'Oh, no, you don't have to come, Faith, really. Stay, have a good time. What happened to your friend from earlier?'

She nodded to the bar. 'She's on the late shift. I'll catch her another time. Besides, I'm wrecked from the dancing and my body deserves nourishment. You know, to counteract all the vodka. Unless you genuinely want to be alone? Which is also totally okay.'

I couldn't remember the last time so many decisions had been totally up to me. And in that moment it was much harder than it should have been to decide whether I actually wanted to stay or leave. *But no,* I thought, *a high note is what I want.*

I nodded. 'I'm done, really. But I'd like the company?'

'Chips?'

'Chips.' When I stood up Faith moved with me, and looped an arm through mine as we headed to the exit of the club. 'Shouldn't we tell the girls?'

She laughed. 'When Lil and Bett head to the smoking area for something interesting, in my experience, it's usually best not to be here when they get back. They'll think we got lucky.'

I thought of the efforts they'd all gone to, to make the night easier, and I gave Faith's arm a quick squeeze. 'I think I did get lucky, actually …'

Chapter 14

Faith and I were sat up in bed and on our second cup of tea when my mobile hummed on the bedside table. She got to it before I did and handed it over, and even that struck a strange chord. *Rowan would have looked.*

I hit answer then speakerphone. 'Morning, Betty.'

'Who did you go home with last night?' she asked without missing a beat. She sounded rough with cigarette smoke and singing.

Faith laughed. 'Morning, Betty.'

'Oh.' She spoke away from the phone, then. 'Nah, she took Faith home ... Not like that, you filthy-minded sod.'

'Lily, is that?' I asked.

Betty spoke into the phone again. 'How did you guess? This silly cow rocks up at mine at the arse end of sunrise because she's managed to lose her keys. It's a good job I was awake, isn't it?'

'Wait, why were you ...' Faith started but petered out. 'Actually, I don't what to know.'

'I was seeing someone out.'

'He was cute!'

'Lily says he was cute.'

'Oh, don't worry,' Faith answered, 'we heard her. Wait, why was Lily up at ... Actually, I still don't want to know.'

'What are you two doing today?' Betty asked, then.

Faith and I swapped a look. We hadn't talked about what we'd do past having a third cup of tea, and maybe going to the café across the road to get egg sandwiches. But if Betty was asking then she likely had something in mind. *It can't be anything too bad, though,* I thought, *it's a bloody Sunday after all.* Faith wrestled my near-empty mug away from me and slipped out of bed to replenish it.

'We haven't really made plans. I don't—'

'Cool, we'll be over in a bit.'

She hit the call end before I could answer. While Faith wasn't around to see, I clicked into WhatsApp again to check for signs of life from Rowan. He'd texted me in the early hours of the morning, long after I'd passed out with my face pressed into Faith's back, to say he missed me and he hoped I was okay. I replied first thing – *I miss you. Did you go out last night?* – but the double-tick hadn't changed colour yet.

*

Faith had been explaining the intricacies of online dating for nearly an hour. In the end, Lily suggested setting up multiple accounts rather than choosing just the one platform. But Faith cautioned against it – 'That's a lot of pressure for a beginner' – so they opted for Plenty of Fish. Tinder was, apparently, universally known for hook-ups and nothing more and they decided between themselves that that, too, was likely too much pressure for someone who didn't know what they were doing – their words, not mine, but they weren't wrong. When they started to ferret through my Facebook profile pictures to try to find something recent that didn't feature Rowan I felt moved to step in.

'Isn't this something I should be a part of?'

Betty snorted. 'Yeah, okay.' There was a long silence, at the end of which she looked up at me from her phone. 'Oh, God,

78

you're being serious. I'm sorry, Edi, I – well, sure, absolutely, you should be a part of this.' She handed me her phone and shifted to stand behind me so she could watch over my shoulder as I typed in details. Faith and Lily took up residence either side of her. *Edi's Angels.* I would have laughed at the idea if it hadn't felt so tragic. 'Okay, we've input your email address and all the rest of it already, so if you hit that button,' she pointed, 'then you can start building your profile.'

I followed instructions, and there appeared a drop-down menu asking: *What are you here for?*

'Casual hook-ups,' Lily answered without a pause and I craned around to look at her. 'I'm sorry, were you looking for a deep and meaningful connection to go with your future husband?'

'She's got a point,' Betty added. 'If this thing with Rowan is a temporary agreement, you won't exactly be dating anyone with a mind to make it into something serious.'

I rubbed at my forehead. 'This is too hard.' And I didn't like Betty's use of *if.*

Faith dropped on her knees so she could sit level with me. 'It doesn't need to be. We're literally only doing this to show you different ways of meeting people. So, put that you're looking to meet new people, and then also tick that you're open to dating. If you get a casual hook-up, great; if you meet someone who treats you better than Rowan, even better.' I turned to throw her a look, but she winked at me, as though trying to soften the blow. 'Does that help?'

Again, I followed instructions and waited for the next screen to appear. 'I think so.' But then the next question posed an even harder dilemma: What are you interested in?

'Edi?'

I looked around. I wasn't sure whether it was Lily or Betty trying to get my attention.

'You okay, babe?' Lily set a hand on my shoulder. 'We lost you there.'

'No, no, I'm fine,' I lied. 'It's just, I – I mean, didn't I already answer this?'

'No, babes,' Betty took over, 'before it was what you're interested in, like casual hook-ups, now it's what you're interested in, like boys or girls.'

'Or non-binary,' Lily added.

'Yep, or that.'

'I …' I didn't know why it was so hard. Boys, obviously. *Obviously?*

'Unless you feel like *really* pushing the boat out with this whole open relationship thing—' Lily squeezed my shoulder '—in which case click *all* and move on.'

'I love that you realise that sleeping with women is such a fucking delight that it can be considered as pushing the boat out.' Faith looked over my head to Lily, who laughed.

'I mean, I don't have first-hand experience. But you seem really happy with it.'

'I personally have zero complaints.' Faith squeezed my knee. 'Boys is fine, too, though.'

'Okay, boys,' I said, as I clicked the option. 'Yep, boys.' The next screen appeared, just like before, and the conversation moved on to what I was interested in, meaning hobbies. Lily and Betty argued over my head – 'She likes reading … Is that an interest?' – and Faith lowered her voice to talk to me.

'Are you okay, Edi?'

I flashed a tight smile. 'I think so?'

'There'll be women on there, you know.'

'I'm sorry?'

'Women. Even though you hit men, there'll be women. It's this weird thing that happens with online dating. You get it a lot when you hit the women for women option. Blokes will have set up a "lesbian account" but with their actual photo, like the sight of some middle-aged hairline leaning in front of a sunset is going to make or break someone's sexual preference. But I've heard that women do it, too, on women seeking men accounts. So, you might match with women.' I don't know what my face did, but she felt the need to build on her explanation. 'I'm just saying when you start looking you might come across women. Like, it can happen.'

I nodded along like I understood, and on the surface I did. But I wondered what Faith was implying. Like a heavy-handed doctor testing reflexes, her comments catapulted me back to my teenage bedroom. The place-memory was alive with the smell of Impulse and breath mints, swallowed and sprayed at leisure after all the crafty cigarettes smoked out of my bedroom window. I could remember the pink walls, the grease of the Blu-Tack stains that just wouldn't come out, no matter how hard Dad and I had tried with them. Then I remembered the window seat, where I'd been when I kissed—

'Reading, dinners out, and watching romantic comedies,' Betty announced.

Faith rolled her eyes. 'What?'

'My interests. They're trying to decide on my interests.'

'Novel concept, ladies, but we could just ask Edi what she's interested in.' Faith stood up and groaned as she moved. 'Shit, I'm old. Tea?'

'Tea.' Lily was the first to answer. 'I'll help.'

Their chatter trailed out of the room as they disappeared, leaving Betty and I behind to tick boxes and tell lies – 'Put that you're interested in the gym.' I added details as quickly as she could come up with them, but I still couldn't get my own head out of the drop-down menus – and why they'd been so hard to find answers for …

Chapter 15

Before

'Should I tell Rowan?' I could feel the heat of panic spreading up my chest and towards my neck. If I'd looked in a mirror, I was sure I would have been greeted with the blotched skin of a bad reaction. Only I couldn't look in a mirror on account of not being able to stand the sight of myself. 'I really think I should tell him.'

A fourteen-year-old Faith was perched on the edge of my bed. She ran a hand through her hair and sighed. 'I don't think you need to do that.'

'But we kissed.'

'I was there, you know.' She laughed but she sounded sad, even as she was trying to smile. 'Look, Edi, you're with Rowan and you're straight and now you know what it's like to kiss a girl. So, what more is there to say? You tell him and it'll cause – well, fuck knows. Maybe you'll lose him.'

I was sitting on the window seat in my childhood room, trying to work out how it had happened. One minute we were on my floor making notes for an English presentation. Then the snow started. We stood and watched until an hour had rolled by, maybe more. Betty and Rowan had texted us both during that time and we'd ignored it. I'd even put my phone on silent – 'They're so needy sometimes.' – and we'd laughed about it all. We later saw that they were texting us to check that we were okay – just in case we didn't feel bad enough already. But into the second hour of standing there there'd been a flurry, and Faith had leaned over to point at a dog in the distance and—

'Edi, it doesn't matter how it happened. It's just one of those things.'

'But I cheated.'

She laughed, but it was a curt noise – like she maybe thought I was being an idiot. 'Shut up, you did not cheat. It was a single kiss.' But we both knew that was a lie; it certainly wasn't one kiss. 'We kissed and it didn't mean anything.' *Oh and there's another fib*, I thought, *unless it didn't mean something to you ...* 'You don't have to tell Rowan. You don't have to tell anyone. Over time it'll just—' she made her hand into a flying object '—drift away and be forgotten.'

'I'm not a bad person?'

She stood up. She didn't ask for a hug, but she held her arms out to offer one and I closed the gap between us. 'Edith Parcell, you are one of the nicest people I know in the world and you always have been. This doesn't make you a bad person or girlfriend.' She moved away and held me at arm's length. 'Take comfort in this: if you and Rowan don't last, this really will never matter.'

'Do you think we won't last?' I hurried the question out in a panic.

'Hypotheticals, Edi, it's all hypotheticals. Here's another for you: if you do last, all the nice things you'll do—'

'It won't make up for it, Faith. Nothing will ever make up for this.'

She hugged me close again. 'Well, we'll see. But you're definitely not a bad person.'

'And …' I hesitated. 'Am I still straight?'

She laughed harder, and I felt the judder of her body go through mine. But she didn't answer.

Chapter 16

Now

I was wearing clothes reserved for date nights – 'And this *is* a date night,' Cora reminded me – but they felt ill-fitting. Although, the longer I waited for NiceGuy2022 – or Jeremy – to arrive, the more I realised that it was the entire experience that didn't feel like a right fit. Jeremy had been the second person to message me on Plenty of Fish; the first man to message turned out to be someone Lily had slept with and ghosted already. 'Why did you ghost him?' Betty had asked, while she skimmed through the man's profile, but Lily only waved the question away. Then Jeremy had messaged – 'Absolutely not a nice guy, don't believe that username,' Faith narrated, as the voice of online dating experience – but we'd got on well enough for me to agree to coffee.

'You could suggest dinner,' Molly piped up, after an hour of stoic silence. She was as on the fence about me dating as I was. But these opportunities were sent to try us.

'Don't suggest dinner.' Betty flat-out refused to budge. 'Terrible idea.'

I dropped my phone like it was burning my hand; as though

I might accidentally type a message suggesting the world's most romantic dinner while Betty was trying to explain why I shouldn't. 'Any advances on why it's a bad idea?'

Faith opened her mouth to answer but Lily beat her to the punch. 'Power dynamic.'

'Absolutely not what she was thinking,' Cora said.

'No, no,' Betty weighed in, 'it was.'

'Hello?' I was holding my phone again by then. 'Do I want to go for coffee or not?'

'Yes!' Faith, Cora, Lily and Betty answered like a chorus.

'Molly?' She turned to face me. 'Do I have your approval?'

Molly came to stand behind me, then, and draped her arms around my shoulders. 'No. But that doesn't mean I don't support you, and it doesn't mean you shouldn't do it.' She kissed the top of my head. 'I'm just in an adjustment period with this whole thing.'

'Well—' Betty snatched the phone from me '—imagine how Edi must be feeling.' Molly looked scorned, and when Betty didn't apologise I wondered whether that had been her intention. 'He's offering coffee at four o'clock on a Saturday. I say go for it, but don't suggest dinner, and definitely don't ask him what his plans are for later.'

'Why shouldn't I ask …' I petered out. 'Do you know what? I won't ask. It's fine.'

The girls assembled to get me date-ready. And their bags of magic tricks had worked wonders because Jeremy's eyes lit up when he saw me – like Lily, when she spots a buffet sign. I shifted awkwardly in my own skin while he looked me up and down. 'Edi, right?' He held out a hand, which I nervously took. 'NiceGu— I mean …' he laughed '… Jeremy.'

'It's so nice to meet you,' I lied and flashed him my best toothy grin.

'Great smile.' He flashed his own and I felt like I'd started a competition in something. He held the door open to the coffee shop for me. 'I have to say, I'm a little relieved that you are who you said you are.' When he followed in behind me I found that I was unexpectedly self-conscious of my own arse. 'You said you're new to the online dating thing? But let me tell you, the number of women I've met who aren't *anything* at all like their pictures is … shocking, genuinely shocking.'

I tried to make sympathetic noises, which was a tricky thing to do when I'd just then realised that Jeremy absolutely was not the six-two build he promised women online he was. 'I think everyone lies a tiny bit on these things, don't they?' We shuffled into a booth at the back of the shop. Although to call the place *just* a coffee shop was a gross disservice to the proprietors who'd tried to make it coffee-shop-meets-sexy with leather seats and low-lit lighting. 'I've never been here before,' I said, taking another look round.

'I bring all my dates here.'

I searched his face to see whether he was joking but there were no signs of it. 'All of us?'

'Mm, not true actually. If the woman suggests going somewhere else, I'll go in for it. But if I've got a free hand, we'll come here.' He took a glance around, then, but soon looked back at me. 'It's good to have a safe space where you know the coffee will be good even if the company isn't, am I right? Although I do realise I'm making myself sound like I date *a lot* which I probably don't, not really.'

'Okay.' I desperately wanted to steer the topic away from dating. Desperately. But—

'You really are beautiful, you know? You have the prettiest face.' The compliment landed with a thud between us and I physically distanced myself from him; suddenly the table space wasn't enough. 'I know looks aren't everything but …' *Dear God, Jeremy, stop talking.* '… don't you think?' I didn't think anything because by then I'd *totally* zoned out, but I nodded all the same. 'Utter ugly Bettys some of them.'

I forced a laugh. 'I have a best friend called Betty and she hates that expression.'

He stared back blankly. Then, as though remembering why we were there, he asked, 'Coffee? What'll it be, flat white? Lemme guess, some kind of non-dairy milk, too?' Jeremy narrowed his eyes and pulled his head back in an expression of appraisal. I wondered whether he'd mark me with a red dot in the corner or a sticker saying SOLD if he liked me enough. 'Oat milk? Flat white with oat milk, right?'

Wrong. 'Perfect.'

I hadn't tried anywhere near hard enough with him yet to panic-text the group chat with an SOS. But things were weird enough for me to send them an update. When Jeremy disappeared to order the drink I didn't want, I pulled my phone out and saw that the girls had beat me to it. There was a string of messages – *I love you and I believe you can do this*, from Molly; *If he gets fresh tell him you're still on antibiotics, works every time*, from Cora; *Betty and I have got you dates into next week lined up. Love you. Don't hate us*, from Lily – and two messages on Plenty of Fish. I took a cautious glance at the counter where Jeremy was talking to the server still, and decided I'd got the time. The first was a short and pointless message from a spammy-looking username – *Hi pretty* – and the second was—

'Oh my fuck.' A penis. An actual penis. I didn't just drop my phone; I slammed it down and pushed it away, as though STDs might be contractable through digital contact. I wanted the offending genitalia as far away from me as I could get it. Which left me open to another problem.

'Oh.' Jeremy's eyes stretched when he saw the screen. He was standing at the end of the table, a red rose in hand. 'Oh, I see.'

'That's not mine,' I hurried to say. 'I mean, it's not *mine*.'

He laughed. 'Well, that would have been a first for me from an online date, I have to say.' He handed me the rose, which I took feeling both like I didn't deserve *or* want it because, *eurgh, isn't this a cheese-fest? Where did it even come from?* 'You said on your profile that you're looking for casual stuff, Edi,' he said as he sat down opposite me. 'I'm not exactly surprised that you've got other stuff lined up. If it makes you feel better ... Oh.' He paused as the server brought our drinks over; he placed my flat white down and I thanked him, but Jeremy said nothing when his own iced coffee – extra cream, extra syrup, I noticed – was seated on the table. That ignorance was a tick against him.

'Thank you,' I made a point of saying again as the server left and Jeremy shook his head lightly and stared, as though it was a strange thing for me to have done.

'Like I was saying, if it makes you feel better, I've got a date lined up for when we're done here, too.' He sipped his drink and smiled. 'That said, I'd rather not see ...'

It was only then that I realised I'd left the offending appendage lit up on the table between us. 'Oh fuck.' I grabbed it, back-clicked then cradled my forehead, 'I'm so sorry.' When I'd stashed the phone out of sight on my lap, though, I couldn't help but swing back to Jeremy and his not-so reassurances. 'I'm sorry, did you say you've got a date after this?'

'I do. Down the road, in fact. Do you know the restaurant Bel—' I don't know what face I made but it stopped him in his tracks. 'Is it weird that I have a date after this?'

Yes. 'I thought you said you brought all your dates here?'

'Oh, she's a second date. It's always a restaurant for the second date.'

'Same restaurant or ...' Jeremy obviously didn't sense the sarcasm in my voice given that he actually answered the question!

'Actually, yeah.'

'Okay.' I sipped my drink for something to do. Comedy, I decided, the moment needed more comedy. 'Well, at least I know you're not going to try to take me home on the first date.'

He raised an eyebrow. 'Let's not be hasty. Plans get cancelled all the time.'

Under the table I fumbled to unlock my phone. I'd deliberately made Faith my last call of the afternoon, so she was only two clicks away in my call log if I needed to one-ringer her. I smiled, neeeearly laughed at Jeremy's comment, then feigned a blush so I could look down and check I wasn't calling Rowan. *Because that would about round this experience off nicely,* I thought with a heavy heart. Faith called back within seconds, though, and I thought she must have been waiting on the handset. I excused myself with fake concern – 'I'm so sorry, Jeremy, I better take this real quick' – and then I made my way to the bathroom.

'Oh my God,' Faith said in a deadpan tone when I answered. 'My period is late and I'm really worried about this guy I didn't have sex with. Be a best friend and come over.' She cleared her throat, then, and added, 'Is that emergency enough?' in a more jovial tone.

'I need an airlift-level emergency, Faith. NiceGuy2022 my ass …'

Chapter 17

By the time Rowan next came over for dinner, I'd been on three dates and received approximately two million messages. Still somehow everything was painfully normal. He even went as far as to suggest sex, or close to suggesting it – 'I thought maybe I could stay over?' – and even though I said yes to the sleepover, I leaned hard against the lie that every woman tells at one time or another – 'I'm on, babe, sorry' – and suggested a film instead.

But for the whole long night while I lay awake next to him, the same thought lapped around: *Has he already slept with someone else?* That is, until the early hours of the morning, when I slipped out of bed to brew tea and find a book to bury my face in, when the thought swapped to something altogether more terrifying: *If I don't sleep with him now, will he just go out and find someone else tonight?* It was, I decided, the worst reason ever to have sex with your partner. So, when he got up, I carried on with the lie. And I said nothing about the three new messages I'd had through to my shiny new dating profile, all before breakfast time and all of which said only, 'Hi'. But at least there'd been no more dick pics.

It was a busy week for us both. He had meetings galore and I had more things than ever pencilled in with the girls, plus an after-work social gathering to battle through; a team-building exercise that HR could tick off. He suggested the weekend and I suggested waiting and seeing. He kissed my cheek – 'It's okay if you have plans with someone' – then grabbed his bag and headed for the door before I could come up with a response. I was too busy with a new thought: *Shit, did he say that because he has plans with someone?*

*

The entire public relations team – myself, Miranda, Helena, Xander, Verity and Max – were gathered together by our manager, Diane, to find out the details of our HR-sponsored treat. These things rolled around once a year and, in my experience, they'd never been anything but awkward, cringe-worthy and time-consuming. But we all made a habit of heading out for a drink afterwards which was, I thought, more of a team-building exercise than anything the higher-ups could throw at us.

'Now remember,' Diane said, envelope in hand, 'I don't know what's happening to you all this evening either.' Diane, as a senior staff member, was lumped in with other senior staff members for their own HR event rather than spending time with us, her team, which never made much sense to me. But I couldn't see how her being on our nights out would have made them any easier either. She lifted the lip of the envelope and slid out an off-white card with the details on. 'Well ...' She blinked hard twice, and my stomach flipped. 'You'll be going to the museum this evening for an after-hours life drawing class.' She said it all in one breath and someone – maybe Xander – let out a curt laugh.

I linked arms with Verity, the one work friend who I would ever voluntarily hang out with outside of work. 'Come on, then, let's see how long this'll take us to blag through.' I tried to sound cheery, all the while thinking: *Awkward, cringe-worthy and time-consuming ...*

But on the walk to the museum everyone's spirits lifted.

'It might be a laugh,' Max said.

We trudged to a side entrance and Max keyed in the door code that had been scribbled in the corner of the invitation card. The chatter continued – 'What are you doing this weekend then, folks?' – while we took off our coats and dropped our bags.

I was midway through fabricating an answer when the person who'd come to meet us – 'If you follow me around this way' – brought us to a stop outside a studio space and the words died on my lips. In the centre of the room, balanced on a wooden stool, there was the curve of a back so smooth-running I thought it might have been moulded. Our very female model was waiting for us and, as Miranda had begrudgingly predicted, she was beautiful. Her hair was a deep brown, tumbling in the loose curls that I could only ever get if the hairdresser did them for me – despite my best homemade efforts. There was a faint tattoo across her lower back, although I couldn't make out the details of it; it looked as though it had been dabbed over with foundation, though, not scarred enough to be a laser treatment. She was busy talking to another woman – older, also beautiful, with grey hair plaited and trailing over one shoulder – but they stopped when we came in.

'Evening, all,' the older woman started. 'I'm Dorothea. I'll be taking the class this evening, and from the looks on your faces I can tell you're all suitably terrified,' she joked, and we reciprocated with nervous laughter. 'This is Winifred, who'll be our model for the night.'

She turned around to introduce herself. 'You can all call me Fred.'

Or, I thought, *I could call you the waitress, from the café.*

*

Little did I know – after being told to appreciate the arch of the back and the curve of the breasts – the most embarrassing part of the evening was yet to come. When we'd all put down our weapons of choice, Dorothea announced that Fred would get her robe and then do a walk around of the room to inspect the works. From the stretch of Max's eyes, I could only guess that his output was as dreadful as my own – which I took great comfort in.

'Well, I'm about to insult this nice lady when she takes a look at this,' Xander muttered along the line of us, and that broke the tension a little further. 'But don't we all feel closer as a team?'

Helena tried to brush the charcoal from her hands. 'Yeah, closer to the pub.'

Like schoolchildren, we chuckled and giggled at our poor efforts. But when Fred reappeared – her hair now in the same messy bun she'd worn when I saw her in the café – we all fell silent and waited for the inspection. She and Dorothea started at opposite ends, meaning the tutor started with me and Fred would reach me last. Dorothea was kind though: 'There are some good shapes here, Edith.' I held on to that – *there are good shapes here, definitely good shapes* – like an affirmation while Fred worked towards me.

She burst out laughing at Miranda's sketch – 'You see me as quite abstract?' – and Miranda soon joined in the laughter, even though 'abstract' didn't sound exactly complimentary to either the artist or the subject.

'Edith, yes?' Fred held out a hand.

'Edi.'

'Fred,' she said, as we shook. 'I know you, right? You're the woman doing research?'

I was grateful for her phrasing; grateful she hadn't made me into the sad woman looking for ways to meet people – despite wearing an engagement ring. 'Ah, I knew I recognised you.'

She laughed. 'A little harder to recognise me with my clothes off?'

It was a joke. I *knew* it was a joke. And yet, my mouth became waterlogged with cotton balls and no matter the witty comeback I thought of, nothing emerged. When uncomfortable seconds had passed, Fred swapped her attention to my drawing and I followed her stare. It was how I saw her: curved and rounded and soft and—

'This is flattering,' she said, still looking at the easel. 'I like this one.'

'It isn't too abstract?'

Another laugh. 'No, Edi, it's … Well, it's quite beautiful.'

'I had a good subject.' It popped out, like a kneejerk reaction, and I was too scared to look at her to see how the comment had landed. Instead, I kept focused on my own work, and started to nod like I'd seen all the tortured artists do in low-budget films.

'I'm glad you think so.' She lowered her voice, then. 'You're researching how to meet people still?'

'I …' *Yes.* But I couldn't say it. 'I'm not really sure.'

'Well …' She dropped a hand into the coat of her robe. 'If you decide you are.' She passed me a small rectangular card, black with white writing: **Fred. Artist.** *Is that her phone number?* 'I hear life drawing classes are another great place to meet people …'

Chapter 18

I carried the card around like a lucky talisman in the days after the drawing class. I'd done it, I kept thinking, I'd met someone, organically, *and* without the girls! But did it count? Rowan and I had talked about meeting other women and men respectively; was this cheating on our deal somehow? And it wasn't until I was midway through this mess of convoluted sexual politics that I realised something even more confusing: I was actually thinking of calling her.

Since online dating had become such a hot topic, the group chat with the girls had become a stream of sordid screenshots. Faith would send the beginnings of a conversation to 'show us how it was done'. Typically, this was followed by a message from Betty or Lily or sometimes both in tandem, as though they'd synced up their bad experiences with men, only their screenshots showed penises – with a well-placed emoji to hide some of the man's modesty, not that any of them looked concerned with that in the pictures. It was the curse of being the cool girl, Betty had told me, that men didn't take you all that seriously because they thought they could do or say anything without you flipping your shit.

Only in a bullshit patriarchy landscape is any of that valid or true, Lily wrote back.

Meanwhile, I responded with my single-word screenshots – 'Hi' – and queries on what I should write back; the general consensus being nothing at all.

Over brunch one Saturday morning, Lily explained through a mouthful of pancake, 'You don't have to write back to these men, Edi. You're not obliged.' She paused to swallow. 'If they want to talk to you then they're going to have to make an effort.'

'Maybe they're nervous?' I suggested.

Betty laughed. 'The fact that I just got another unsolicited dick pic as you said that is too well-timed for words. That's the universe, that is.' She dropped the handset on the table. 'It's also enough to put a girl off her bacon.'

'I realise this is a dumb question,' I started, not knowing whether that was in fact true. 'But what's a woman meant to do with that? Like, those pictures, I mean. Do men think women will fall over themselves like a Lynx advert and go flocking to their—'

'Edi, I beg you not to finish that sentence.' Faith looked about ready to heave.

'I assume we're meant to swoon,' Lily answered, and Betty came in swift with support.

'Swoon and ask them to ping their location.'

Molly waited until both women were chewing again before she asked, 'Can I be the unpopular one and ask how things are going with Rowan at the minute?'

Lily rolled her eyes but Cora nudged her. 'It's a valid question.'

'Okay, I think?' I took a swig of orange juice to buy myself time. 'He's told me he's flirted a little and that it's been nice to have that …' I pulled in a greedy mouthful of air. Flirting is nothing, I reminded myself, because look at what I'd done already. Then, as though that early flicker of guilt weren't uncomfortable enough, I thought back to the woman's business card burning a hole in the front pocket of my backpack. 'Yeah, that's all he's said about all this, really, only that it's been nice. But that he also misses us being as close. I guess, I don't know, I think I've put some distance between us since all of this started.'

Faith squeezed my hand. 'Which is allowed.'

'No, I know. It's not exactly an organic situation, is it?'

'Babes, is there any chance at all of you letting yourself enjoy this a bit?' Betty used a softer than usual tone. 'I'm being serious now. He might miss you, there might be distance, yada yada, but if you're both going to make the most of this, you need to actively be putting yourself out there, you know? Men won't just come to you.'

'No …' I lingered over my agreement. *But women might.* 'I think I'll just see what happens, Bett. I tried the online thing and Christ, it's rough. Like, Rowan will howl with laughter when I work up to telling him about it. And I know everyone thinks I need to throw myself in that bit more, but …' From across the table I saw Lily's head snap up like a meerkat who'd spotted a keeper. 'What?'

'Nothing. Finish what you were saying?'

'Only that I'll just let it happen, that's all. I'm not forcing anything.'

'No.' Cora wiped her mouth. 'But is that what Rowan's doing?'

Lily, who had been looking behind me this entire time, dropped her gaze. She rested an elbow on the table and covered her face. Meanwhile, Faith, Betty, Molly and I all craned to look around. And there was Rowan. His housemate Monty had walked in ahead of him, holding hands with a woman I didn't recognise. He'd never been the serious dating sort, not in all the time I'd known him, but he had a smile slapped on and he was sharing laughs with the woman like they knew each other well. Rowan trailed in behind him, walking next to another woman – only next to her, admittedly – but they were suspiciously close. She was taller than me, taller than Rowan, too, and she had blonde hair that looked to have been straightened, with the occasional whisp of frizz starting to break free. She wore jeans more fitted than any I owned and a loose T-shirt that looked …

'Oh God.' It came out before I could swallow it. 'I think that's Rowan's T-shirt.'

'It doesn't mean anything,' Molly rushed out. She spoke at such a speed that I wondered whether she'd been ready with the answer since this madness started. 'Maybe she slept with Ian, or Monty, and grabbed Rowan's T-shirt for convenience.'

'Sure,' Betty agreed but her tone was flat, 'then she came for breakfast with him.'

Faith spoke quietly. 'Do you want to leave, Edi?'

Yes. 'No, no, not at all,' I lied. 'This is fine. This is what we agreed. This is …'

'Look, I'm going to be the horrible one and just point something out here.' Lily gestured behind me with her fork and moved it side to side; I imagined her shifting focus between Rowan and his squeeze. '*This* is more than flirting, I can tell you that much for free.' Molly opened her mouth to disagree but Lily only shifted the focus of her fork, then. 'I know you want to be a cheerleader for love and that's great, but Rowan is still out for breakfast with a girl wearing his shirt and *no one* is going to do that on a first date.'

Molly looked scolded. 'Being angry isn't going to fix anything.'

'I'm a woman living in the twenty-first century.' Lily speared a piece of pancake on her fork. 'It's my birthright to be angry.'

Betty clicked her fingers three times. 'Can we focus on Edi for a second? It's her fire, after all.' She lowered her voice and spoke just to me. 'What do you need, lovely Edi?'

For my Rowan to be my *Rowan again,* I thought. But I couldn't bring myself to admit it aloud to them all. Instead, I grabbed my bag and felt around for my phone. 'So, I turned off notifications because it was just buzzing at me all the live-long day, but maybe there are some messages.' I clicked into the dating app. 'And maybe we could, I don't know, do some swiping. This guy seems nice.' I thrust my phone under Lily's nose.

'Fuck-boy. Swipe left.'

'How do you even know from a picture?' Cora asked, and Lily shrugged.

'It's a gift.'

'It really is.' I noticed then that even though Betty was joining in, she was also still staring behind us, 'Lily can smell a fuck-boy from a mile away.'

'Is she gorgeous?' I didn't turn around to look. But I trusted Betty to stare for me.

'A hundred per cent would not swipe right,' Faith rushed to answer. 'I'm a better judge of these things than Betty is and let me tell you, Parcell ...' She tucked an arm around me. 'I'd swipe right on you, whatever dopey picture you had set on your profile.'

I leaned against her. 'You're being kind.'

'Honest,' Molly said, 'she's being honest.'

'Yeah, Faith's wanted to swipe right on you for as long as I've known her.' Lily threw a blueberry in her mouth and winked. 'Trust me, we've talked about it.'

'She's not wrong.' Faith was busy cutting into a poached egg, which meant I couldn't see her face. And I couldn't tell from her tone whether she was joking. Something turned over in my stomach, though, and I let the conversation carry on around me.

'What about this one?' I eventually said, extending my phone into the centre of the table.

Betty spluttered a laugh. 'Fuck-boy who I've slept with. Left. Next!'

Chapter 19

Gwen was the only person in the world, apart from the parties involved, who knew about Rowan and Skye. I'd found her through a local counselling service and, even when things had started to get better, I'd kept a foot in the door with our sessions. It was the closest I'd ever come to investing both time and money into my mental health and well-being, and it didn't seem like the right day and age to go giving that up. I called her after I'd seen Rowan with the girl who he told me he didn't really know that well – 'Just a friend of Monty's' – because of course I asked him about it. Like any woman in a misfunctioning adult relationship, I'd sheepishly sent a text in the early hours of the morning two days after I'd seen them together. He said they'd fooled around – 'But that's allowed, right?' – and that he was sorry I'd found out that way.

Since then, he'd sent four WhatsApp messages asking whether I was okay, called twice and turned up at my front door once. I'd been on my way out – to see Gwen, funnily enough – when I bumped into him on his way to me.

'I can't talk, Rowan, I'm really sorry.'

'Edi, come on. What's the rush?' He grabbed me and turned me towards him. He looked truly worried. 'Look, I'm not so sure this is okay, babe, not really. I feel like … I don't know, I feel like maybe you're just going along with this and—'

'Rowan, I said I can't talk.' Then, I said the one thing I knew would answer all his worries – with more worries. 'I've got an appointment with Gwen …'

*

It had been maybe six months since I'd last seen her. The first fifteen minutes of my appointment went to explaining that I was now engaged – and sleeping with other people. 'Well, not sleeping with other people yet but we've both got the option to, if we want to and …'

'And do you want to?' she asked gently.

I sighed. 'I don't know, Gwen, I … I thought it was a good idea, but it's just been one worry after another since it all started. Seeing Rowan with that girl, it just felt like Skye all over again except now people know about it and I have to be okay about it.'

'Why do you have to be okay about it?'

'Because …' I pushed out a deep breath. 'Because I told him this was okay.'

'And …'

'I told him this was okay because if I hadn't done, I'd spend the next two years half-planning a wedding and half-wondering whether the man I was going to marry really wanted to sleep with other women,' I said, answering a question she hadn't quite got to. 'That's why I did it, because if I hadn't, would he have cheated again? And, if I hadn't, would he spend our whole married life wondering what he'd missed out on by not screwing around more?'

'Give me a deep breath,' she said and I followed the instruction instantly. 'Then talk me through these reasons one at a time. Your first reason to agreeing to it, was that because you were worried Rowan would just wander around wanting to sleep with other women?'

I thought hard and stared out of the window. I wanted a slow-paced instrumental to kick in from somewhere so I could pretend I was the lead in a smushy romance movie – instead of the lead in what felt like a bloody cautionary tale. 'My first reason is because I was worried, am worried, have always been worried that Rowan would ... will cheat on me again.' By the end of that explanation I was speaking into my lap; I couldn't look at Gwen, or her city-scape view. 'It felt, feels like Rowan was ready to cheat again, but instead of cheating, he went ahead and just asked whether he could cheat. And I said yes, so now it isn't cheating.' There was a horrible swell building in my chest.

She narrowed her eyes and nodded. 'And how are we feeling about Rowan at the moment?'

'When I'm with him, I love him.'

'And when you aren't?'

I inhaled hard and exhaled a long stream of feeling to stop it coming out as tears. 'When I'm not, I find that I'm getting angry. Angry that he suggested it, and angry that I agreed. And I'm *still* wondering what the hell he expects to get from this.'

'I've heard a lot of wondering and thinking so far, but there's also a lot here about what Rowan wants.' She stopped then, as though she'd asked me something, and when I didn't answer she pressed on. 'What about what you want?'

'From this situation?'

'Maybe. But why don't we go a little further back than that? Let's think about the engagement. The proposal. You seemed happy when you thought about it?'

'I was – am happy about it. We've been together for so long and now it's ... I don't know, it's an official thing, isn't it? Something that let's everyone in the world know that we're in this forever.'

'And that's how you feel, like you're in this forever?'

The question felt too big for the compact room we were sitting in. I looked out of the window again, as though a blimp might float along with an answer tailing out the back end of it. Lacking that, though, I said, 'I don't know anymore.' I sank back against my chair as the admission tumbled out of me. 'This is just jitters, I do know that. It's just, all this – the messing around and the seeing what's out there, I don't know, maybe it's made me worry that Rowan isn't in this forever?'

Gwen nodded along with my self-analysis. 'But again, that's about Rowan; that's his needs, his wants. What if it turns out you're not in this forever?' She still spoke gently.

'I don't think that will happen.'

'No but humour me, what if it does? What if you waltz out of here, straight into some strapping young thing ...' I blinked away a flashback of the curve of Fred's waist. 'Dates later and you decide actually this is the person for you. It's a connection like nothing else you've ever known. Would you stay with Rowan, still, just because you'd once thought it was forever?'

'I don't ... I mean, I can't know the answer to that.'

Gwen shifted forwards in her seat and leaned over, so her forearms sat on her knees. 'Edi, relationships change and grow and evolve, all the time. In fact, it's part of being in a relationship that we allow these changes to happen. Your relationship with Rowan seems to have forked slightly and it's leaving you, understandably, in a position that you're not entirely sure how to move forwards from.'

'What are the forks?' I asked, even though I felt like I should know.

'To me, as an outsider at least, the forks seem to be that you might think about sitting Rowan down and explaining to him that maybe, despite the agreements that were made, you're not altogether comfortable with how this new situation is developing. Another thing to consider, Edi, is that you didn't set a time limit on this situation, or at least not one that you mentioned?'

'Three months,' I answered flatly. 'But, I don't know, that's a long time.'

'So, let's consider another option. What if Rowan decides to suggest an open relationship on a permanent basis?' The question stunned me; I hated her use of that phrase. But I think Gwen spotted my kneejerk panic. She reached out towards my hand but didn't quite touch me. 'It's another hypothetical. Let's concentrate on the forks that are already there for now. The second fork, then, if you decide you really can't press pause on the situation, is that you go along with it. What would happen if you put yourself out there a little? If you did what Rowan is doing, even? Would it be the worst thing in the world?'

There were hypotheticals coming at me like teenage boys at a house party and I found I was physically shaking my head at Gwen's ideas. 'I've *put myself* out there, believe me. I've had dick pics flung at me left and right; I've had coffee; I've been *ghosted* by people I haven't even seen. I …' I felt a sudden outrage at the men I'd met and not met since the girls started to tart me out online. Then I reached down under my chair and pulled out my backpack, tore Fred's business card from the front pocket and slammed it on the table between us. *Let's get it all out then,* I thought. Gwen leaned forward with a raised eyebrow to inspect it.

'Okay, tell me about Fred.'

I spoke to the windowpane. 'Fred's a woman.'

'Okay, tell me something else about Fred.'

I explained how I'd met Fred the first time, then the second time in an altogether more compromising position. Gwen asked kind questions about whether I'd felt anything like a spark, whether there were certain thoughts or feelings I couldn't shake from the encounter – encounters.

'Is it only since she gave you her card that you've been thinking about her?'

'I mean …' I thought back. *No, I'd thought about her before that, too.* 'Okay, if I'm being completely honest then yes, I thought about her before that. But she was the first person to flirt with me without an avatar and a username, and Christ, I wasn't even sure she was flirting.'

'But since you became sure, since this—' she tapped the card '—you've thought about her more?' I nodded. I couldn't bring myself to admit it out loud – although I didn't exactly know why. 'Edi, now, you don't have to answer this, but this is a safe space; I have to remind you of that. Have you ever had these sorts of thoughts or feelings about a woman before?' Again, I nodded; again, I couldn't admit it out loud. But the question sent me catapulting back to the smell of Impulse and the taste of strawberry lip balm. 'Okay. Well, that's okay, Edi. Sexuality, despite what some people think, can exist on the same sort of scale as gender. It can move, evolve in the same way our relationships do. Not everyone experiences it, no. Some people feel their sexuality is very much fixed. But some people don't. And both of those experiences and viewpoints are valid and allowed. There's nothing wrong with either lived circumstance.'

'Rowan says he could never be with a man.'

'Well, that's Rowan's narrative.' She waited for me to look up. 'What's yours?'

'I don't know what it makes me, if I call her.' I couldn't bring myself to look at Gwen. But I knew that I needed to tell someone – and I was paying £90 for the privilege of the back-to-back appointment, so I thought I should at least put my privilege to use. 'If I call her, do I stop being straight? Do I start being something else? Do I need to have a sit-down with my parents?'

'Is this something that you've considered before?' I threw her a quizzical look. 'Your sexuality: exploring it, identifying it?' The question was enough to make me look away again, but I nodded – a hearty, honest nod. 'Recently, or, let's say, in your teenage years?' I thought the question over; rolled the memories around.

'I think you can probably take out the or,' I admitted. 'It's more, and.'

'Hence the confusion you feel over Fred?'

Confusion felt like an understatement. Still, I nodded again.

106

'Do I need to start ticking a different box on equality forms? Like, is that the decision I'm *really* making here?'

Gwen let out a soft laugh. 'Edi, what are you planning on doing with the girl?'

'That depends on how the date goes.' I snorted, and Gwen laughed along with me.

'That's more like it.'

'I'm just worried, and Rowan is—'

'A grown man, who initiated this agreement. You didn't place limits on it. You certainly didn't place gender limits on it. And that isn't a criticism,' she leapt to explain, as though spotting a stir of worry in my expression, 'but if you're going to do this – explore different wants, different needs, different people – why shouldn't exploring different genders be a part of that, if that's how you want to explore your options in this time?'

I counted out the ticks of the clock until it hit half a minute. 'I don't have to tell him?'

'Did he tell you about the girl he took to breakfast?'

'Well, yeah.'

She raised a finger. 'If he told you when you asked, that isn't telling you.'

'Oh.' I sank back further in my chair. I wondered whether, before the session timed out, I might find a way to origami myself into the crack between the backrest and seat. 'What if …'

'What if you have a really good time?' Gwen smiled. 'What if you find something you really enjoy? What if you find some-thing you don't? What if …' She petered out, shrugged. 'What if anything, Edi? What if you leave here today and decide gender is fluid, sexuality is fluid, Rowan isn't for you, Rowan is all you want? Life is all about what-if questions.'

It sounded like something Lily would say; only she'd find a way to swear more. 'I should call Fred?'

Gwen squinted. 'Should is a quick route to guilt. Do you want to call her?'

The clock hand did another half cycle before I answered. 'Yes.'

'Then yes, call her. And …' She set a hand on either armrest and pushed herself upright. 'Maybe you can let me know about the date in our next session. No pressure, but you're always welcome.'

'Thank you. I …' I sighed. 'Just thank you.'

On my way out of Gwen's office building I fumbled for my phone with my free hand, while the other clung on to Fred's card for dear life. I was tapping the screen in time with my hurried steps down the stairs and, when I arrived on the pavement, I was dialling. It rang out three times before she answered.

'Good afternoon, Faith speaking. I'm pretending to work here.'

I laughed. 'Good, so you're free? I think I need some advice …'

Chapter 20

Faith said she could come over to mine after work. I told her I'd provide the refreshments, and she said that seemed a fair trade. But beyond telling her I needed advice, I hadn't given her much information about what had happened. I'd just slipped a large pepperoni into the oven when she texted to say she was outside, though, so I brushed myself down, took a deep breath and headed to the door. Faith gave me a kiss on the cheek as she walked in, with a bottle of white wine in one hand and her phone in the other. But as I moved to close the door, another body blocked it: Lily.

'Hey, babes.' Another kiss, and she followed Faith in the direction of the kitchen.

Faith had been a strategic decision when it came to selecting friends for the job of teaching me how to interact with love interests, a task I hadn't had to manage, ever. Mine and Rowan's relationship had already been cemented by the time either of us really knew what making an effort looked like. Sure, there were flowers and nights out and surprise trips away. But when it came to the intricacies of wooing someone, my knowledge started and finished at, 'Will you be my girlfriend?' which seemed a bold move given that I'd only met Fred twice. And seen her naked once.

I blinked away the memory and followed the girls. 'I didn't realise Lily was coming.'

'This one thought you might need a straight perspective,' Lily answered, as she crouched down to look through the window of the oven. 'One pizza? Boy, you really didn't think anyone else was coming.'

'I'm sorry ...' I could feel my chest flushing; I was minutes away from the red blotch of panic creeping up my neck. 'A straight perspective?'

Faith was ferreting through cupboards to find glasses. 'In case this is about a romantic issue. Ah!' She finally found the right one. 'Which I assumed it was. Wine?'

'Please.' I could have snatched the bottle from her and upended it. But I waited until there was a glass in front of me before I started to explain anything. 'So, someone gave me their number and I really need help on what to do next.' Once their low howls and giggles had abated I carried on. I could feel the heat of my chest, though, and I thought my cheeks must match in colour. 'Fred. Works at the museum. Also sometimes a model ...'

'I'm sorry, a model?' Lily leapt in.

'... and definitely a woman.'

Faith dropped her phone with a thud. 'Okay, you've got my attention.'

'Lily?' I said, worried, questioning.

'Edi?'

'Are you ... I don't know. Are you okay?'

She threw Faith a quizzical look and then glanced back at me. 'Yes, are you?' There was a long pause where no one spoke at all. Then, like a car backfiring, Lily erupted with a sharp burst of laughter. 'You were worried about telling me.'

'Well, yeah,' I admitted. Faith was a safe bet for this confession. But I hadn't known how anyone else might react. The girls had been amazing through everything in my life. A crisis of sexuality, though, I'd thought might be a crisis too far. That said, I'd been through this with Faith when she came out to me at twelve, and it wasn't like she hadn't had a prior brush of this panic with me – another memory that I had to blink hard to get rid of. Lily looked sincerely confused – hurt, even. 'I'm sorry, Lily. I …' I crossed the kitchen and ran my hand under the cold tap, before pressing that palm to my forehead, throat, chest. 'I'm sorry. I hardly feel like I'm thinking straight at the minute.'

Faith snorted. 'Probably a good thing.'

'Oh, oh,' Lily started to laugh, 'quick thinking for you.'

'Cow.' Faith picked up her phone the second it dinged. 'Score. Shallwetea25 is looking for something similar to me and she's in the local area. What about this one?'

Lily glanced over. 'That is definitely not her real picture.'

They bantered back and forth as though I wasn't standing in front of them – having a minor meltdown over my sexuality, conscience, life. And while Faith swiped left, left, right, supported by Lily's instructions and laughter and scepticism, I felt the heat move from my face to my stomach, and the sensation was altogether more comforting than the worries I'd started out with. I crossed the room and pulled them both towards me, an arm around each of them.

'I love you.'

'Oh, Parcell,' Faith spoke into my neck, 'I've waited so long—'

'Faith, she's having a moment, don't ruin it.'

I let them go but placed a palm on each of Lily's shoulders and kept her at arm's length. 'I'm sorry that I thought I couldn't tell you.'

'Oh shush.' She reached behind me to the counter and grabbed the bottle of wine. 'Tell me about Fred now, would you? What kind of model?'

I half-laughed. 'Life drawing model.'

Faith dropped her phone again. 'You've seen this woman naked?'

I hesitated. 'Yes.'

'Then what the hell do you need me for?'

I recounted the first round of flirting – 'Oh, it's *that* woman?' – and explained the life drawing class had been a happy accident, orchestrated by work. But that since Fred had given me her card, the closest I'd come to using it was wedging it between the pages of whatever book I happened to be reading. I'd typed messages, I admitted, but nothing I could bring myself to send.

'Out of curiosity,' Faith asked, when I came up for air, 'both times you've seen this woman, you've been wearing that?' She glanced at my engagement ring, and I nodded. She made a noise. 'Interesting.'

'Bad interesting?'

'I don't know. Not bad, I wouldn't say. But she must have assumed you're fair game, even though you're obviously … Hm, interesting.'

'Faith, what are you – you're killing me. What kind of interesting is it? We didn't go through this with the online dating. No one coached me; Betty just took my phone and ran with it!'

Lily tapped Faith's arm. 'Don't scare her. No, Edi, not bad interesting. It is interesting, obviously, but look.' She linked arms with me and matched my stare on the business card that sat between us all on the kitchen worktop. 'I know you and Rowan have had a certain flavour of relationship for a little while. But there are other flavours out there, you know, babes? Some people have lots of flavours on their plate at once and that suits them. Some people have a favourite flavour that they always stick with. Are you with me?'

Faith sighed. 'For the cheap seats at the back, she's trying to say this woman might not give a shit that you're engaged. Maybe she's banking on you having an open relationship.' She picked up her phone again and started to scroll. It was a miracle the woman didn't have repetitive strain injuries already. In that moment, I *hated* the open-relationship term. I'd hated it when

112

Gwen had used it, too, but I hated it even more now. That said, if it meant that …

'So, I shouldn't mention it?'

Lily deferred the question to Faith, who made a show of thinking about it. 'No. She will.'

'You're certain?'

'No, Edi, of course I'm not certain. But, if you're wearing an engagement ring, it's not like you're lying to the woman's face, is it?'

'Isn't it a lie by omission, though?' I turned and looked between them. 'Not telling someone something just because they haven't asked, doesn't mean you're not lying.'

'Christ on a cracker, Parcell.' Faith snatched the business card. 'Give me your phone.'

I'd talked myself into a corner where the only logical move I had left was to follow someone else's instructions. I passed the handset over, and let Lily top me up with wine while Faith did whatever it was she planned to do.

'Have you told Rowan?' Lily asked, her voice low, as though shielding the question.

'No. He didn't tell me about the girl – girls, who even knows. I haven't mentioned the online dates either. But I don't think, like, I can't imagine that when he suggested this, he thought this would be how it shaped up,' I explained and Lily nodded along. 'I don't know how he'll react to something like this.'

'Okay, babes. But … you do know that not knowing someone's reaction to something isn't a reason not to tell them whatever the thing is? Especially if they're your partner, actually. Like, I know you have us lot, and we're here for anything. But Rowan should also be a kind of go-to person for the big stuff.'

'You think I should tell him?'

Lily kissed my temple. 'I think you should consider telling him that you're dating people. Because I think Rowan needs to know this isn't one-sided. Whether you tell him one of the people you're dating is a woman? Well ...' Lily glanced over at Faith who was typing furiously. 'For now, though, you're in her capable hands. And you can trust Faith when it comes to dating women because she's definitely better at it than Rowan is.'

'Damn straight I am.' She handed me the phone back. 'She's on WhatsApp. She's gorgeous.'

'Lemme see.' Lily snatched at it before I could. 'Oh, Edi. You have done *well*.'

'Right? I'm a little jealous, Parcell.'

'Shut up, the pair of you,' I warned. But I couldn't keep a straight face. I grabbed the phone back from Lily and looked at the conversation screen, which had been taken over by a picture of Fred. Her hair was loose, messy but in that chic way, and she looked to be mid-laugh. Christ, I thought as I clicked into the conversation proper, I hope I can make her laugh like that. I read the text twice over – *Hi, it's Edi from the museum. Still putting together that list on where to meet people. How does Benny's sound?* – and I smiled. 'Thank you.'

'You're welcome.'

'Oh, fuck, the ticks went blue.' I dropped the phone. 'The ticks went blue.' I leaned over the worktop to look at the screen. 'She's online. She's online and she's typing.'

Faith laughed and went to the oven. 'Lil, I'm getting this pizza out. Check the fridge for more wine?'

Lily's glass was midway to her mouth but she paused and glanced at me. 'Christ, she'll need it.'

Chapter 21

Fred was fast to reply to messages, which was one of many things I liked about her. We swapped texts back and forth to arrange for a dinner date – three days on from when Faith first texted her for me – but throughout the days in between we managed to keep up conversation often, too. She would text around her shifts and her modelling, and her 'other work stuff', which I strategically side-stepped asking her about. I reasoned that, worst-case scenario, I at least had that in my back pocket for the date. We'd planned for dinner but Fred had said she was waiting to hear back about a modelling gig – *Cut-throat industry. Being naked for middle-class artists. Haha. Xx* – so we left it until the day before to pin down a time.

The day before happened to be an evening with Rowan, though, and throughout the night – while intermittently grabbing my phone to reply to the woman I hadn't stopped thinking about for days on end – I felt a new burden brought on by the whole thing. I flitted from *Christ, what are we doing …* through to *Living our best lives, that's what …* in the space of half an hour – before again shifting back and forth between the two. Eventually, though, I changed tune to *Is this right …* when Rowan excused himself to use the bathroom and my first thought was that it meant I could at least reply to Fred's message. I hadn't really been present throughout the film and a half we'd watched. But I wasn't convinced that Rowan – who'd replied to his share of messages, too – was entirely switched on either.

'Have you seen *Orange is the New Black*?' he asked, when he came back into the room.

I lifted my legs up for him to sit back down on his side of the sofa, then laid them out across his lap. 'Not that I can think of. Why?'

He shrugged and grabbed the remote. 'It's about a load of women in prison. It seems like the sort of thing you and the girls might be into.' I watched him click around the Netflix screen. 'I'm not sure I'm bothered about this second film, babe, are you?'

I couldn't tell him a single thing that had happened in it. 'Not really.' My phone buzzed and I snatched it up straight away. 'Did you want to try a series instead?'

'That prison thing has quite a few seasons, I think. Maybe five, something like that?'

I whistled. 'Are you sure we're ready for that sort of commitment?' I'd meant it as a joke. But when he didn't answer, something in me shifted. Then I remembered who it was I was texting … 'Hey, how's everything going, Row? Like, with the dating thing?' I locked my phone, to put a stopper in the text I was midway through typing. Fred had asked how I was spending the evening and, while Rowan knew that I could, potentially, be dating other people right now, I hadn't yet got to the point of explaining that to the woman I'd be dating.

He looked uncomfortable. 'Are you asking if I've been seeing people?'

'I guess? I'm more asking whether it works for you.'

He put the remote down and reached over to grab my hand. When he squeezed, I felt my fingers pinch around my engagement ring. 'I don't feel like we're as close, Edi, if I'm honest.' I opened my mouth to rush in with a reassurance, but he interrupted my words while they were still just breath. 'But I'm secure enough to know that relationships change and, I don't know, there are always going to be times where we're closer, or more distant. Right?'

I stalled. 'Right.'

'You don't seem convinced. But I just mean, we both want this time, and we're doing our best with it. If either of us felt like it wasn't working, we'd say.'

He seemed so sure that I found myself nodding along in agreement. *But is it working?* I was sitting with my feet in my fiancé's lap while I was texting another woman. *Is this what engagement does to people?* I wondered. But when Rowan let my hand go and felt around for the remote again, I took it as a sign that our conversation was closed. Still, there was one last thing I needed to push.

'Have you told me about everyone you've dated?' I asked. He'd only mentioned two girls so far. Betty had seen him out with someone last weekend and in a diplomatic way had told me they looked 'cosy'. The description she gave, though, of a redhead with a slim build, didn't match either of the women I knew about. I realised, then, that I wasn't asking him whether he'd dated anyone else. I was asking him whether he was a liar.

'Babe.' He reached over but this time with his other hand, so he could keep the remote ready. 'Of course I have. I'm not out there playing the field every weekend, Edi, just … I don't know, seeing what comes up. Like you are.'

And he *was* a liar.

I flashed a thin smile and reached for my phone.

'So,' he started, 'how are we feeling about a series? Or, if you're not in the mood for anything new, we can flit back through our watched list and … Is everything okay?'

I looked up. 'Course, why do you ask?'

'You've been on and off that thing all night. But you look all serious.' *I'm concentrating,* I thought, but decided it was something I was best off not admitting to. 'Are the girls okay?'

I shot him a look. 'I think so?'

'I assumed …' He nodded at the phone. 'Group chat?'

'Oh.' Before they'd left me, days ago, Faith and Lily had asked again whether I'd tell Rowan; I'd asked them in return whether they thought I should. Dating another woman felt a little like colouring outside the lines of our agreement. Even though nothing had been set down in the ground rules – which were by then tacked to my fridge with a photograph magnet of a more monogamous couple than we could claim to be now – to say whether we could or couldn't date people of the same sex.

'Do you think he'll be funny about it?' I'd asked them both.

Lily's lips had bunched up to one side as she'd thought it over. 'He might be into it.'

Faith was less convinced. 'A bloke like Rowan? Edi, beaut, don't think me rude, but he probably doesn't even think you're dating anyone, never mind dating a woman. Blokes like him—' she kept phrasing it that way, as though Rowan was of-a-type '—they make these suggestions with themselves in mind and I'm telling you now that it won't cross his mind that you'll do better at this than him.'

'It isn't a competition,' I'd told her and she laughed, but then Lily had weighed in.

'When it comes to men and women, babes, it's *always* a competition.'

'It actually isn't the group chat,' I answered eventually, even though my internal narrator was screaming protests against the admission. 'I'm just making some plans for the weekend.'

'Fair enough.' He turned back to the television. 'Hot date?'

If someone asked what was wrong with his question, I couldn't have explained it in a word. But it was, I thought, fractured with the beginnings of a laugh. He didn't quite smirk. The question was thrown out there with such disinterest, though, that it occurred to me Rowan – with his perfect looks and his girls lined up around the block – honestly thought he knew what my answer would be.

Not for the first time, then, it crossed my mind whether Faith was right – whether he was enjoying this partly, largely even, because he thought I wasn't doing the same as him. And in the seconds after he'd asked, while something like rage started to simmer in my stomach, I felt spite rise up like a kind of bile.

'Yep.' I deliberately waited for his head to snap around, in time to catch my smile, before I went back to typing my message. 'I don't really fancy the commitment of a series either,' I said, staring at my screen. Because unlike Rowan, I wasn't ready to be a liar.

'Who?' he asked, and I thought it might have been the first time all night that I'd had his full attention. 'Anyone I know?

It seemed a strange question. 'I mean, I'm not about to date one of your friends or colleagues.' I tried to sound jovial. The lie by omission was back in the room, though, and I was quickly trying to weigh up the possibilities for how the rest of our talk might play out from here. *It'll be your call,* I thought then, *it'll be your call and let the chips fall where they may.* 'Someone I met at a work thing,' I said, glancing down at another message. 'Fred.'

'I see.' I heard the click of the remote and then the opening hum of the *Brooklyn 99* theme tune. 'This okay?'

And that was the only question he asked for the rest of the night.

Chapter 22

I stayed on FaceTime with Faith for as long as it took for me to get ready. When I left the flat, we swapped to voice call instead.

'You look amazing, you are amazing, this will be amazing,' she said, with the conviction of an experienced yogi master chanting an affirmation. 'What do you need? Animal pictures? Wait, I must have something cute on my camera roll now … Oh, I've got a text from Lily.' She let out a curt laugh. 'She wants to know why you FaceTimed me and not her.'

'Tell her it's nothing personal.'

'I'll tell her it's because she's straight,' she said, and I could already hear the taps of the message.

'She'll hate that.'

Another laugh. 'I know.' There was a long pause while Faith finished typing. 'Sent. Now, do we have a code in place?'

'For what?'

'For if Fred the model isn't all that good on a date and you want out.'

'Faith, out of me and Fred, I find it hard to believe … Ah shit, shit I'm here and she's inside. I can see her.' I came to a stop outside the bistro where we'd agreed to meet. It was an early dinner after all, because of what turned out to be a lengthy work commitment for Fred, and Green's dining area was a sparse enough landscape for her to stick out a mile. Her hair was styled into what I thought must be her trademark messy bun, and she was wearing a button-up shirt-dress in dark denim. I wondered whether that was a practical outfit, something easy to take off for later. *Oh, Christ alive* … I swallowed hard at the thought. 'She looks amazing.'

'*You* look amazing, Parcell. Take a belly breath for me, lemme hear you.' I sucked in a greedy mouthful of air and pushed it out in a slow stream. 'Yeah, that's the shit. It sounded like a good one. Can I get another? I'll do it with you.' She matched my inhale and exhale down the phone. 'Now, shit hits the fan, and you send me literally any emoji at all, and I will call you and cry about my period. Deal?'

I laughed. 'Deal.'

'Knock her dead.'

Inside the restaurant I found Fred laughing with a waiter who looked like he might have fallen in love with her. She stood to meet me when she saw me, though, and when she pressed a kiss against my cheek the young man's face fell in disappointment.

'Can I get you a drink?' he asked me, his tone flat.

'What are you having?' I looked to Fred.

She made a questioning face. 'Edi, drink whatever you fancy.'

I tried to make a show of thinking it over when really, I had my response ready and waiting: my go-to drink for stressful situations. 'White wine, please, medium-dry, large glass.' When the waiter was out of earshot, I said, 'You look beautiful.'

She smiled. 'Thank you, you gorgeous woman, you don't look so bad yourself.'

Gorgeous. Christ, she thinks I'm gorgeous. I ignored the compliment. 'You've been here before?'

'Once or twice. How about you?'

'Nope, first time,' I admitted, 'first time for everything tonight.'

She narrowed her eyes. 'I don't think I follow … Oh, *oh*.' Her eyes spread and she cupped a hand over her mouth. Faith had told me not to tell Fred that this was my first time dating a woman, but the honesty had slipped out, as though the confession had been stuck in my teeth this whole time. When she moved her hand away, though, I was showered with relief to see she was smiling. 'Well, let me tell you, Edi, you are in for a treat.' She winked and handed me a menu. 'We're going to have an amazing time ...'

And it turned out Fred wasn't a liar.

*

Another hot topic of conversation in the group chat titled 'Let's get Edi gay-ed' – which consisted of me, Lily and Faith – was whether I would, firstly, wear my engagement ring on my date; secondly, whether I'd explain the situation. Faith and Lily had fallen on opposing sides of not telling and telling respectively. We'd all agreed on the middle ground of wearing the ring but waiting for Fred to initiate a conversation about what the ring meant – assuming I still knew. Over the course of the afternoon into early evening, though, I became more aware of my ring as a nervous tick. Whenever Fred asked something that made my cheeks flush – which seemed to be happening every ten to fifteen minutes – my right hand would reach for my left, and I'd spin the ring around one, two, three times as I answered. Worse or better still – I couldn't quite decide – I thought she'd noticed. But not said anything.

She checked her watch. 'We'd better ask for the bill.' She turned and hollered the waiter who, having watched Fred from the corner of his eye for most of our dinner, came rushing over at speed. With what I thought was a forced smile she batted away his final push at flirting with her – *I'm right here, chap, but okay* – and then gave me her full attention again. I hadn't realised I was back to spinning the ring until she reached over the table and grabbed my hand. It was our first skin-on-skin contact, and I felt like something was going to fall out the bottom of me – but in a *very* good way. She smiled. 'Do we need to talk about the ring thing?'

I hesitated. 'You're not interested?'

'In your potential spouse? No. In you? Very.' Another smile, notably less forced than the one she'd flashed the waiter, though. 'It's not lack of interest. But I'm single, I'm allowed to be here.'

I pulled in a greedy amount of air and said, 'I'm engaged. But my fiancé is worried that we rushed into the whole thing, maybe. We're together, but we're sort of seeing other people for a little while, to see what happens.'

'Fiancé with one e, I assume?'

'Yes.'

She half-laughed. 'Of course.'

'I don't think I—'

She held up a hand to pause me. 'So, just so everyone knows where they stand. I'm allowed to be here and you're also allowed to be here.' She said it with a questioning intonation at the end, so I nodded. She squeezed my hand then, before moving back to her own side of the table. I pushed down the rising want to reach out after her. 'Whereabouts do you live?'

It felt like a rapid subject change. 'Over in the Quarter.'

'Okay, then.' She stood up and grabbed her bag from under the table. 'I'll pay and then walk you back.' I opened my mouth to object to the offer but she powered on. 'Hey, if this is your first date with a woman, the least I can do is get the bill and get you home safe.' She walked away, then, before I had time to object any more. But her absence did at least give me time to get my shit together into something that made me look less like a stuttering mess. *Is this what dates with women are like?* I wondered, while I pulled on my cardigan and grabbed my own bag. 'Ready?'

'As ever.' I walked out ahead of her. When I reached for the door, though, I froze in my tracks as I felt what I thought was a light tap on my arse.

Fred cosied up behind me, then. 'You'll have to forgive that, Edi, it was more for the waiter than it was you.' She stepped around me. 'I'll get the door.'

We fell out into the street like a pair of howling teenagers on WKD for the first time. Fred apologised several times over – 'I'm a bit of a pain for things like that, Edi, I am sorry' – and she explained that when it came to heteronormativity, she couldn't help herself. And that's exactly how she phrased it. For my sins, I wondered whether Rowan even knew what heteronormativity was. *His assumption that I'm on a date with a man tonight, that's what* … and I laughed along with Fred as she continued to explain herself, only leaving me room to occasionally jump in and explain she really didn't need to.

'It was fun, being like that,' I admitted.

'Well, I'm glad. You'll get it a lot.'

I swallowed my nerves. 'Light taps on the arse?'

'If that's what you're into.'

We came to a stop outside my building and I was sincerely grateful because I had well and truly maxed out on courage for one night. 'This is where I get off.' She laughed, and it took me a beat to understand why. 'Oh! Oh, I didn't—'

She leaned in and kissed me square on the mouth. 'It's the wine. It gives me a dirty mind.' Then she put a healthier distance between us. My lips tingled – everything did – and I felt as though all the words had been drawn out of me. 'Thanks for letting me buy you dinner, and for letting me walk you home. It's been a genuine pleasure, Edi …'

'Parcell,' I filled in what I thought her blank was. Praise be to the gods that I still knew my last name. 'Thank you for tonight. It's been kind of amazing.'

She started to back away along the pavement. 'Kind of? I'll up my game for next time.'

I laughed – from nerves; from amusement; from wanting to fill the quiet. 'Take care now.'

'Text me some time if you'd like? Not in four days, though. I can't wait that long.'

'You'll be first on my list after I've told my friends that I wasn't murdered.'

Fred laughed and turned away, then, and quickened her pace along the walk back towards the main city streets. I wondered whether she'd be late for work, but she didn't strike me as the sort of woman to worry about it. I pushed into my building and ran up the stairs like a teenager on a cross-country course. By the time my key was clunking in the front door lock, I'd already pulled up a fresh message to Faith and Lily: *Home safe. She said NEXT TIME. xxx*

Chapter 23

Rowan didn't ask about the date. But he did send flowers, and suggest a cinema night, and offer to cook dinner – 'You come to me, let me spoil you' – in the days after I'd seen Fred. She and I were texting every day and it felt disloyal – but there was an unceasing sting of excitement in it all as well. I decided, then, that when I went to Rowan's for dinner I would ask the unthinkable questions: *What are we doing, and how long is it really going to last?* I appreciated his new efforts, but I was less appreciative of the fact that he was only making them because he thought I was out there, dating – in short, doing exactly what he was doing (with a woman who I knew would turn his head, which made it all the worse, or better, or both).

After our cinema date he walked me home just like Fred had, except he'd held my hand and kissed me hard and asked whether he could come up. My phone had vibrated with three new messages in my back pocket, though, and they probably weren't from the girls. 'I've got an early start,' I'd said. But we made plans to have dinner the following Monday. And that's when I'll talk to him, I thought. That's when we'll work this all out …

*

The city was always quiet on a Monday. So, instead of ordering an Uber, I walked the twenty-minute stretch from my front door to Rowan's. The boys would probably be out, I thought, given this invitation. We'd have the place to ourselves to talk and maybe – just maybe – I'd want to stay over.

The buzzer for Rowan's building was broken, again, so I walked straight in and pressed the button for the lift. The mirror at the back of the space gave me a final opportunity to look myself over. My hair didn't quite have the same lift as it had when I'd left. But city air will do that to you. Still, I smiled at my reflection and told myself for the umpteenth time that I was making an effort. I'd turned it into a mantra as though reminding myself of something. *But what?* I sighed and stepped out into the hallway, rushed along with the clicks of my heels for company, and tried to actively avoid thinking that godforsaken phrase. *At least you're making an …*

I pounded the front door with more force than it required. And Ian answered.

'Edi.' He seemed surprised. 'How's it going?'

I mirrored his shock, though. 'Ian, you're … here.'

He laughed. 'I live here.'

'Who is it?' someone shouted. But it wasn't Rowan's voice.

'It's Edi,' Ian answered, and seconds later Monty appeared behind him.

'Edi, you're—'

'Here,' I finished, and tried to laugh. 'I think we all know I'm here now.'

Monty laughed, too, but it sounded nervous. 'How come you're here?' They both shifted awkwardly. Their figures were too large for the doorway, though, and with each shift they knocked together slightly. 'Rowan isn't here,' Monty finally said. 'He's out.'

'He's …' I exhaled hard. There was a sicky feeling in my throat. 'It's our date night,' I said, and I saw their shared look of sincere panic. The realisation hit me like an early period; the shock of the stomach cramps and the horror of not having a liner, of having to walk home with your innards on your outwards and … 'Oh.'

'Edi …' Monty nudged Ian to one side. 'Fuck it, come in, would you?' He gestured me in through their doorway. 'We're making chilli, okay? Would chilli be okay? Just come in.' Monty ushered me into the living room with Ian not far behind us. When I'd landed in the centre of the sofa, Monty spoke over my head. 'She likes wine. Would you see if we've got any?'

'Should I text Rowan?'

'No,' Monty snapped. 'Actually yeah, yeah text Rowan and tell him he's a prick.' He landed next to me on the sofa and put his hand out flat, as though it were an offering. I rested my palm on top of his and he closed his fingers around mine. 'Edi, I'm sorry. He said he was going out for dinner, some girl or another. We just assumed—' Ian coughed sharply from behind us. 'Okay, whatever, *I* just assumed that you knew.'

I shook my head. 'We made plans. He told me … He was going to cook dinner.'

Ian appeared with a glass of white wine. 'It might taste like piss. But it'll do the trick.' I accepted the offering and laughed. 'And we've got chilli. Like, fucking loads of the stuff.'

My nose prickled with incoming tears, but I tried to swallow them back and laugh instead. 'As long as it's better than Rowan's cooking.'

Monty snorted. 'Roadkill is better than that. Ian, get back in the kitchen and make this woman a real meal.' Ian followed orders without another word. I realised, then, that even though I'd accepted the wine glass with one hand, I was still holding Monty's hand with the other. I went to pull away and he squeezed. 'Hey, this is okay.' Another squeeze. 'Do you want to talk about how much of an arsehole he is?'

'That depends.' I took a generous swig. 'Are you going to tell me how many women there are?' He looked uncomfortable, but he didn't flat-out refuse. 'I get it, there's a bro code and all—'

'Oh, Edi, fuck the bro code. I know what I'm about to say is going to land him in shit.'

'So there are lots of women?' I shook my head. 'Maybe not lots, but more than he's told me.'

'Given that he didn't tell you about the one tonight,' Ian answered as he reappeared with a bowl in each hand, 'I'd wager that yes, definitely more than he's told you.' He handed a bowl to each of us, then rushed back to the kitchen to get his own. 'I'll make a deal that Monty won't make, because Monty doesn't want to be the bad guy. I, on the other, don't mind being an accidental arsehole.' He paused to spoon chilli into his mouth. 'I'm going to tell you what Rowan has told us, about the women he's seeing, and about your … situation, let's say? I'm *only* going to tell you stuff that he's told us.'

I didn't catch his meaning. But Monty did. 'Ian and I have no reason to believe Rowan might have lied to you. It's not dishonourable to relay things we've been told.'

Ian tapped my knee, then, to get my attention back on him. 'Take a deep breath, okay?'

Monty made panting noises around his first mouthful of hot chilli. But he made a college effort at trying to talk, still, even if it did make him look like a nervous chimp. 'I genuinely have no idea how many women Rowan has slept with, nor how many he plans to sleep with before this is over. But I have seen an eye-watering number of women join us on nights out. Your turn.' He clicked his fingers at Ian.

'Wait.' I stopped the big reveal when something bigger caught my eye. There was something tucked out of sight behind the armchair in the corner of the room. 'What is that?' I didn't wait for them to answer. Instead, I crossed the space and ferreted about to retrieve what looked like a whiteboard that had been drawn up as a scoreboard – with Rowan's handwriting on it. There was a shaky green line that ran down the middle, creating two columns. At the top of the left-hand column it read 'Player One' and on the right—

129

'It isn't what it looks like,' Ian said.

'Good.' I turned back around to face them, still with the scoreboard in hand. 'Because it looks like a tally chart for something and I'd hate to think it had anything to do with what we're talking about right now.'

'Edi, I—'

'Monty, don't,' I stopped him. 'I don't think I'm ready for this part of the truth yet.' I looked at the board again. Player Two, whoever they were, had clusters of five tallies collected together; four lines crossed out with a fifth across the middle. I scanned the column but I didn't have the stomach to count them up. Meanwhile, Player One, whoever they were, looked to be lagging with hardly a cluster. I didn't look at either of the boys for a second longer, but I did ask, 'Can you just tell me, is one of these Rowan?' They stayed silent so I looked up in the end, just in time to see them swapping panicked expressions. 'I'm not going to ask which one of them is him.' I tried to laugh. 'I think that's the thing I'm not ready for. But, now I've seen it, I think it's important that I—'

'One of them is Rowan,' Monty announced and Ian slapped his arm. 'What?'

'The code.'

'Fuck the code. She's right in front of us!'

'I thought you didn't mind being an arsehole,' I said, aimed at Ian.

He laughed, then, and rubbed at the back of his neck. I recognised the gesture from Rowan. 'I mean, it's one thing being an accidental arsehole.'

I huffed. 'You people and your omissions.' I landed heavy, then, on the very armchair that had been shielding the board, which I let fall to the floor. My forehead felt as though I'd been on a bender with Betty and I thought how preferable that would be to this. 'Okay, you've lost track of the women coming on nights out with you. Rowan is either excelling at the sport of shagging around or—' I gestured to the board '—well, seriously falling behind. What else is there? I'm not asking anything. You're just telling me what you've assumed I know.'

'Fair is fair.' Ian tried to sound light. 'But what Monty knows is what I know. I haven't been keeping track of the women he's dating, getting to know, whatever he's calling it. He keeps saying he's in no hurry, that he's got plenty of time. But he's like a dog with two dicks, Edi, it's got to be said.'

He's in no hurry, I parroted back to myself. 'Wait, he's got plenty of time?' They swapped looks, then, as though my question had reignited their panic. 'How long has he said we're doing this for?'

'I think we need to draw a—'

'No, Monty, tell me how long.'

Chapter 24

Three days and twenty-one missed calls later, I strolled out of work to find Rowan leaning against the wall opposite my office building. There was a heavy flow of traffic between us, and I felt a stab of gratitude as car after car went by, which gave me time enough to think of a reason for not answering his calls. *Because he's behaved like an arsehole,* I decided, as I finally padded from my side of the street to his. But I couldn't bring myself to say it. I flashed a tight smile and gave him a shrug.

'Player Two has entered the game,' I said as I came to a stop opposite him.

'Did you think I'd just stop calling in the end?' he asked, leaving my comment unremarked on. I wondered whether the boys had told him the extent of our talk. I still didn't know whether he was player one or two; only that he was definitely becoming a player. And I didn't like that on him. 'Or were you just too busy with Fred to answer my calls?'

I physically recoiled at his use of her name. A stab of guilt moved through me as I thought of Rowan worrying about me with another man – who was actually another woman. But I corrected myself. *Does he look like he's feeling guilty to you?* I shook my head by way of answering my own thought, but Rowan took it to mean I was answering him. When he spoke again his tone was flat, annoyed almost.

'Edi, you can't ghost the person you're engaged to.'

'No, but I can remove myself from a situation until I'm ready to deal with it.'

He laughed. 'You sound like Lily.'

'Please.' I matched his spiteful huff with one of my own. 'Lily would have slept with Ian or, maybe even *and*, Monty, if she'd arrived for a date with you to find you were on a date with someone else already. You're on shaky ground to throw accusations my way, Rowan.' He looked genuinely taken aback and my kneejerk reaction was to fact-check what I'd said. But yes, Lily would have reacted much worse. Yes, he had behaved poorly. 'I needed time.'

'You could have told me that.'

'I thought you'd infer it, on account of me ignoring you and all.' I made to walk off. 'It's been a long day and I'm going home. Are you walking with me?'

He pushed himself away from the wall. 'Sure.' His tone was still flat and, even though it brought with it a stab of something like guilt, I thought back to Fred walking me home days before; the offer of walking her home next— 'Can we talk, then?' Rowan cut my thought off. 'About what happened, I mean.'

It was easier doing this mid-walk, I decided. I didn't have to look at his face. From experience, I knew it would break any resolve I thought I had. I pulled in a big breath. 'Is there anything you want to say, about what happened the other night?'

'I'm obviously sorry.'

'But you haven't said you're sorry.'

'Well, I am.' He stopped and pulled me to face him. The shift in movement made me wince with feeling. It had always been the most hurtful thing in the world to see him hurt. And he did look hurt. But— 'Edi, I *am*, I'm so, so sorry, because it shouldn't have happened and I should have ... Shouldn't have. I don't know.

133

I should have been keeping better track of plans and priorities and … I just need to be better.'

I frowned. 'Better at what?'

'All of this.' He gestured at nothing at all with one hand while he rubbed at the back of his neck with the other. 'All of this juggling.'

'Who was she?'

'What?'

'Who was she?'

'The girl?'

Are you stalling? I narrowed my eyes. 'Is it someone I know? Is that why you're repeating everything back to me?'

'No, babe,' he sighed. 'It's not a stalling technique. I'm just surprised, confused, maybe, I don't know why you'd need to know that.' *Maybe because you needed to know when I was the one scoring a hot date?* I wanted to point out the hypocrisy of it all, but I wasn't about to derail my own interrogation. 'Okay. Okay sure, she's a girl I met on Tinder. We said we'd go for a drink and we happened to be leaving work at the same time, and …' He rubbed at his forehead and swallowed so hard that I heard a glug in his throat. 'And I forgot that you and I had plans. I told the lads I'd be late home, that I was out for dinner, and then I went to meet the girl.' He grabbed both of my hands in his, then, and I wanted to pull away. 'It, she, all of this, it doesn't mean anything, Edi. Remember? It's just us messing around and flexing our muscles and ourselves and—'

'How many girls have there been?'

'Girls that I've dated, or like, had a date with?'

He was nervous. I recognised the sly looks to the side; the audible dry mouth; the near crack in his voice straight down the centre of his question. And I actually laughed – but only lightly. 'No, Rowan. I think I'm asking how many girls you've slept with.'

'Edi …' He paused and took a deep breath. 'I don't think I understand.'

'Did I stutter?'

He laughed. 'No, I mean … Isn't this what we agreed to? We're meant to be out with other people, we're allowed to be, and sleeping with other people, we even put that in the ground rules for all of this, when we first started it. Didn't we? I mean, I didn't … I didn't imagine that part? So, the ghosting me thing, is that about me double-booking you, really, or is it about me sleeping with someone else? Because, babe, I don't mean this in a shitty way, but if it's about the second one, then I'm only doing what we said I could.'

What we said I *could …* I parroted his phrasing back to myself and felt my face fall into a frown. 'So, if I'm sleeping around that's fine, too?'

Another laugh. But when I stayed deadpan he suddenly became more serious. 'Well, are you?'

'Don't answer a question with a question. You know it's bad form.'

'Okay, then sure.' He threw his arms up in a defeated gesture. 'It's fine if you're sleeping with other people. This is what we were missing, Edi, this freedom—'

'The freedom to double-book a date – is that what you were missing out on, Rowan?' He looked annoyed again. And I was annoyed that I wanted to apologise for that. Instead of apologising, I launched an even bigger question. 'And how long will you be needing that freedom for, exactly?' His head snapped up and his eyes narrowed. *You know that I know.* 'Remind me, is it three months, or is it more open-ended than that?'

I saw his head twitch and I wondered whether he was listening for the crack of ice. He must have decided to step carefully because he answered, 'We agreed three months.'

'And yet …'

'Look, I don't know what the boys told you—'

'They *told* me what you'd already *told* them, so don't come down on Ian and Monty like they're the ones who are out of order here, when *you're* the one telling people we're taking *not*

135

three months, in fact, but up to *six*!' The weight of the reveal had nearly crushed me when the boys told me days before. But after sitting quietly with it – and ignoring Rowan's calls long enough to help me think – I realised it was less about the change of duration and more about the not-telling-me; more about there being *another* lie. If anything, I was a little worried that I wasn't worried *enough* at the prospect of a longer break – or maybe it was more time with Fred that I wasn't so worried about. I shook the idea away; *another fire, for later and/or with the girls.*

'Edi, I'm so—'

'Let me guess …' I held up a finger to stop him. 'Sorry?'

He sighed. 'What do you need right now, Edi? Do you need space? Do you need for us to stop doing this?'

Even though I understood what he was offering, I didn't like his reason for offering it. It didn't feel like he wanted for the break to be over – only for this conversation about the break to be over. The expression he wore was the same one I'd seen during Saturday food shops and trying-on sessions in New Look. He didn't care; he'd just had enough. And somehow, in this mess of a situation, he'd been able to make it sound like *he* was sacrificing something for my benefit: sleeping around; using Tinder; double-booking dates. It didn't bother me that he was doing everything we agreed to, I realised; what bothered me was how easily he'd taken to it – and worse still, how long he wanted to swim in the shallow waters of pretending to be single. *And* when he was planning on telling me about it!

The reasons for doubting him piled on, making it impossible to pick just one thing to be angry about. But I wasn't an angry person – and I'd *never* been the angry girlfriend before. I thought back to Skye and the hurt that had spilled out from that, but had it been anger? Because it certainly didn't feel like whatever had elbowed between us now.

'I need some time,' I said, looking down the road and deliberately away from him. There was a riptide of nerves and bad feeling in my belly. 'Not six months' time, but time.' The girls would be proud of the dig.

'To think about whether you want this to stop?' he pushed.

But I did look at him, then, because part of me needed to see his reaction when I said, 'Yes. And then to think about what I mean by "this".' In a snap he opened his mouth to answer, but I knew him well enough to know that nothing good would come from a kneejerk response. 'Don't. You asked me what I needed and I've told you. I can get home from here, thanks.' I leaned forward and kissed his cheek. 'Tell the boys I said hello.'

I turned and hurried and hoped he wouldn't catch up with me. When I rounded the first corner onto a fresh street, I realised he wasn't coming – and I didn't even know how I felt about that. What I did know, though, was that this wasn't Skye take two. I was allowed to call the girls; I was allowed to tell them everything. 'It's my fucking story, after all,' I said to no one as I fumbled to free my mobile from my coat pocket. Before I'd even got the screen unlocked, though, an incoming call flashed up: Betty.

'Bet, am I glad that you—'

'Women, assemble,' she interrupted me. I could hear chatter in the background. 'Patrick and Molly have gone south, and Thursday is the new Friday anyway. You in?'

But work ... was my first thought.

But a hangover is a sickness ... was my second.

'I'm in.'

Chapter 25

Through the traditional means of a twenty-first-century group chat, Betty managed to call us all together to one bar, at one time. She cautioned us privately though – in another group chat, minus Molly – that it would be best if we didn't mention what Betty was referring to as, 'the fuck-boy situation'. It was inevitable, though, that Molly would get drunk enough to confess all, so we knew it was only a matter of timing. We were five drinks in – apart from Lily, who was seven in, despite her protests – when Molly started to slur her worries and disappointments. Betty interjected now and then with a correction, as the only person to have received this original story earlier in the day as it unfolded – in the harsh light of sobriety, too. But Molly looked to largely keep to the script of what had happened.

She and Patrick had been sleeping together and dating – Molly thought – exclusively. Only Patrick thought he and Molly had been sleeping together in the non-exclusive way. *Jesus, what is it with Rowan and his friends?* I threw down enough wine in one go to make my throat burn. Faith squeezed my knee and asked for the fourth time if I was okay and for the fourth time I lied and said I was. Horrible as it felt to admit, the situation with Molly was at least a good distraction.

'Like, were there loads of girls or one other girl?' Cora asked, her words clanging together. She gestured to nothing at all with her beer bottle as she spoke. 'Because it might be just the one.'

'Does that make it better?' Betty snapped back.

Lily laughed. 'If anything, doesn't it make it worse?'

'Fucking hell!' Cora threw her hands into a defensive gesture. 'I only asked.'

'There were other girls,' Molly started, then stalled and placed a hand flat on her chest plate. She took two deep breaths, universal drunk speak for, *I might be about to vomit ...* but then she picked up, 'He said it's just lads being lads. Some fucking, I don't know, some disgusting competition with him and someone. I think he said one of the others. But *then—*'

'Moll, wait,' I interrupted her. 'What do you mean a competition?'

'Boys being ratbag, arsehole boys,' Betty answered. 'He said something to her about being quids in on a bet with a friend about, I don't know, being a fuck-boy?' She waved away anything more, as though what she'd said were a complete explanation of something. *Oh, but there's so much more to this now,* I thought, as I leaned back in my own chair and gulped air down like it were shots of something stronger. *Because Patrick might be Player One/Two.*

'But it's the latest of them all that I saw him with,' Molly picked up. '*Then* he goes, he goes, I didn't even sleep with that one!' She lowered her voice to match Patrick's tone in a way that would have been comedic under other circumstances. But despite us all being three sheets to the wind, we knew there was nothing funny about it. 'I saw him and her, cosied up, talking like they went back bloody years, while he was out with a group of the others.'

'Babes ...' Lily leaned over to hug her.

'I bet she wasn't even anything special,' Cora added, and I saw Lily throw her a warning shot. It was one of Lily's least favourite things: one woman taking it out on another. But Cora wasn't taking it back. She shrugged. 'I'm just saying.'

'She was beautiful,' Molly said. 'Beautiful, with one of those pretentious, glamorous artsy names.' She exhaled slowly while Lily rubbed the spot between her shoulder blades. 'Fucking Grass or Cloud or—'

'Skye?'

Molly looked at me. 'That was it.' She tried to click her fingers. 'Skye.'

*

When I asked Lily for a cigarette, that's when my cover was blown. She said, 'Course, babes, I'll come with you ...' and led me into the smoking area, with Faith close behind. They even went as far as letting me spark up and inhale a blissful drag before Lily snatched the cigarette away.

'Right, that's your fill.' She pulled on it herself. 'What's going on?'

My kneejerk was to continue in my protests, but Faith held up a finger. 'Be. Honest.'

'Rowan and I had a massive shitty discussion about the whole shitty situation with dating other people. He's been sleeping with other people already and, fuck, I don't even care about that because we agreed it. But he's telling the boys bullshit about how long this is all going to last and I hate it now; I hate who this is making him; I hate how *easy* it is for him to be sleeping with other people and for him to *welcome*, so fucking freely, *more* time to be doing that. Do you know?' I looked from Lily to Faith and back again. 'Do you get it?'

Lily pulled me into a hug. 'I know, babes.'

'Who is Skye?'

I pushed away from Lily and shot Faith a look that would worry Death. 'What?'

'Skye. The woman Patrick didn't sleep with. Who is she?'

'How should I know?' I looked to Lily for support but she shook her head.

140

'No, Edi, I saw your face, too.' She rubbed my shoulder. 'I'm just too nice to ask.'

Faith snorted. 'Sure, okay. But who is she, Edi?'

'Belly breath, babes, a big belly breath and then—'

'Rowan slept with her.'

'Ewwww.' Faith recoiled.

But Lily guessed. 'You don't mean recently.'

I shook my head. 'A couple of years ago. He told me soon after it happened. I told him we'd work through it, which we did.'

'Edi, babes, why didn't you tell us?' Lily pulled me into a one-armed hug so she could be close but also search my face for an answer. I could feel the weight of Faith's stare, too.

'I didn't want you to think badly of him.'

'Oh, beautiful girl.' She pulled me tighter then. 'I have *always* thought badly of him.'

I spluttered a laugh into her chest before I righted myself to talk to them again. 'But, I don't know, now Patrick might be hanging around with this woman and – is it a coincidence?'

Lily guessed again. 'Or has Rowan been hanging around with her, which is how Patrick ended up hanging around with …'

'Exactly. I didn't want to push Molly but did she say anything, to either of you, I mean? She mentioned the guys being all together but she didn't say whether Rowan was one of the group she saw and now … Do I push this? Do I leave it, what?'

'Edi …' Faith rubbed at her forehead. 'You know you deserve better than this.'

It wasn't a question, I knew, but I tried to muster a nod all the same. 'I think I thought it would be harder for him. Or maybe he'd at least see that meeting people and dating them isn't exactly how he thought … Fuck it, I don't know. I just thought he'd realise he had it good already.'

'Textbook.'

Faith backhanded Lily's arm. 'Don't bring your feminist textbook bullshit into this.'

'Okay, but when this isn't as raw as it is now, we're going to have a serious discussion ab—'

'Lily,' I cut across her. 'We can have a serious discussion whenever you want. As long as it isn't right now.' I felt tears prickling behind my eyes and I wondered whether she could see them, given the speed at which she backed down. 'Fuck it, maybe I should drunk-dial Fred and booty call her or something.'

Lily laughed, but Faith was outraged. 'You absolutely cannot do that.'

'Yeah, yeah,' I agreed, but I pushed away from Lily and pulled my phone out all the same. 'I know I'm only doing what I'm berating Rowan for doing, yada yada.'

Faith snatched my phone. 'I don't give a hoot about Rowan.' Lily snapped her fingers in agreement. 'You can stroll right in there, meet a man and take him home if that's going to ease some of this. But so help me, Edi Parcell, the first time you have sex with a woman is going to blow your fucking mind and I will not let you be drunk for it.'

None of us had noticed Betty filter out to meet us.

'Oh.'

I felt my stomach clench as she shifted eyes from me to Faith and then Lily, before settling on me again. There was a cigarette dangling from her mouth and a lighter clasped between half-raised hands. And I felt the prickle of tears even more so then.

'Betty …' I started, but she closed the gap between us and kissed my cheek.

'Literally could not give less of a shit.' She leaned back and sparked up. 'Who's the girl?'

The tears poured out of me, then, but they were paired with fierce laughter. I sobbed against Faith's shoulder – a little with sadness but mostly with joy – and fenced questions from Betty – 'Big knockers?' – that I knew she was only asking to lighten the load of … everything! When I'd finished, Faith unleashed me into Betty's clutches for a full cuddle and as she pressed her hands flat against my back to pull me to her, she whispered, 'You deserve better than where you're at right now, babe, that's all I'm going to say.' And I found that I was crying again. The arrival of Cora and Molly halted the share-time, though, and we flocked to tending to Molly's every need for all of ten minutes.

Cora was the one to break the tension between us. 'What did we miss?'

Betty winked at me and exhaled a stream of smoke. 'Edi is thinking of shagging a woman.'

'No bloody wonder.' Molly rubbed at her bare arms and made a show of shivering. 'Any chance the non-smokers can migrate towards the dance floor and the smokers can join us when they've finished with their …' She waved her hand in Lily's direction. 'Vice.'

Lily tilted her head back and released a plume of smoke over us. 'Everyone has something.'

'You're not wrong.' Cora pushed through the group to link arms with me. 'Mine happens to be booze, though, and it's Edi's round, so if I just steer you …'

'That's it?' I stood rooted and looked around the group. 'That's actually it?'

'What, do you want a flag rolled out?' Molly joked.

Lily exhaled hard again. 'They actually have a flag.' Her voice was still thick with smoke.

Faith snorted. '*They?*'

'I feel like we're getting off-topic here,' Betty added, and Faith threw her a look of surprise. For Betty to steer a conversation towards where it was meant to be, was nearly unheard of. Unless there was something she really wanted to say. 'Babe, if you mean, *that's it*, about the woman thing … I can't speak for the others, mind you—'

'Although you often do.'

Betty nodded. 'Sure, what Lil said. I can't speak for them now, but I genuinely couldn't give less of a shit if I tried. And I say that with sincerity and love.'

Cora squeezed my arm. 'What she said. *Now* will you buy me a drink?'

I looked around at their stunned expressions. They seemed less surprised about the woman reveal, and more surprised at my worry about the woman reveal. Since the first date with Fred, I'd drafted a hundred different conversations – Cora keeping her distance, Betty assuming I wanted to sleep with her – where I explained my feelings and fenced their questions, most likely of all the real tough nut of: 'So, does this make you gay now?' A question I'd asked myself at least once a day since I met Fred; twice a day since she'd walked me home.

But, among the questioning glances that bounced back from my friends' faces, there wasn't even a flicker of something that looked like judgement. They were all face-value women; never in our friendship's lifetime had I known Betty or Lily not say what they meant, or what they happened to be thinking (to a fault). So here they were, then, making a literal safe circle around me – and whatever it was I was going through – and despite the shit of the day beforehand, with them, all I felt then was love.

Chapter 26

When I woke up the following morning, my inbox was a mess of *I got home safe. xx* and *Are you back yet? xxx* as we checked in one after the other. There was also a message from Betty from only three hours earlier – *Called George. Still not best man material. Love you babe. Bx* – and another from Faith – *Proud of you Edi* – but nothing from Rowan. Had I expected there to be? I rolled over in bed and starfished until I took up both sides equally, and I thought, *This is what life would be like* … It didn't matter that my mascara was (probably) down my cheek; nor that I'd definitely drunkenly stripped off on the way from the front door to the bedroom, meaning the place was littered with clothes. It wouldn't matter, either, if I got drunk in the middle of the week whenever I felt like it, or if I brought someone home or called someone who …

Empowering as the starfish position might have felt initially, my hand quickly flew to my forehead with the half-memory of something – 'I'm going to call anyway … No, no I don't care' – and it left me grasping about for my phone.

'Bollocks.'

And there Fred was, right there in my call log. One outgoing at two-thirty in the morning which she maybe hadn't even answered.

I clicked in to check the timestamp for the duration: ten seconds. *A voicemail at worst,* I decided before I clicked out again. Then I double-checked WhatsApp, although I hadn't seen anything there when I'd checked in with messages from the girls. I allowed myself an air-punch of joy, too, when I saw that I hadn't messaged Rowan in my drunken stupor either. But just to be sure, I clicked into my text messages to check and—

'Double bollocks.'

Not one; not even two; but *three* messages to Fred. I scrolled through them slowly and took belly breaths as I read them: *Hry Beautifull. I hppe thsi doesnt wake youu. Jusr anted to llet you kno I was thinkiing about you toniht. Be grate to see you soon.* – and I decided after the first message alone that if the worst possible outcome was that Fred now thought I was a tad illiterate when drunk, that was fine. I could handle that. I could one hundred per cent talk myself out of that. The illiteracy only continued well into message two – *Soz pressd send to soon. Call m yeh? Well get drinks/drinner/something. It's Edi btw. Xxx* – and I wondered whether anyone even used those abbreviations anymore! I was surprised 'great' hadn't had a figure eight in it somewhere.

'Still, Edi, if that's the worst …' I spoke aloud to steady my breathing as I scrolled to message three, one eye closed at the prospect of finding yet more spelling mistakes. 'Oh, but it's so much worse.' I groaned and threw my head back into the pillow, swamped with a desperate want for my bed to swallow me entirely and let me avoid whatever would spill from the embarrassment Drunk Edi had caused me. But the pillow resisted any wishes for suffocation, despite the weight that message three was bearing down on us both: *Been outout w/ girls tonite. Feels dead weird not to txt youu to let yu know Im home. I miss you.*

Having never made such a monumental dating cock-up before in my life, I decided the only thing to do was immediately call Fred to apologise, explain the message was meant for Rowan, and then apologise again (in case that explanation somehow made things even worse). I navigated through to my outgoing display and hit the green phone next to her name, then I waited. And I waited. And—

'The person you're calling can't answer at the moment ...'

'Oh, *triple* bollocks!' At least I resisted the urge to leave a blundering voicemail message. *But wait*, another thought came to me as I thumbed to my WhatsApp listings, *maybe she hasn't even read the messages yet?* There was no way of knowing with Average Joe texting, which made the situation both better and worse all at once; it was now Schrodinger's monumental cock-up instead. Still, I steeled myself and started to type a message to apologise – on WhatsApp, so everyone involved knew when it had been read – and I was midway through drafting something long-winded and heartfelt when the buzzer for my front door sounded. The noise went through my hungover head like an ice pick to the eye – which was a procedure I thought might actually help me at that moment. I took great care in locking the screen of my phone before I threw myself out of bed and headed for the door.

'Morning, babes.' Lily looked bright as a freshly sprung bulb and I hated her for it. The only thing that abated my flicker of jealousy at her obvious lack of a hangover was the fact she'd brought coffee with her. 'This one is strong and this one is—' I snatched at the strong one. 'All righty, then.' She nudged the door closed. 'I'm assuming hair of the dog is out of the question?'

I held back a retch. 'Lil, how are you so fine?'

'Years of arduous practice. Are you packed?'

'I'm sorry?'

'Packed. Like, to go. Cora has work until lunchtime but that's—' she checked her watch '—only about an hour away now. So, I thought we could grab her on our way out of the city.'

'Lil, I've no idea what you're talking to me about.'

She laughed, a sincere and schoolgirlish giggle, like I'd really tickled her, and the sound was enough to make me smile, too, despite the ice pick still searing through my forehead. 'Edi, babes, you really do need to drink more. Well, not drink more, but, you know, get better at handling what you drink.' She steered me towards the bedroom. 'Molly was still sad over that pillock when the night was out, so Betty suggested a night away.'

'And we all agreed?'

'We *all* agreed.' She landed on my bed and sipped from her takeout cup.

'But we're going tonight? So soon?'

'Do you have plans?'

'No, I guess I don't. Where are we ...' I petered out when I saw the shake of her head.

'No idea. Drunk Betty booked it, last-minute Air-wotsit. She's turned it into a secret mission of sorts. Apparently we're to set off north, and she'll send us details along the way, ending in a postcode.' Lily rolled her eyes. 'I knew her James Bond kick would ruin us all.'

'Speaking of being ruined ...' I opened my underwear drawer and pulled out two pairs. 'Betty is in no fit state to drive. She texted me like, three hours ago and it didn't sound like she was decent.'

'When is she ever?'

I laughed. 'That's fair.' I stuffed the underwear into a bag and crossed to my wardrobe. Everything in me wanted to pull out the soft jumpers, curl into a ball and call it a day. But instead, I reached for the green and white floral-print dress, cut just above the knee, that I felt both sexy *and* comfortable in. Because balance. I folded it over and tucked it into the bag.

'Take a cardi.'

'Is that your way of telling me you love me?'

She frowned. 'Well, yeah. I'm not just going to come right out and say it.'

'So you're driving me and Cora. Who's driving Betty?'

'Faith.'

I felt like a traitor, but my stomach turned at the thought of Molly moaning about Patrick for a car journey. 'And Molly?'

'Also with Faith.' Lily let out another little laugh. 'Out of all of us, Faith will need a drink the most by the time we get to where we're going. Molly is weirdly beat up over the Patrick thing, don't you think?'

'A little?' I added a black cardigan to my bag. 'But maybe she's got a lot invested?'

Lily shrugged. 'She's of an age, I suppose.'

'What, you mean *our* age?'

'Well, yes, chronologically. I more mean Molly is a settling-down type, which is absolutely fine; cannot lean on that hard enough. But she's on the wrong side of twenty-five and she hasn't met the man she's going to marry yet, and I think, I don't know, women like Molly are conditioned to feel bad about that, aren't they?' she asked, like it wasn't a sociocultural question with a crushing weight attached. 'She'll meet someone when she's good and ready, or she won't and that's actually fine as well. But because she lands so hard on the must-get-married mentality, when she meets someone she sometimes goes all in.'

'Are you turning Molly into a textbook case?'

'No, babes.' She took a long swig of her coffee. 'Society did that.'

There was a sting to what she'd said, even though it was nothing I disagreed with. It sent me catapulting back to thoughts that I still wasn't sober enough to grapple. 'Do I have time for a shower?'

She checked her watch. 'Sure, I'm not your keeper.'

I kissed her on the head on my way out of the room, but she caught hold of my hand and pulled me back. 'You absolutely don't have to answer this.' I suddenly felt a desperate need for a nervous wee. 'But are we going to talk about what you told me and Faith last night?'

I opened my mouth, as though there were an immediate answer there. But nothing came.

Lily leapt into my silence. 'I know it was a long time ago, and maybe that's fine. Maybe you've dealt with it and you're over it and talking will only drag up a bunch of things that you'd rather not deal with.' I made a face like even I didn't believe her. 'No,' she carried on, 'I somehow didn't think so. Are you going to ask Rowan about her?'

I tilted my head from side to side as though rolling the thought around. Then I remembered the text – the one he hadn't even asked me to send, because we were busy not talking. But when had he last asked for a 'home safe' text anyway? 'I messaged him last night to tell him I miss him.'

'Oh, Edi,' she answered, in a sad tone.

'Don't worry, though, I somehow managed to send it to Fred instead.'

Her hand flew to her mouth in time to conceal her smile but a laugh ruptured out of her. 'Oh, Edi.'

I sighed. 'Right, sod you, I'm going for a shower now.'

She tapped my backside as I stood up. Her laugh still hadn't quite settled. 'Away with you, you smell like booze and bad decisions.'

Chapter 27

Cora didn't take her sunglasses off until an hour into the journey. She'd stayed prostrate on the back seat for much of the time before that, only letting out the occasional groan whenever Lily hit the brakes without warning. Her hangover championed my own. When the shades were off, though, she stuck her head in between our seats to catch our conversation. But Lily immediately stopped talking.

'Because that isn't suspicious.'

'We weren't talking about anything interesting,' Lily lied.

'Good, I love things that aren't interesting.' Cora glanced between us both. I was looking out of the window, but I could see her head shifting about in my peripheral vision. She looked like an observer at Wimbledon. 'Well?'

'We were just talking about Rowan,' I answered, still looking out of my window. While Cora had been sleeping off her fourth shot of tequila from the night before in the back seat, Lily had gently ushered me to the topic of Rowan – and Skye. *Do I tell Cora?* I thought, then, *Does it matter who knows?* I pulled in a deep breath as though I were about to speak but I still didn't know what would come out. So I was especially thankful when I opened my mouth and—

'I'm sleeping with Hamish.'

'What?' Lily and I answered in unison. I felt the steering tug on the car. 'Concentrate on what you're doing,' I told Lily, 'I'll deal with this.' I craned around to get a good look at Cora. She dropped back against the seat, then, and she was looking out of the driver's side window. 'Are you out of your bloody mind?'

'Yes,' Lily answered, 'yes, she bloody is.'

'What did I just say about concentrating?'

'How can I?' She rested her elbow in the open window of the car and made a fist to lean her head against. 'After a shock like that?'

'Oh, shut up,' Cora finally protested. She leaned forward again. 'Like you haven't slept with a who's who of bad decisions. You could put together a compendium on it. Besides, he's good at what he does and he doesn't want anything serious. He got checked before we—'

'I should bloody think so!' Lily interrupted but Cora carried on as though she hadn't.

'He got checked before we slept together and he tells me he isn't sleeping with anyone else.' She shrugged. 'I really don't see the problem.'

I saw Lily's mouth drop open and I knew a mouthful of problems were only seconds away from filling the car. But I set a hand on her shoulder to at least delay the tirade. 'He tells you he isn't sleeping with anyone else? Does that mean, what, you're exclusive?' Hamish was known for having sex with anyone who didn't shake him off; he'd never been selective about the women he'd taken home. For him to settle down with anyone seemed …

'Christ no.' Cora laughed, as though I'd suggested something really ridiculous. A curt and surprised sound. 'I'm also telling him that I'm not sleeping with anyone else. But we're about to get drunk on a girls' night so …' She petered out, and I wondered whether sleeping with someone else was an objective for Cora on this night away. 'Look.' She leaned closer to me then, cutting Lily out with a strategic turn of the shoulder. 'You've got something you're scared to tell me. I had something I was scared to tell you. But you still don't have to tell me whatever it is you don't want to tell me.' She laughed. 'I'm just making this a safe space, in case you want to.'

Cora had always been the middle ground of the friendship circle. She wasn't quite Molly enough for marriage and domestication, but also not quite hard-edged enough to make it her lot in life to tear the patriarchy down, one man at a time, like Lily. Still, no matter which side she fell on at any particular time, I knew her reaction would be ...

'That utter bastard!'

... as soon as I'd told her about Rowan and Skye.

'Edi, babe.' She craned into the front of the car to hug me at an awkward angle. 'Why didn't you tell us?'

'Because she didn't want us to think he was an utter bastard,' Lily answered, deadpan.

'He was so sorry.' And he really had been. The weeks and months after Skye were, strangely, some of the happiest we'd had. Every promise Rowan made – every night out with the girls, lunch with my parents, shopping trip, weekend away – he came good on. At the time it didn't even feel like he was serving a punishment, only being kind. 'He did his time for it, or, I don't know, he did *some* time for it. I think if it happened again now ...' I trailed off and a half-laugh, half-huff escaped out of me. 'Which of course it won't, because now he doesn't need to cheat, now he can just walk right out there, pick up a woman, and tell me about it over the dinner that *I* make for him the evening after.' I felt a riptide of anger move through my belly with such a force that my hand flew to my core. 'At the time he blamed it on being young and stupid.' Another huff fell out of me. 'I don't know what his excuse is now.'

'Hey.' Cora rested a hand on my shoulder. 'Babe, you okay?'

'He was just so sorry.'

Lily reached over to squeeze my knee, then. 'Try to breathe for me, would you?'

And all three of us sucked the air right out of the car together, and exhaled it back out.

'Anyone need a wee break, or you know, a McDonald's?' We were hurtling towards a sign that marked up the next service stop as being three miles away. 'Cora? You must have a stonking head still – don't you think food would help?'

Cora licked her finger and then held it upright, as though assessing the winds of probability in the car. 'Yeah, yeah, I feel like I could go for some fries. Side of mozzarella sticks, maybe. McFlurry, too, if you're offering.'

'I'm offering to pull over is what I'm offering.'

'Fine, whatever, my treat for Hamish,' Cora joked in answer then added, 'Mind you, out of this secret swap I feel *very* short-changed. Mine is infinitely more embarrassing than yours.'

'When Edi was seventeen she got so drunk that she weed herself on the way to a bush that she'd actually planned on weeing in.'

'Lily!' I slapped her arm. 'I can't believe you told her that.'

'Oh come on, she's sleeping with Hamish, we've got to give the girl something.'

'Yeah but—' The sound of my mobile cut me off. 'This is probably Betty calling to tell me that Faith has blurted out the time I—' *Fred*. 'Oh my God, Lily, it's her.' My phone had pulled in Fred's WhatsApp display image and the sight of her set me reeling with warmth. 'Do I answer?'

'Do you *answer*?' Lily was reaching for my phone. 'Cora, get the—'

'Cora, you dare.' I cautioned her with a raised finger and she threw her hands up in submission. 'I can do this.' I exhaled hard, pulled in hard. 'I can do this,' I said again on my out breath, then I tapped the answer key before I could convince myself that I in fact didn't have a sodding clue what 'this' was – or whether I could do it. 'Hello?'

'Put her on speakerphone,' Lily snapped in a whisper and I followed instructions, lest she or Cora start another wrestling match for the phone.

'I miss you too. Thanks for having let me know you were home.' *Oh fuck. Oh fuck, oh fuck, oh—* 'Wow, that joke landed harder than I thought it would.' There was a giggle of laughter at the other end of the line and next to me Lily made a poor show of stifling a snort of amusement too. It felt as though my stomach had been pumped full of bubbles, the small and joyous kind that happened if you squirted washing-up liquid at the right angle. 'Are you hugging a toilet bowl still or have you recovered? I thought I'd leave you a few hours to make sure the alcohol was *really* on its way out of you.'

'You're ... Wait, you're okay with me?'

There was a long pause. 'Did I miss something?' Her voice still sounded light, like she was smiling. 'Edi, please, do you think you're the first woman to ever get pissed and text the wrong person on the way home? At least it wasn't anything indecent. Unless you count emotion as indecent but, I don't know, you don't strike me as the type for that.'

'This feels too easy,' I pushed. Lily slapped my leg and I batted her away. 'You're really okay?' I heard Cora sigh in the back seat. I wasn't looking for an argument – but I had to check there wasn't one there. With Rowan I usually found them days later, hidden down the side of the sofa or rotting at the back of the fridge; he'd always liked to let these things fester. But Fred ...

'Are you in a car?' she asked, a rapid-fire change.

'Yeah, my friend is driving, though. Girls' night away, all very sudden.'

'Sounds dangerous.' She dropped her voice and I realised then that there was someone else with her. 'Sure, I'll be maybe a minute. Hey,' she spoke to me again, 'what's the occasion for the girls' night outta town?'

'A friend is pining over a guy.'

She laughed. 'The friend isn't you, is it?'

Cora let out a loud, 'Ha!' before slamming her palm over her mouth. Lily reached into the back to slap at her legs.

'Not even,' I tried to carry on like there wasn't a small war breaking out in the seats around me. 'I'll have you know I'm being held hostage here, practically kidnapped.'

'I'm about to go into work, so why don't you call me when you're home?'

'Wait, where's my sympathy?' I tried to sound beat up in the hope that it might carry as flirting. *Does this count?* I wanted to ask the girls but there wasn't the time or means. I just had to hope that—

'I'll give you sympathy over dinner when you're home.' *It's flirting.* 'My place?' *It's really flirting.* 'Don't do anything I wouldn't while you're away.'

'Well, what does that rule out?'

There was a pause of a few seconds. 'I'll tell you over dinner.'

Fred hung up, then, and Lily and Cora fell over themselves in a chorus of whoops and laughter, with the climax of a loud whistle rising from the back seat.

'Okay, okay,' I tried to talk over them, 'I think that's enough.'

'Not even close,' Lily said, 'you just bloody wait until we tell Betty.'

'Betty?' Cora squeezed my shoulder again and gave me a wink. 'It's Faith I can't wait to see. Christ, she'll be so proud.'

Lily made a show of sniffing hard; she forced her breathing jagged and said, 'God, don't they just—' a huff and a sniff and a splutter '—good God, they just grow up so fast …'

Chapter 28

Before

Faith was red in the face from laughter. She'd been complaining of a stitch in her left side for five minutes, but Betty had persisted – 'What? I don't think it's an unfair question' – which only made Faith laugh all the more. By the time Cora and Molly were waddling back into the living room, laden with trays of snacks and glasses of wine, Faith was panting out of an open window.

'We either missed something good or terrible.' Molly sounded nervous. 'Which?'

'Hilarious,' Faith answered. She was still breathless. She let out an 'oof' sort of noise while she fanned herself, pulling winter air into the warmth of the room. 'Betty would like to know the intricacies of female sexy time.' She tried to keep a straight face but there was a smile cracking through every other word. 'Apparently she's curious but not *curious*-curious, only like, straight-woman curious.'

'I don't understand what's so funny, if I'm honest.' Betty looked to me for support but I'd tried hard not to get involved. The more interested I appeared, the more likely it was that I'd be accused of being curious, and I wasn't sure what my face would do if that happened. I wasn't *curious*-curious either, I was sure of it. But not sure enough for the conversation to feel comfortable.

'Bett,—' Molly handed her a glass '—don't you think you're just being nosy?'

'I mean, no nosier than the rest of us are being when we talk about sex with men.'

'She's got a point there.' Cora threw a cheese ball into her mouth. 'If Lily were here—'

'If Lily were here instead of getting busy with her post-grad boy toy, she'd *definitely* want to know more about it,' Betty interrupted.

Faith slammed the window closed, then, and moved back to her beanbag next to the radiator. 'Lily doesn't need to ask me. She's worldly enough to know these answers for herself. And no—' she held a finger up in response to Betty's dropped jaw '—I'm not accusing Lily of being a big lez, or even a little one, I'm just saying she's read the right books.'

'Okay, well gimme a reading list.'

'Are you allowed to say "big lez"?' Cora asked around another cheese ball.

'Gay rights. *I* can, but you can't.' Faith's phone pinged and it pulled her attention away from the conversation.

'Is it her?' Molly asked.

'It is.'

I couldn't help myself. 'Who?'

Faith made me wait until she'd stopped texting before she answered. 'Okay, you know Barker's Pool Hall down in the city centre …'

I already knew what was coming. She was texting Audrey. She was the new bartender who'd joined Barker's around a month earlier. Audrey went to our university, lived off-campus with her older-than-her boyfriend – who, rumour had it, had left his wife for Audrey six months back – and she was what I thought male writers must mean when they described a woman as drop-dead gorgeous. But she was nice with it. The few times I'd spoken to her – usually when it had been my round to buy – she'd asked how I was and how studies were, and she'd tilted her head in a way that made her look sincerely interested in my responses (even if she was being paid to ask the questions in the first place). She had a smile that warmed my insides and hair that I felt both jealous of and something else entirely towards – but I'd tried my utmost not to think too hard about the latter.

'She's with someone, though, right?' Cora asked.

'Ack, come on. How bothered is she if she's texting me?'

'Walk me through it.' Betty lay on her front but propped herself up on her elbows. 'You what, focus your sights on a woman and then lay a careful plan to seduce her out of straightness?'

There was a murmur of giggles from the group. Faith only cocked an eyebrow, though. 'Please,' she said, already reaching for her phone again. 'Straight is an abstract idea. There aren't straight women. Only women who haven't met Faith.'

It was met with further squeals of laughter from the group. But there was a homing pigeon banging around in my chest. And I was too bothered by it to laugh along.

Chapter 29

Now

When the two-day hangover from the girls' night out had cleared, I decided to text Rowan. I desperately wanted to mention Skye – to ask how she'd come hurtling back into our lives with such convenient timing. *Assuming she ever even left,* I thought as I typed, deleted, typed again. I didn't want an argument over text; I didn't want an argument, full stop. But I couldn't not speak to him forever. So I sent a neutral message – *Hey Row. I hope you're okay. Thanks for the space. I've been thinking. Or trying to think. Ha. Let me know how things are? xx* – and he'd dodged a written reply entirely, opting instead for a call.

'I was so glad you messaged.' He sounded glad, too; there was a breathlessness about him, as though the relief were a physical feeling, and the reaction set me back. 'Edi, look, about everything that got said—'

'Is Patrick sleeping with Skye?' I let it out with an urgency, as though before that it had been trapped wind. There was an uncomfortably long silence after, though, so I added, 'Or are you?' I tried for a defiant tone, one that friends would be proud of, even though off-screen I was shitting a brick – boulders, even.

After another too-long silence, he only said, 'No.'

I let out a breath I hadn't realised I was holding. 'Rowan, I'm choosing to believe you for literally one reason, and I'm going to get it out there, and then we're going to be done with it.' I thought I heard his lips part but I didn't leave the space for him to jump in. 'You could be sleeping with Skye. As in, according to the deal. So I'm trusting you to be honest because right now there's nothing actually wrong with doing it.' It was a lie. A dirty great whopping lie. But once it was out there, there was no going back.

'She's friends with Hamish.' He sounded genuinely sad. 'I don't even know how they know each other. She and I, as soon as we saw each other, we made out we were meeting for the first time. The lads, they don't know.' I nodded along while listening, but when he stopped, I found that I had nothing at all to say. I didn't know whether I believed him. But I didn't have the evidence not to. As though sensing a breaking-off point to move away from the awkwardness of it all, Rowan then changed the subject entirely and asked, 'Anyway, I heard you had a night away with the girls. How was that?'

We managed idle small talk for fifteen minutes: he'd been out with the boys; caught up with work emails, despite it having been the weekend; then fenced a call from his parents. 'Speaking of which, do you remember they're visiting?'

No, I thought, *because I don't think you told me …* 'You told me they were coming?'

'Yeah, like, a week or two ago, I definitely mentioned it.' His tone was blurred with annoyance around the edges. 'Anyway, they're coming next week. You'll be around, right? They're booking us in for dinner so I'll let you know when I hear from Dad. Probably looking at Thursday, though, or Friday.'

'Okay, sure, I'll keep those nights free.'

'You're a star, babe. Any plans for tonight?'

I was midway through rolling on a pair of tights. 'I'm having dinner with Fred again.'

There was a lull. 'Good,' he finally said. 'Good, that's going to be good for you.' I could hear he wanted to ask more, and I wondered whether he would. 'Let me know when you're home?'

'I always do.' *Even when you don't ask.*

Fred came down to the front of her building to meet me. She was wearing skinny jeans with a loose-fitting polka dot blouse and she laughed when she saw my dress. 'My God, we're already co-ordinating.' She kissed my cheek, light enough for my breath to catch. 'You look amazing, Edi. Anyone would think you're making an effort.'

I laughed. 'Please, this is how I dress every night.'

'Coming up?' She held the door open. 'I've taken a wild guess on dinner …'

For the second time in a two-hour window, I made small talk with someone. Only it felt easier doing it with a relative stranger than it had done with Rowan – and I tried not to lose my head over that. *Lose your head over it tomorrow,* I coached myself in between answering Fred's questions about my work, and listening to her answers about her own.

'I should hear back about the exhibition project soon anyway.'

Her job – away from the café, which she brushed off as nothing – sounded ridiculously interesting: creative and expressive and intense. I realised that from the short bursts of time I'd spent with her, I'd probably describe her in the same way. She set a hand on the base of my back to steer me the right way along the corridor to her front door.

'I hope you're hungry. Stuff will be done in half an hour or so.'

The front door was a bright and bulbous red, but everything behind it was white. The hallway, the rooms I could see branching

162

out from it, the open-plan sitting room right at the end of the walk; the walls were all a brilliant white. There were splashes of colour everywhere, though, lighting the space up like a paint chart: the colour blocks of blue on the wall; the teal lampshade; the scarlet sofa that came into view as we walked towards the living area. It was a grown-up space.

Fred must have read something into my silence. 'What did you expect?'

'I have no idea.' I looked around like a child stepping into a National History Museum: *And here we have a replica of the lesbian, at home in her natural nesting space.* 'Is white your favourite colour?'

'Good question.' I heard something clunk and when I turned to find the source I spotted the kitchen, tucked out of sight on the other end of the large living space. Everything was so open. 'Are you in the mood for red wine or white wine?'

I panicked. 'What goes with the food?'

She laughed. 'Beer?' She pulled out a bottle and reached next to her to pull two wine glasses from a shelf well-stocked with them. 'We'll start with white and see how we feel.'

'Is that how you decided on decorating the place?'

'Sort of.' She brought the glasses over and landed heavy on the sofa, so I matched her. 'I like having things that I can add to. White is clean, neat, it makes me feel like the whole flat is a gallery. Plus, it makes it easy to swap and change things around here.'

Opposite us, there was what looked to be a single line drawing framed and positioned pride of place on the jut-out of an old chimney breast. The portrait was impossible to miss. It showed a woman's body, I realised, after looking for longer than I maybe should have. The hips were wide and the thighs were thick and there was something—

'She's caught your eye?'

I smiled. 'Sorry.'

'Don't be. I love it when people stare at my work.' She sipped her wine. 'Well, and my body.'

Heat gripped my cheeks and I was painfully aware of turning a colour that matched the sofa. 'It's your … I mean, it's your work, a self-portrait?' She murmured a yes. 'It's really beautiful, Fred.'

'Well, I think highly of myself.' Her tone was light, relaxed, and it was starting to brush off although my cheeks were still blooming roses.

'That's how you see your body?'

She stood and looked at the drawing, then tilted her head from one side to the other, like someone inspecting it for the first time. 'Shaky lines, bold curves.' She nodded. 'Strong.' Without another word she disappeared behind me and, I guessed, into the kitchen. 'Now, you're banished from turning around while I get food sorted because I'm a sucker for suspense. But take a look about the place, why don't you? You can try to guess which work is mine.'

I stood up, covered my eyes and said, 'Yes, boss.'

'Hm,' I heard, then, although her voice was nearly a whisper. 'I like that.'

The heat in my face flared, and I wondered how much of my hand might be covering the creep of red. Fred would probably call it crimson or bloodshot or magenta. To keep my cool – whatever was left of it – while I walked around the flat, I tried to name as many colours as I could that meant the same or similar to red. *If nothing else I'll impress her with my palette,* I thought while I stared over a distorted bouquet of sunflowers that was framed and hung in another part of the hallway. Beyond the white, I realised, nothing else had to match. The colour-blocked blue was close to the burnt orange and then, when I took brave steps into the bedroom, I found teal and purple and greyscale – none of which matched the green in the bathroom.

'Ready when you are,' she soon shouted, and I felt the dip of something in my pelvis.

I traced my way into the open space of the living room and

rounded the corner to the kitchen, where the table stood loaded with food. There were slices of what looked to be garlic and herb flatbread, bowls of pasta soaked in different sauces, and were those vegetable spring rolls? Fred kept quiet for a second while I took in the sights of rice, small pots of curry, and – *Christ, is that a cheese board?*

She crossed the space to meet me. 'Beyond what you ate for dinner the other night, I was kind of shooting in the dark. But statistically, there must be something here that you like.'

I sighed and felt a sink of something drop from my chest and settle between my hips.

'I think I'd like you?'

Fred narrowed her eyes and waited a second, as though giving me the chance to take it back. But when I didn't, she pulled me by the waist, leaned in and kissed my jawline. 'That, I can do.'

Chapter 30

The bed shifted next to me, which woke me up, and it took a handful of seconds to realise where I was. The room was brightly lit, both by the white of the walls and by the sunlight streaming in; Fred had sheer curtains, which I hadn't noticed the night before. I was facing away from her, and I took a quick glance towards the bedside table next to me in search of a clock. There wasn't a clockface to be found, though there was a steaming mug. She settled down behind me, then, and kissed my bare shoulder one, two, three times before moving away.

'I hope you're a tea drinker,' she said, as I pushed myself upright in bed next to her. I bunched the bedsheets up around my unmentionables – as though I had any left. 'I took an educated guess and left the bag in until it stewed.'

I smiled as I reached around to grab the drink. 'That's exactly how I take my tea.'

'You don't have to be polite.' She set her mug down and extended an arm out. 'Fancy doing the cuddle thing?' I didn't answer, only moved a few inches closer and tucked myself into the space between her torso and her arm. She gasped. 'Look at what a good fit you are.'

I laughed and, despite nerves, turned and set a kiss just beneath her collarbone. 'Thank you.'

'Jesus, after last night I should be thanking you.' I half-laughed but half-cringed. *God, it had been*— 'Seriously, Edi,' she cut my thought off, 'that was your first time?'

I looked up at her. 'Are you going out of your way to be nice?'

She kissed my forehead and softly squeezed my shoulder too. 'I don't know whether anyone has ever told you this, but you're actually quite easy to be nice to. Plus, I had a great time, Edi, seriously. And, Jesus, I remember the first time all too well. So first off, you smashed it straight out the gate, at the risk of sounding like a horny teenager there ...' I laughed at her comparison – even though that was exactly how I'd felt with her the night before. 'Second off, you're going to worry whether it was okay and whether you knew what you were doing. But you definitely did.'

'God.' The word came out in a groan. 'Am I that desperate for reassurance?'

She moved away, then, and reached around to get her own mug. 'Pre-emptive. Have the compliment, just in case.' She sipped at her tea. I stole a glance across and saw that she took hers the same way I took mine. 'I like a woman who knows what she wants, what she likes.'

Is that the type of woman I am?

'Now, what do you *want* or what would you *like* for breakfast?'

At the mention of food my stomach growled like old machinery and we both laughed. 'There's so much leftover food in the kitchen.'

'Mm. There were better things on offer. I'm not sending a woman home hungry though. Do you have a favourite place for breakfast?'

'You mean, to go out or ...'

'You don't want to be seen with me?' She sounded playful, and from her profile I could see a growing smirk.

In the harsh sunlight of day, though, my horny teenager had been replaced by a desperately insecure one. 'I was more worried, I mean ... Do you want to be seen with me?'

'Have you *seen* you?' She turned around and set a kiss square on my mouth. 'Who wouldn't want to be seen with you? Raid my wardrobe for clothes, though, why don't you? If I take you out for pancakes in that dress people will think we're in a *Pretty Woman* situation.'

I laughed. 'Are you saying I look like a sex worker?'

'No.' She upended the mug and drained it. 'I'm saying you look like a leading lady.'

*

Fred styled my hair into the messy bun look that I'd come to associate with her. It was piled on top of my head with loose strands escaping and when she was finished she patted my shoulders – 'Beautiful' – and kissed the back of my neck. My back arched and she laughed, as though she'd expected the reaction. She handed me an oversized shirt and a belt to wear.

'Ah, I don't know if black tights will work,' I said, slipping the shirt on. 'Do you have leggings?'

She looked from my feet to my pelvis. 'Don't wear anything else.'

'I …' I rubbed at the back of my neck. 'I don't have the legs for that.'

'For what?'

'For not wearing tights.'

'Sure you have legs.' She was flicking through her wardrobe to find something for herself. Her bare back was facing me; the only thing covered was her bum, with a pair of patterned briefs. While I'd hidden myself in swathes of bedsheets, Fred had spent the last half an hour waltzing around the bedroom like she was there alone; naked and unashamed, and occasionally dancing to the Betty Who track that she'd put on repeat 'to set the day up'. She wiggled her bum again, then, half-dancing but half-flipping through clothes still. 'Edi, I can see where this is going,' she carried on, still not facing me, 'and take it from someone who spent *a lot* of time looking at your legs last night.' She turned. 'You've got the legs for anything.'

I didn't argue, only blushed, buckled the belt up, and waited patiently on the edge of her bed while she tugged on cut-off jeans and a T-shirt with a small rainbow emblem on the upper right of it.

'Ready, beautiful?' She held out a hand for me to take. 'Pancakes? Because Thom's does a gorgeous pancake stack and after last night, with work this afternoon, I'm in a place for some carbohydrates. What do you say?'

I laughed. 'I'm in.'

Everything about it somehow felt familiar – even though there was so much neither of us knew. Thom's, it turned out, was a fifteen-minute walk away and the crisp air of the morning blew away any dreamy eyes and cobwebs left over from the night before. Fred spoke to me like I was someone who knew her life and the characters in it – 'Then Mum and Dad moved, took the dog with them down to Devon one weekend and decided, actually …' – so I tried to do the same with everything I told her. But there was a sticking point when I realised just how much of my life revolved around—

'Should we call him Rowan or hubby?' she interrupted a stream of information where I'd tried to disguise his importance – but I'd obviously failed quite dramatically.

'Rowan will do.'

'Just here, hon.' She gestured across the street and grabbed my hand as we crossed the road. 'So you and he have been together for …'

'Ever,' I finished her sentence.

We came to a stop outside the café. 'But now you're …'

'Apparently sleeping with other people.'

She cocked an eyebrow as she reached for the door. 'Well, good news for me. Maybe not such good news for him. You're a bit of a catch, Edi.'

I opened my mouth to brush the compliment away.

'It wasn't a question,' she cut me off. 'Just a statement. Now, in you go. If we're going to talk about your fiancé then I'm probably going to need more carbohydrates.'

Her tone was jovial and her smile as wide as it had been throughout the morning. There wasn't a flicker of a sign that she was uncomfortable. *But how can I know?* I recycled the thought, sandwiched around flashbacks of all the times Rowan had been upset about something – and told me what it was three days later.

'Hey—' Fred poked her head around me '—are you still with me?'

'I think so?'

She stopped and turned me around to face her. I thought she might kiss me, right there in the middle of the dining area, and I didn't know how I felt about that. 'We absolutely don't have to talk about the fiancé stuff because it's genuinely none of my business.' She waited until I nodded, albeit a little reluctantly. 'If you want to talk about it, that's also fine, because I'm a big girl, and I clocked that ring the first time I met you. Plus, if you *really* need something to set your mind at ease, my last girlfriend was married.' I opened my mouth to interject but she pressed on. 'And no, you're not my girlfriend, but I figured post-sex might be a good time to talk about whether you're still planning on getting married to him now you know how good gay sex is.'

I could tell from her tone that she was joking again, and a laugh escaped. 'Thank you.'

'Jesus, for what? Compassion is free. Pick a table, would you?'

Mid-laugh still, I set myself back on track to find a free table at the back of the room. I was so focused, though, that it caught me completely off-guard when someone said—

'Edi?'

I jerked around. 'Monty.' *Fuck.* He stood to hug me and I leaned into him.

'Look at you.' He pulled away and looked me up and down. 'You look amazing.'

'Doesn't she just?' Fred cut in. 'Nice to meet you.' She held out a hand and Monty looked startled; by her good looks, by her confidence, maybe by both. But he still took her hand and introduced himself. 'Monty, nice name. I'm Fred.'

His eyes stretched wider then. '*Fred* Fred?'

'I mean—' she sounded amused '—you can just say it the one time but sure.'

Monty laughed, too. There was a soft pink blush creeping up his face. 'Sorry, ah, Rowan has mentioned you.' He glanced at me, then, and I wondered what reaction he was searching for.

'Oh, he has, has he?' Fred seemed genuinely pleased with herself – as though she'd shattered the glass ceiling by gaining notoriety. She looked at me, too, and winked before turning back to Monty. 'What is it that Rowan knows exactly?'

Monty rubbed at the back of his neck. My gut reaction was to leap in and save him from the awkwardness of it all. But something about Fred's wicked humour must have rubbed off because *I* also wanted to know what Rowan thought he knew about Fred. 'He hasn't said too much. Just, you know, that Edi was having dinner with you, and sort of seeing someone called Fred. Only didn't mention you were so—'

'Female,' Fred interrupted him and laughter spluttered out of me. 'I get that a lot.'

Monty soon joined in the humour. I saw him physically relax. 'Sure, that makes sense.'

But then I felt panic stab me like an early period pain. 'Shit, is Rowan okay? I was meant to text when I got home.'

'Ah, he's fine. He and Ian had a lads' night in last night. Did their make-up, got drunk.'

'Besides,' Fred added, 'you can still text him when you get home.'

I risked a quick look at Monty who, mouth agape and one

eyebrow raised, now looked like the love child of shock and pride. He gave me a nod. 'I see. Well, ladies, go on ahead and enjoy your breakfast.' He leaned in for a second hug and, speaking into the ear away from Fred, whispered, 'Good on you, Edi.'

When we were sitting down, Fred looked over her menu while I fidgeted with mine. And as though sensing my worry, she said, 'I'm not going to be offended if you text him. Especially if he's a worrier.'

I apologised profusely and wrestled my phone out of my bag. *He isn't a worrier but—* There were two messages: *Home yet babe? Getting late. xxx* and *Guess you're still out. But lemme know when you're back. Bloody love you. x* – and a voicemail that I decided against listening to. There were ripples of guilt moving through my belly. But I tried hard to counter the feelings by making a tally of the number of pancakes Rowan might have eaten with women by now. Besides, it had always been me who instigated the 'home safe' text; half the time he didn't reply so I couldn't see why this time he'd—

'Edi.' Fred reached across the table. 'Are you okay? You've gone really pale.'

You. I forced a smile. *This time it's about you.* 'I'm fine, sorry.' I flashed a tight smile and back-clicked out of my WhatsApp. But before I could stash the handset away another message came through. This one wasn't from Rowan, though, instead it was a GIF from Faith: Two women kissing. And she was still typing …

Definitely saw you with Fred. Too early in the day for a date. Stride of pride? xx

Followed by the emoji of a rainbow flag.

Chapter 31

Monty told Rowan he'd seen me – 'Yeah, just said you were with one of the girls' – and I felt a jumble of relief and disappointment that he hadn't told Rowan everything. It maybe wouldn't have hurt him to know he wasn't the only one having sleepovers with new friends. 'He always says he can't tell the difference between them though,' he added, and laughed along. I was facing away from him while he talked, ferreting through drawers to find a pair of skinny jeans that didn't stink of cigarette smoke (Lily) or regret (Fred, who I'd seen another three times in the last week, and slept with another twice). In the end I turned around, threw my arms in the air and announced, 'I'll just wear a dress.'

Rowan moved towards the small chest at the bottom of the bed. 'Black tights or natural?'

I smiled. *See, he knows everything . . .* 'Black.' But then a memory hit. 'Actually, none.'

'You'll go with trousers?'

'Nope. Bare.' The dress dropped down over my thighs and into place, quickly enough for me to catch an expression of surprise. 'What?'

'You never do that.'

'Well . . .' I smoothed the fabric out on a pale blue number that would look good with the late afternoon tea we were having. 'Maybe I can still surprise you.'

He crossed the room and caught me by the elbow, then pulled me closer for a kiss. 'Maybe I'm not all that keen on surprises.'

Well, I thought, *maybe that's just tough luck …*

*

The tea rooms were prim and proper and everything I'd expected from Rowan's parents. They were sitting uncharacteristically close when we arrived, like a real-life couple. But they shot apart when they saw us – as though they'd been caught doing something unseemly – and one after the other they pulled Rowan into a hug to greet him.

Gregory turned his attention to me soon after – 'Edith, fantastic dress' – before dropping back into his seat.

Penny hugged me but somehow managed to make the gesture a distanced one – 'Edith, so lovely you're here this time' – which I took to be a jibe about my absence during Rowan's trip home, like I should follow wherever he led.

I flashed her a tight smile and sat down. I crossed my legs then and, noting Penny's glance, I suddenly felt desperately self-conscious at having them on show at all. I pushed out a deep breath through my nose and thought of Fred – 'These legs, Edi, I'm telling you' – and her friendship (*is that what we're calling it?*), her compassion towards my least favourite parts. I ran a hand down my own thigh as though brushing something away, then I reached across to Rowan's clasped hands and grabbed a hold of one.

'Penny, you're looking so well. New hairstyle?'

'No.' She primped her hair one side then the other. 'But thank you, Edith. Your hair looks …' She trailed off, tilted her head one side and then the other. 'Effortlessly chic.'

'Well, certainly effortless,' I joked. 'I spent so long picking out the dress that I didn't leave enough time for the hair. A friend of mine is trying to get me into these messy buns—'

'Your natural wave suits you. Classy.' She leaned forward to reach for a teacup. 'You and my Rowan make quite the picture-perfect couple when you're dolled up like this.' I noted the ownership – *my* Rowan; not ours – as though I'd snatched something away from her alone. When she put the cup back in place she smiled, looked at Rowan, raised an eyebrow and then looked back at me. 'Rowan tells us that you're on a sort of break?'

'Penny!'

'Christ, Mum.'

I turned to face Rowan. 'A break?'

'You know what I mean, Edi, we … you know, the deal.' He stretched his eyes in urgency. 'I told Mum and Dad we were a bit open-ended at the minute, to give us a break from wedding planning, too, and to let us both, I don't know, breathe a bit or something.' He smiled, like he'd rescued the situation – but he'd actually made things a bit bloody worse. *Breathe?* I parroted. *I'm stifling you?*

'Of course.' I looked back at his parents and tried to relax my expression into something they might believe, then held my left hand up and flashed the ring. 'Still very much engaged. But we're both young, as you've pointed out yourselves, and there's no need to rush into a wedding, is there? Not when we can enjoy being engaged for a bit beforehand.'

Penny's own expression relaxed – as much as it possibly could. 'Well, now that's settled. I was worried we'd have to cancel the announcements and all sorts.' She said it like it would be a real travesty and her worries became a small weight sitting in my lap. 'Everyone knows and is delighted, of course. But we'll save that talk for another time, perhaps?' She looked at Rowan, who nodded. 'Now, are you two hungry? We've only ordered two pots of tea so far. Gregory, why don't you take Rowan up to choose something for us all? I'm sure Edith trusts him to choose for her as well.'

It wasn't a question, so I didn't answer. But I thought – shouted, internally: *No. I don't.*

'Edith, are you okay with Rowan choosing?' Gregory asked, and I wondered whether this common courtesy had been filtered out in the genetics somewhere on the way to Rowan; his mother's influence, perhaps.

'Of course. Penny and I can catch up.'

When Rowan and his dad had disappeared out of earshot, though, I realised this private catch-up had been exactly what she'd wanted. Penny shifted forward in her seat to lessen the distance between us and, in a voice notably quieter than before, asked how I was.

'I'm well, thank you. Work is—'

'Edith, I'm not asking about your livelihood. I'm more interested in your relationship with my son.' She looked past me, and I thought she must be checking where Rowan and Gregory were in the queue. 'This break. His idea, was it?' She spoke with a certainty that unnerved me.

'It was but …'

'But you're fine with it?' I hadn't even told the lie and she already didn't believe it. She leaned back a little but kept her voice hushed. 'Gregory has been a good husband, Edith, I won't pretend otherwise. A good provider; there when I needed him to be through the most serious matters in life. But …' She hesitated, then looked up and swallowed hard before continuing, 'Loyalty hasn't been his forte throughout our marriage.'

'Oh.' I felt my body deflate around me as I sank back in the chair. 'Oh, I … Penny, I'm—'

She held up a hand. 'Don't be sorry, Edith, it was my choice. But given my time again …' She petered out and, rather than looking behind me, seemed to find a distraction in the distance somewhere. She smiled then, in the most genuine way I'd ever seen her manage. 'Given my time again, with the advice of someone who had lived experience, I'm not sure I'd make the same decisions.

Which I suppose is what everyone my age says about everything they've done.' There was a light laugh as she leaned back in her seat. 'It's something that happens when you're old.'

'Nonsense.' I dismissed her self-deprecation in a kneejerk reaction and she looked surprised. 'You aren't old, Penny.'

She looked me up and down. 'Maybe it's just that you're so beautiful, young.'

I felt my cheeks bloom into small roses. Penny had been kind, accepting when I was younger. But the longer Rowan and I were together, the more distance there was carved between me and his mother. People had told me it was normal and I'd accepted it without question. But this kindness from woman to woman, I thought, this felt much more normal now.

'Thank you, Penny. I appreciate the honesty, and—'

'I've always liked you, Edith.' *I'd appreciate finishing a sentence, too,* I thought. But the compliment stunned me quiet. 'You've got … I don't know, something about you. Grit. Gumption. Don't let anyone dilute that down, will you?'

I held her look for a second. I was sure something passed between us. Some older-woman wisdom, trickling down into the next generation about to make their mistakes. 'I won't.' Rowan dropped hard in the seat next to me with a landing that made me jump. I added, 'I promise,' to Penny who nodded, before letting the men overtake the conversation.

'Promise what?' Rowan asked.

'I was asking Edith whether she's going to turn into one of these hideous brides that lets the wedding become her main focus in life.' Her detached tone was back then, and I realised whatever intimacy we shared had been stashed away – for safekeeping, though, where no one could try to change what had been said.

I smiled. 'And I promised that I won't be that woman.'

Chapter 32

In the days after, I threw myself into work with a vigour I hadn't felt for months. By Wednesday, I realised it was a coping mechanism. I used my mid-morning coffee break to try and consider what for: the new sexual experiences and the questions they were bringing about; the old relationship; the woman-to-woman advice from Penny that I'd carried like a small nugget of gold in the back pocket of my jeans in the days since we'd spoken. It could have been any number of things. *Or a hideous mixture of them*, I thought with a groan as I poured coffee, sipped two mouthfuls, then poured again to top up what was missing. I was looking out onto the city, like I might find answers written across massive Post-it Note displays in the windows of other high-rise buildings, when Diane caught my attention.

'Everything okay, Edi?'

I turned. 'Of course. I needed a screen break.'

'Boy, you're telling me. I feel like meetings make the world go round these days, but when you're meeting people up and down the country ...'

'You're not really meeting them, you're Skyping them.'

She nodded. 'Got it in one.'

Diane had always been a kind manager to work with – or

178

rather, work for. As the company had expanded, we'd seen less and less of her. But she occasionally popped by the communal coffee station for no reason at all beyond the chance to rub elbows with one of us. I moved out of her way and gestured to the half-full pot. 'Don't let me bogart the caffeine.'

'Actually, I was hoping to pin you down for a chat, if you've got time?'

Any distraction is a welcome one. 'Absolutely. What can I do for you?'

'Lucille, she ... Actually, do you know Lucille?'

Only by reputation. I swallowed hard. Lucille was Diane's boss, and she was known about the company for the best and worst reasons: dedicated, respected, terrifying. 'I haven't met her, no.'

'You'll get on just fine. She's having an office day today and she's asked whether you're available for a meeting, which you aren't because I checked the team calendar.' *Christ, where is this going?* 'But I've shifted your meeting with Nicola to Xander's diary so you can pop along this afternoon and talk to her about a few things. Now, I can see your face and I want to reassure you from the off that it's nothing to worry about.' She reached across and patted my hand. 'The opposite, I'd say. Half past two suit you?' She didn't wait for an answer before thanking me and hurrying out at the same speed she'd miraculously appeared at.

I turned back to the window. I sipped again. *Great, another thing to worry about ...*

*

The front of Lucille's office was floor-to-ceiling glass, allowing everyone to see her daily goings-on. She was on the phone when I got there, so I lingered awkwardly outside and waited to be ushered in. In the seconds that ticked by, I found myself stealing hooded glances at her. I'd only ever seen her through a pixelated image, on her LinkedIn profile and our company's website. But neither of those had done her justice. She was gorgeous. Not Fred-gorgeous, either, but intimidating-gorgeous. She wore a pale blue suit with a white blouse underneath, and high heels that implied she wouldn't be going far from her desk. Her hair was a platinum that's impossible to maintain – unless you've got the time and money for it – and it was cut in an angular bob, longer at the front than the back. Straightened to within an inch of its life, too.

Her actual face, though, was harder to get a read on. She didn't wear much make-up but what she did wear would have rendered Betty weak at the knees with jealousy. Every now and then she arched an eyebrow, as though whoever was on the phone had either shocked or impressed her. *Impressed,* I decided, *she looks far too controlled to be shocked by anything.* Without any sign that it was coming, then, she slammed the phone back into its cradle and looked my way. She'd hardly taken a breath between ending the call and beckoning me in.

'Edith?'

'Edi.'

'Edi.' She smiled. 'Lovely to meet you. I'm sorry to have kept you outside.' She didn't stand, but I leaned over the desk and offered her my hand to shake anyway, and she arched her eyebrow again as she reciprocated the gesture. 'Take a seat.'

I did as I was told. 'It's lovely to meet you.'

She was looking at open folders on her desk as she spoke. 'I'm grateful you could make the time.' She shuffled papers and looked at me. 'Now, you've been with us for some time and you've got a glowing record from all of your superiors. But are you happy here, Edi?'

Is this a well-being check-in? 'I enjoy my work, absolutely,' I said, baffled by the mere suggestion that anyone might ever say otherwise when faced with a question like that – being asked by their boss. 'I certainly don't have any plans to leave,' I added.

She nodded, and looked away from me, like she was considering something. 'Well, I'm delighted to hear that.' She handed over the paperwork she'd been reading. 'We're looking to restructure some of the teams and yours happens to be one of them. Diane is wasted at her desk as it stands so she, and she's aware of this, will be moved to a more forward-facing position so she can engage with clients out and about, interviews, developing PR plans in the field. I won't bore you. But we'll be looking first and foremost to replace her, but secondly to make it a more pronounced managerial position. You'll oversee the team you currently work with, and another three teams besides that. Ahead of this happening, though, we'd like to give you the opportunity for proper managerial training. Just to hone those skills that you've been flaunting already.' She winked – *oh my God, an actual wink* – at me between breaths. 'Now, tell me, Edi, how does that sound so far?'

Terrifying. I cracked into a toothy grin. 'I mean, amazing. Is there a catch?'

She shook her head. 'No catch. We'll look at a pay increase, too, of course, for the extra work you'll be doing. Diane will want to talk to you about the workload distribution, though, so that might be something best saved for when you've discussed your duties with her?'

'Okay.' I nodded, still smiling. 'Absolutely.'

She leaned on her elbows and rested her chin in the palm of one hand. 'Questions?'

'When does all of this happen?'

'Ah, of course.' She leaned back. 'Diane has a twelve-month changeover period to finish up outstanding work, but for six of those months you'll be shadowing her. So, the start date is fluid. But the paperwork you've got outlines a number of modules, available through the city centre university, so if you want to take a look through that and liaise with Diane about your choices then we'll look to get you signed up for the next start date.' She glanced over at her screen. 'September, by the looks of that email.'

'Perfect. Okay. That's all perfect.'

'Edi.' She stood, then, and held her hand out. 'It's been a pleasure.'

I'll say, I thought, matching her gesture. It had been the exact thing to turn a ridiculous few months into something salvageable. If I'd been talking to Diane I would have said so. But Lucille looked ready to rush me out at break-neck speed, so I thanked her another two times and hurried out of the office, clutching the paperwork to my chest like I was holding government secrets.

I took the stairs back to my normal floor, to give myself time to calm down, take deep breaths, and dance about like Chandler Bing post-orgasm. I threw my arms out, kicked my legs, grabbed my phone and typed a text: *AMAZING NEWS AT WORK. Got a second? xxx*

But I was dumbstruck. *Who should I send this to?*

Chapter 33

Order of importance: I texted the group chat to tell the girls, then I called Rowan. He was supportive and delighted – 'Jesus, Edi, that's amazing!' – but not enough to immediately take me out to celebrate – 'I'm shit, I know, but I've got stuff tonight that I can't get out of. This weekend though?' – which I tried to be understanding of. In fact, I tried so hard to be understanding that I managed to convince myself it really was fine (even though it really wasn't) and instead of doing anything to mark this drastic change in my career (super drastic, some might say), I just got myself together and went home. Alone. I landed heavy on the sofa that evening with a sigh and decided the least I could do was order myself a takeaway. I was a click away from Just Eat when the phone hummed alive in my hand: Fred.

'Hi,' I answered, 'this is a nice surprise.'

'Got a second to talk?' She sounded light, happy. It was infectious. 'I wasn't sure if …'

'Not at all. I'm alone and all ears. What's going on?'

'I had good news and I wanted to share it.' A heat spread across my abdomen and I found myself smiling like a desperate teenager; it was a look Fred brought out in me quite often. 'I've had confirmation of an exhibit, Edi. Like, of *my* work in an actual *gallery*.' Her excitement mounted the more she added – 'They're confirming details, and then, Christ then …'. I felt a shared excitement for her. I was on the edge of my seat by the time she'd finished. 'Isn't that bloody brilliant?'

'Yes, God, absolutely. Congratulations.' I decided to tell her, then. 'This is serendipity.'

'You have news?'

'Promotion.' My smile inched a little wider when I heard her gasp. 'Training courses, pick of managerial modules, head of multiple teams.'

'Okay, how are we celebrating?' she asked, her voice full of happy jitters. But then she sank a little and said, 'I'm an idiot. You'll be with people.'

I assumed she meant Rowan. I'd done my utmost not to be the woman-moaning-about-her-partner-while-having-an-affair. It was a tired role. But from Fred's facial shifts whenever he came up in conversation, I knew she had thoughts on it all. In the interest of holding everything together as it was for a little while longer, I used my best breezy voice and said, 'He's actually working tonight.'

There was a long pause. 'I'll be downstairs in thirty minutes.'

*

The bar was heaving with people. It had taken Fred so long to order two glasses of wine that by the time she'd elbowed her way to the front of the queue for the bar, I'd seen her change tactic and order a bottle instead. I'd been perched in a dimly lit corner on a high stool, leaning awkwardly on the table next to me and trying to pretend that this atmosphere, on a date night, felt normal. Mine and Rowan's date nights had long ago devolved into dinners at home and films on Netflix; the girls were more likely to take me to a bar. But Fred had suggested celebratory drinks, and I was too excited in her company not to go along with the idea.

She bumped her way through the swaying bodies, set two glasses on the table and leaned in to kiss my cheek before sitting down herself.

'To us,' she said, when our glasses were half-full. 'For being beautiful and successful.'

I laughed. 'I'll toast to successful.'

'Edi ...' She paused to take a mouthful. 'Why do you do that?'

'Do what?'

'Put your appearance down all the time.'

I'd never been called out on it by a love interest before. I'd never *had* a love interest before, apart from Rowan, I thought but then I shook the idea away. The girls had always told me I was beautiful. But that's literally in the job description of being a good friend. Molly could arrive pockmarked with a PMS break-out and her hair half-curled from three days ago and I would have told her she looked beautiful; I would have done the same for any of them.

I shrugged. 'I just don't think I'm all that special.'

'So ...' She lingered, looked at her glass. 'Why should I have sex with you, if you aren't all that special?' My eyes stretched and she laughed. 'I'm not asking you to actually explain why I should have sex with you. *I* already know why I should have sex with you. But why do you think it?'

'My quick wit and sparkly personality.' I used the flattest tone I could manage. 'I'm a fucking delight to be around.'

She laughed again and then hopped off her stool. Her stomach was close enough to brush against my knees when she stopped in front of me. 'This okay?' She gestured to the proximity and I nodded. 'Good, so, walk me through this. Rowan, and yes, I'm going to talk about Rowan.' I felt a flare of nerves but I also didn't want to stop whatever was coming. 'He's *never* called you out for putting yourself down the way you do?'

185

I thought. 'Well, yes. He tells me I shouldn't.'

She narrowed her eyes. 'How does he tell you?'

He usually tuts and tells me to stop. I sighed. 'Is there a right answer to this?'

'Yes.'

'Okay, well, I have a weird feeling I'm going to say the wrong one.'

Fred smirked. Her head dipped slightly, and her hair fell forward, and the whole movement made me want to kiss her. But I didn't have the time. She came to stand alongside me instead, draped an arm around my shoulders in a display that could have looked like friendship, and with her free arm she made a sweeping gesture in the direction of the room.

'Pick someone.'

'I'm sorry?' I craned to look at her expression, but she was staring into the crowd.

'Pick someone who you find attractive.'

It was hard to pick out anyone at all, between the mass (mess?) of people and the deliberately dim lighting that set the mood of the place. There was one man, though, who stepped aside to let a woman walk ahead of him. *Manners, apparently that's what I find attractive.* But rather than admit that aloud to the outrageously beautiful woman who was still touching me, I kept looking. After an uncomfortable length of time, I finally pointed to someone: a man around my age, dark hair that was faded into a longer cut on top; he was wearing black jeans and a T-shirt under a blazer, smart but not too smart.

'Him,' I said, and then dropped my arm quickly in case he turned.

Fred tilted her head one side then the other. 'Okay. Let's say I buy it. Go and talk to him.' She ushered me from my seat as she spoke. 'Say hi, ask him to dance.'

'Are you mad?' I turned around to face her, then, my back to the crowd. 'Why?'

'Because you find him attractive, and we're in a bar.' She made it sound like the most obvious explanation in the world. 'Why wouldn't you talk to him?'

'I mean, to start with he's a solid eight and I'm definitely a four in the right ligh—' She cut me off mid-word with a kiss. And I didn't care who could see. When she pulled away my mouth stretched into a smile. 'What was that for?'

'I sensed you were about to say something you shouldn't.' She kissed me again, but only quickly. 'You're a goddamn ten, Edi, and, frankly, I don't think you've made the most of this open relationship deal. If Rowan is out there doing ...' She waved the end of the sentence away. 'Do you know what, arses to him. It genuinely does not matter what Rowan is out there doing. It matters what *you're* doing, how *you're* playing this.' She turned me around with an urgency to face the crowd. When she spoke again, I could feel the heat of her breath just under my ear and it was doing terribly distracting things to me. 'Now, pick a woman.'

I laughed. 'Why a woman?'

'Why not a woman, Edi?' She reached across the table to grab her glass, but stayed behind me still. 'Why not anyone at all in this room?'

'Did you do this?'

'What?' she asked and took another sip.

'Experiment.'

'Once upon a time. But I've never been with a man if that's where this is going.'

'So, why should I be with a woman?'

'Because you might want to be? Because you can be?'

'Why do you think I need this, Fred?' I felt myself getting defensive, as though this were a mangled rerun of the car-crash conversation with Rowan that started all of this. There was the same confused knot in my stomach, rising part-way to my throat. 'Wait,' I started, an uncomfortable worry rising, 'are you trying to get rid of me?'

'Oh …' Another kiss, but this time on the cheek. 'Make no mistake, Edi, I *am* taking you home tonight. But you don't want me permanently.'

'Why?'

'Edi, come on. Who actually ends up with the first person they have sex with?' She slammed her palm to her forehead as soon as the question was out. It was the first time across several dates that I'd seen Fred flush in the cheeks, with what I guessed was embarrassment. 'That wasn't … I didn't …'

I kissed her, then, to ease her floundering. 'It's okay,' I replied, and it was. Because even though the question should have hurt, somehow it didn't. It only felt a little like being told something that I already knew.

Chapter 34

Before

Faith's first girlfriend had just left her for a boy, and it was the talk of the college. The ex-girlfriend and the boy she'd 'turned straight for' made no secret of their relationship. They turned up to college not two days later, hand in hand as though the girlfriend's foray into lesbianism had been exactly that – a quick adventure.

'I don't even mind,' Faith had said, although the mascara tracks sort of undercut her point. 'Like, we're teenagers, we're allowed to experiment. But did we actually need to go ahead and tell our families and shit?' She stuffed another mini muffin into her mouth and spoke around the dough. 'She came out, you know? I was slow and understanding and, like, I literally didn't give a shit.' She sighed. 'She didn't need to tell anyone she was with me. It could have been a secret.'

'But, Faith—' Betty stroked her hair '—would that have been better?'

I thought back to my own flicker of interest in Faith; how we agreed that no one needed to know – Rowan included. 'A little,'

189

I answered, even though it wasn't my place. 'If no one knew that it had started then there wouldn't be anyone to tell when it was over either.'

Faith let out a shudder-sigh again. 'Exactly.'

There had been another girl – only one. She and I met while I was on holiday with my parents. We were in Devon, and she was the surfer stereotype who strolled out of the water with such grace that I would have fully believed anyone who told me she was born with a fin. She flicked her hair in one direction then the other and set droplets of sea flying around her; it looked like a special effect. It wasn't until hours after I'd seen her like that that I saw her again in the restaurant we were eating in that evening; she seated us, and I spent the rest of the night looking for her. There had been another handful of times when I'd seen her over the trip. She started to say hello in passing and that was enough to turn my young heart into a maraca; loud and all shaken up. On the last day I upped the ante from a hello – 'Be seeing you, then' – and then I stashed her in the box of feelings that never happened, alongside Faith, my occasional doubts about Rowan, and how beautiful Mel C looked when she finally left The Spice Girls.

If no one knew, I recited as I rubbed the spot between Faith's shoulder blades, *then there was nothing to tell.*

It was hours later when I was tucked up against Rowan in his parents' living room. They were away again, and we were making the most of an empty house by pretending we were grown-up enough to own property. Rowan had sat on the kitchen counter while I'd cooked dinner; he'd set the places at the dining room table; I helped myself to half a glass of wine. We borrowed adulthood for evenings at a time.

'I just can't believe she'd be so brazen about it.' I was still nursing ill feelings towards the girl from college: Ingrid. 'Christ, even her name makes me angry.'

Rowan half-laughed. 'Babe, don't you think you're getting a bit involved in this?'

'What do you mean?' I pushed away and balanced on my elbow to get a look at him. 'If one of your friends had been dumped for another girl, do you think you and the lads would be okay with it? Let's say June decides to chuck Hamish, which she absolutely should—' he opened his mouth to disagree but I pressed on '—and then a day later she turns up with Faith and pretends Hamish never happened, like, she was never even *with* a boy. That's okay, is it?'

He seemed to put some real thought into it, then said, 'I'd die if you left me for a woman.'

'You're so dramatic.' I leaned back against him. 'You seemed to think it wasn't a big deal a second ago.'

'Well, now I've thought about it and it is.' His voice was hard-edged and I nearly reminded him that I wasn't *actually* leaving him for another woman – or anyone for that matter. 'Besides, it's different for men when stuff like that happens. Everyone is straight, so, someone turning gay is major. But not everyone is gay, so, turning straight is just going back to what everyone else is doing.'

I rolled my eyes so hard that I thought I caught sight of my own grey matter. When I didn't answer for a few seconds, he gave me a little squeeze.

'I take it you don't agree?'

'With what?' I asked, because playing dumb usually helped with these things.

'With what I just said about it being harder for men.'

'Honestly, Rowan, I don't think I agree with much of what you just said.' I shifted away from him, then, and leaned back against the opposite end of the sofa, leaving my feet in his lap instead. 'Maybe it's best if we just leave it?'

'No.' He frowned. 'No, I want to know what's so wrong about what I just said.'

'I mean, to start with, that's absolutely not how sexuality works.'

'Oh, Edi …' He used *that* tone; the one that implied I was

either being stupid, or on the cusp of it. But I was too deep into a psychology and sociology module to doubt myself over him. 'I know you think you know stuff—'

'And this is why I didn't want to talk about it.'

'Hey.' He started to rub my feet. 'I just mean, you only know it from your side, like I only know it from a guy's side.'

'Okay, well, from a basic biology and brain chemistry side, sexuality isn't socially conditioned. Our brains are attracted to lots of different things, including the same gender.'

'Are you trying to tell me something? Is that what you're driving at here?' he asked. His tone was jovial but there was still a riptide in my stomach. 'I know you and Faith are close and all—' he dug his thumb into the heel of my left foot '—but are you *that* close?' He winked at me. 'Because if you are then I can get behind it for a while, you know, if—'

'Don't worry, babe.' My voice was heavy with sarcasm. 'I know you'd die if that happened.'

He laughed. 'Point taken. Come on, though, imagine being left because you've turned someone?'

'But wouldn't you just want me to be happy?'

He made the same face as before, and I could see how much brain power the question required from him. But he soon shook his head. 'No, Edi, I think I'd just want you to be straight.'

Chapter 35

Now

The waiter took the card machine away and handed me the receipt with a flat smile. Betty had been making socially inappropriate comments in earshot all evening – 'So, I'm having my smear test right ...' – because she had no concept of the socially inappropriate. But it had started to get to the poor chap somewhere around an hour in – 'Only arseholes expect you to have sex without a condom these days' – and his face, at least, hadn't quite recovered from these separate waves of shock. I'd been so embarrassed that when the card machine asked if I wanted to leave a tip I'd sincerely considered it, until I realised a) Betty could actually talk about whatever she wanted in public with her friends and b) she was definitely right about the condom thing.

'Thanks ever so much,' I said, and smiled. *My tip? Be less judgemental.*

'So, can we have a quick check-in before you leave?' Molly asked.

'About?' I shrugged on my coat as Lily cleared her throat.

'How the sex is with Fred.'

Cora reached across the table to backhand Lily's upper arm. 'That is *not* what we want a check-in over.'

'Ah, actually—' Faith raised a finger in protest '—I'm certainly curious.'

'I also wouldn't mind knowing.' Betty spoke through a mouthful of food.

'Perverts.' Cora looked from one woman to the next before landing back on me. 'They're all bloody perverts.'

I nodded. 'No more or less so than they always have been, though.'

'We didn't talk about sex this much when Edi was having sex with Rowan,' Molly added, weighing in on Cora's team. It was the crass versus the controlled and I laughed.

'In their defence, though—' I stood up '—maybe sex with Fred is just more interesting.'

There was a chorus of amusement and applause from one side of the table – Lily, Betty, Faith – while the opposing seats flashed wide eyes before a slow fade to a laugh.

Cora nodded, then, looked at Molly and shrugged. 'Well, that's fair.'

Faith tipped her head back to look up at me behind her. 'It also answers Molly's question.'

'I didn't get to a question.'

'No, but you did want to ask how things are with Rowan and, or Fred,' I weighed in, then raised an eyebrow and blew two kisses across to Molly and Cora. 'The deal is ongoing. Apparently we're both free to date who we want; we're still engaged; we still love each other.' I parroted the explanation out, but my level of conviction wasn't quite right. I saw Cora flash Molly a look that I thought was a warning not to push, and Molly's shoulders dropped, as though she were deflated – or beaten at something. 'Honestly? I don't know where I'm at with Rowan. We're seeing each other a bit less than we were, but that's not through lack of trying.'

'On your part,' Lily added.

I hadn't said it, no. But it wasn't an unfair addition. 'Yes, on my part.' I shrugged. 'He's busy, I guess, I don't ...' I rubbed at my forehead. Over the last few weeks the girls had done a great job of asking all the safe questions, but I couldn't blame them for wanting to know more – or, if nothing else, wanting to at least know whether I was okay with the hidden 'more' of mine and Rowan's relationship. But the truth was, I didn't have more to tell. Whatever he was thinking about our engagement, he hadn't spent enough time in a room with me to say. But who wants to admit that out loud? 'I'm sorry, I—'

'You have somewhere to be.' Betty stood up, then, and kissed me on the cheek. 'I'll walk to the door with you anyway. I need the loo.' She gave me a gentle push. 'If the waiter swings around, does someone want to grab another bottle of red?'

Cora and Faith said, 'Yes,' in unison, and Betty and I giggled our way to the exit.

'It's none of our business,' she said, when we came to a stop. 'No, but—'

'But nothing,' she interrupted again. 'It's none of our business. We're not here to know the ins and outs, we're just here to support you through them.' She gave me another kiss on the cheek. 'Tell Fred we said hello. Text me tonight when you get home safe? Or, you know, when you get wherever you end up.' She winked and walked off then, and I hurried across town to meet the woman who would take me home that night ...

*

Fred came back from the bar with an orange gradient drink in a tall glass, topped with an umbrella.

'Sex on the beach?' I asked, after the first sip.

'That sounds like an offer.'

I laughed. 'I meant the drink. I think sex on the beach is actually uncomfortable.'

195

She waved the comment away. 'It's different with a woman.'

'You say that about everything.'

'Have I been wrong so far?' She moved a little closer. 'I think the sex on the beach thing is at least worth putting on the table.'

'Now *that* sounds like an offer.'

'As soon as my blood alcohol drops enough ...'

I closed what little space was left between us, then, and kissed her square on the mouth. It was a newfound bravery that had slowly unfolded. Between the girls' logic – 'Who gives a shiny shit what anyone else thinks?' – and Fred's gentle persuasion – 'Sweetheart, you've got a hall pass. Use this time wisely' – I was well beyond the point of worrying about friends, colleagues, or anyone else catching us mid-contact. Rowan hadn't been worried – as evidenced by the number of messages I would still get on the average week from concerned (read: nosy) bystanders who had spotted him out and about – so I'd tried to filter out my own concerns. Still, it was one thing doing this with other men. But Rowan's thoughts on another woman might be—

'Are you with me?' Fred squeezed my arm. 'You looked miles away then.'

'I'm sorry. The girls were asking questions tonight. I feel like their worries are floating.'

'About me?'

'About Rowan.'

'Ah.' She took a long swig from her drink and I wondered whether she was buying time. 'Okay, give me some guidance, lady – do you want to talk about this or ...' She petered out and nodded to the dance floor. 'Do you want to get your arse over there and have a little grind on me?' She took another sip. 'There's no right or wrong answer, incidentally. Of course, I know which one *I* would prefer. But if you're not in the mood to talk about Rowan, then I guess I could stomach a dance.' Her smile cracked through the final words, and I bit back on a laugh as well.

'Dance with me?'

She held out a hand, palm up. 'I would be honoured.'

Fred and I had talked about Rowan, while tangled in bedsheets and tired from the night before – or sometimes the afternoon, only earlier. She was soft with me like that; not always, but when I needed her to be. She hadn't commented much, other than to say he was mad for risking the loss of a good partner: 'Mad or very cocksure,' she'd once added, but she hadn't expanded.

She eased my drink away from me and set it alongside hers on a nearby table. When 'One Drink Away' by Cher Lloyd kicked in, Fred grabbed me closer to her. 'God, let this song be a prophecy,' she whispered to me while we danced and we fell over ourselves with laughter. Her body knocked against mine in a way that I'm sure Lily's, Cora's, Faith's must have done at one point. But there was a kind of heat starting up, from knowing I'd seen those thighs unclothed; that I'd probably see them that way again before the night was over. I could feel a physical shift somewhere. It might have been arousal, I thought. But as Fred pulled me into the most sexually charged hug I think I've ever had on a dance floor, it occurred to me that this excitement – this charge – might just be something like freedom …

One song faded out to another and soon the room was flooded with Lady Gaga's 'Free Woman' – and I took it as a sign. I eased myself away from Fred long enough to guzzle down what was left of my drink, leaving a sandy mess at the bottom of the glass, and then I turned back to her with my arms stretched wide to welcome her in. Body to body we backstepped to the centre of the floor and swung ourselves about like teenagers on an A-level results night. It was somewhere in this twirling that the mess of other bodies cleared the way enough for me to see him.

I'd told him I was out that night – with Fred again. He'd only grunted in response and then told me he was staying in – with the boys. I tried to work out the lie: had he planned a night out with the other woman all along, or had someone swiped right at the last minute? Either way, they looked comfortable – close.

Fred led my arms in an excited jig, but I still couldn't help but watch for a second longer: while he brushed hair away from the woman's face; while he kissed her cheek with a tenderness that meant they couldn't possibly have had sex yet.

Fred came to a stop, when she realised what I was watching. She tucked an arm around my shoulders and pulled me to her – like I thought Lily, Cora, Faith must have done once. 'Are you okay?' she shouted above the music.

I glanced her way but then looked back – and in that time he'd seen us. Rowan stared at me through narrowed eyes, as though he couldn't place me. I wondered what it must be like to see me so far out of context. But it was clear when the realisation kicked in. He looked like something had physically stung him: his eyes spread wide; his forehead creased; his mouth parted as though he were about to speak across the ocean of bodies between us. He said something to the woman he was with – who was also looking our way – and then forced his way through dancing forms to close the distance. I spotted behind him that the woman's eyes were still fixed. *Are you expecting him to come back to you?* I wondered, closely followed by, *Do you even know who I am?*

Fred eased away from me. 'I shouldn't be here for this.'

'Wait.' I grabbed her hand and tried to bring her back to me. 'Why shouldn't you?'

'Edi—' They both spoke at the same time, and it struck me how different my name sounded in each mouth. Fred smiled – an awkward nervous smile that I hadn't seen on her before – and, I think, laughed, although the sound was hardly audible thanks to the soundtrack of Little Mix's 'Confetti'. Rowan only stood there.

'I thought you weren't out tonight,' I shouted to him.

He raised an eyebrow in answer and looked between us. 'Where's the infamous Fred?'

She opened her mouth but I got there first: 'Here.'

I'd never quite known what people meant when they said someone scowled at them. But when he looked back at me, looked me up and down, and then went back to his narrow-eyed stare, I thought, *This must be it*. He didn't say anything, but when I opened my mouth to speak again, he silenced me with a shake of the head. He threw Fred the same up-and-down look he'd given me before he walked off – leaving the woman across the room alone with her cocktail. She bunched her arms into a shrug and turned her attention elsewhere. *And that's how much you matter to these women*, I thought with my own shake of the head.

'Hey …' Fred rested a fingertip against my chin and pulled my face to her. 'Are you okay?'

'I am, actually.' And I really meant it.

Chapter 36

Cora danced around my kitchen to 'Don't Kill My Vibe' by Sigrid while I ate peanut butter straight from the jar. She kept taking strategic pauses to glance at the pregnancy test on the table between us. When she started to dance again each time, I knew it mustn't be quite cooked. Meanwhile, I couldn't bring myself to look at the test window for fear that there would be one too many lines waiting there. I swallowed another mouthful of butter and caught Cora's eye.

'How are you dancing while this is happening?'

She paused, panted, and dipped her finger into the open jar. 'Don't mind me.' She licked her finger clean and then landed hard in the seat opposite me. 'How do you want me to be acting?'

'I don't know, like you're worried?' I snatched the jar back and picked up where I'd left off. 'Besides, isn't this more a job that you should call Molly for?'

Cora spluttered a laugh. 'Can you imagine Molly on a pregnancy scare? If you weren't free, it would have been Betty or Lily.'

'Pah, why them? They're the least matern— Oh.'

She clicked her fingers. 'Got it in one. Freedom to choose what you do with your own body? Those pair live for this shit.' The song came to a natural close and suddenly Cora's bolshie attitude fizzled out, too. She exhaled hard. 'Fucking hell, now I *have* to look.'

I put my hand over the test. 'Does Hamish know this is happening?'

'No.'

'Do you know what you'll do if – you know?'

'No.' She pulled in a long belly breath. 'You're touching something that I've peed on.'

I took my hand away. 'That's what friends do.' I grabbed her hand, then, and leaned forward to look at the test before she could. 'We have a winner!' I held the dry end and flashed her a single line in the small window. With my other hand, I held up the paperwork with a clear picture of a negative result printed at the top.

'Oh fuck.' She dropped her forehead to the table. 'Fuck, fuck, fuck, thank fuck.'

I laughed. 'I thought you weren't nervous?'

'Oh, sod off and give me the peanut butter.' She yanked the jar away from me. 'And wash your hands, you filthy—' The sound of my doorbell cut across her. 'You're expecting someone?' she asked, a coated finger midway to her mouth.

I wasn't. But when I opened the front door there was Monty. There was something uncanny about the figure of him hovering outside; I realised he'd probably only ever been here with Rowan before then. And that brought to the forefront a quiet panic.

'Is Rowan okay?'

'Completely. Nothing has happened; everyone is safe.' But he hesitated. 'Can we talk?'

'Come in.' I stepped back. 'Cora's here.'

Saying her name must have summoned her; she arrived in the hallway, already shrugging her cardigan back on. 'Cora was here, now she's going.' She flashed Monty a sympathetic smile; it somehow said: *Sorry your friend's an arsehole.* 'Monty, always a pleasure.'

'Likewise, madam, likewise.'

There was red creeping up his cheeks that made me think things weren't quite as okay as he'd said. Still, he held himself together and stepped aside for Cora, who wandered down the corridor humming Sigrid on her way. Minutes ago her relief had been contagious. But now …

'Can I get you a drink?' I asked, leading him into the kitchen. 'Tea?'

'Milky, one sugar,' he said, and then rushed to add, 'but only if you're having one.'

I filled the kettle in quiet and flicked it on to boil. 'Can't have a serious talk without tea.' When he didn't say anything to contradict my assumption, I realised I'd be needing a strong tea myself – maybe even a black coffee. I rubbed hard at my forehead and then set about finding cups, grabbing a spoon, pulling milk from the fridge. 'What's he done?' I turned to face Monty, then, because we couldn't avoid it any longer. I couldn't hurry the water along.

'I really don't know what I'm doing here, Edi.' His voice broke halfway through the comment, and I worried for a second that a tear or two was about to loosen. *Christ, how bad things must be …* 'I'm worried about him. How much he's drinking, how much he seems to be abusing this …' He hesitated. 'This situation. He's like a virgin on death row.'

I laughed, but then a wave of sadness hit straight after. 'I see.' The kettle whistled to a boil behind me and I was glad of the call. 'He and I aren't seeing each other much.'

There was such a long pause that I was about to turn around and check Monty hadn't passed out from panic. But as milk collided with tea, I heard him faintly repeat, 'I see.' I wondered what Rowan had been telling them all. Monty's delay made me wonder whether we were all hearing the same stories – or whether Rowan and I were now on a six-month-to-forever-long hall pass at the never-end of which we'd ride off into the sunset in a carriage pulled by unicorns. I smirked. *But maybe even Rowan has a limit when it comes to lies,* I thought as I set a cup in front of my guest. 'Thank you.' He wrapped his hands around it. 'This is really hard because I don't know how much you know.'

'It's fine.' I took a seat opposite him. 'I know how much I know, but I don't know how much of what I know is the truth.' I half-laughed. 'Does that make sense?'

He nodded. 'I think so.'

'Monty, whatever you tell me, I'm not going to tell him that you've told me.'

His shoulders dropped. 'He'll know one of us has told you.'

'He won't. Rowan is a terrible liar, even now. Which is probably part of why he doesn't want to see me. No poker face.' I fact-checked myself, though, because he did have a face for lying when he needed one. 'Actually, he does have a poker face. But he's clumsy, and that's kind of enough.' I sipped my tea. 'Fred and I saw him out a few nights ago.'

'You both saw each other is my understanding of it.'

Here we go. I sucked in a breath. 'I wondered whether he'd tell you.'

'Only me,' he rushed to add; Monty obviously thought it still mattered who knew. 'He hasn't told any of the others.'

'I'm actually not all that worried about people knowing. Unlike Rowan, I've only slept with the one other woman and that seems a lot more decent than however many he's brought home to you and Ian.'

Monty flashed a tight smile then stared into his mug. He pushed out a long breath before he spoke. 'Remember Leonard? He was at your engagement shindig and, I don't know, friendships reconnect and all that, so he's been spending the odd night out with us since then. But Rowan ... he slept with Leonard's girlfriend.' I didn't – couldn't – answer. So he carried on, 'The night he saw you out with Fred.'

So it's probably my fault, I thought as I sipped my tea to buy myself a second. 'Wait, he was out with someone when I saw him. Was that her?'

He shook his head. 'He left you, bumped into her, saw an opportunity.' I swallowed another mouthful of tea and winced at the heat; it was a good enough distraction for a second, though. 'Edi, I'm sorry, I don't know – Christ, should I even be telling you this?' I only shrugged; I didn't have words yet. 'Apparently he'd got a bet going with Patrick. Leonard and this girl, they're not serious, not really, and rumour had it she was about to bin him anyway so Rowan and Pat decided—'

'I'm cutting you off.' I gazed into my mug as I spoke. *If I look at you I'll cry.* 'I think it's better for everyone that I don't know the end of that story, Mont.'

'Understood.' He took a sip of his drink and when he lowered the mug I could see a slight tremor of nerves that made me feel sorry for him.

'Look.' I reached over and grabbed his free hand. 'I know blokes don't really do the caring thing, but there's genuinely nothing wrong with it.' I squeezed. 'I know you're not doing this – I mean, I know you're not here in malice or competitiveness. You haven't whipped a ruler out. You're here because you're worried. I don't know what they tell you at boy school, but you're doing okay.' I tried to sound light rather than accusatory, but all the while I could hear Lily chanting statistics on toxic masculinity in the background. I pulled my hand back then and added, 'Say whatever more you're comfortable saying. But if you're uncomfortable because of a "should", then power through with it.'

'Why?'

'Should is a guilt word.' I sipped my tea, and quietly gave myself a point for growth. I needed to remember the moment as one to share in counselling.

He smiled. 'You're kind of brilliant, Edi.'

I tried to channel my inner Fred, Lily, Betty. 'I've been told.'

'I don't know how many women he's slept with now.' I held

my breath – more shots fired. 'I don't think he knows how many women he's slept with.' Second round. 'But this with Leonard, this is a final straw, really it is. I understand why this was a good idea and, Christ, all of us thought it was amazing that you were even into it, but, providing you're ready for it to stop because, I don't know, you might be doing just fine with it all, in which case shoot me down …' He looked up from his mug and stared straight at me like he was waiting for an answer. 'If you're ready for it to stop then I think you need to tell him that, and tell him it has to, because, Christ, this whole fucking thing has brought out an ugly shade in him, Edi. He needs you to be the sensible one.'

It all sat between us for what felt like a long time before I answered. 'But doesn't he always?'

Monty gave me a sad smile and reached across the table to take my hand. We finished our teas in quiet.

Chapter 37

The longer we went without talking, the more often I found myself thinking: *So, this is what life would be like*. I tried to call Rowan three times after Monty left but there was no answer and, as the day went on, no written replies either. He'd been on WhatsApp – curse the person who invented that feature – and I'd even gone as far as typing out a message on there, too, but I resisted the urge to hit send. *He doesn't want to talk to you*, I reminded myself as I muted the handset and carried on with what was left of the afternoon. In a manner that felt like a shitty remake of *Groundhog Day*, I found myself repeating the same process the following morning – and the morning after that. On the third day, though, it wasn't the thought of Rowan not wanting to talk to me that put me off; instead, it was the timestamp for when he was last online. Four hours earlier: 3.28 a.m.

I threw my phone down on the table and set about making breakfast. But the wave of gratitude I felt when the handset started to ring was embarrassing. I leapt on it like it was a gold-dusted chocolate bar, gifted to me in the midst of a rowdy bout of PMS. 'Oh, but of course it isn't him.' I hit the green key. 'Mum, you're calling early—'

'I saw you were online on the WhatsApp so I thought I'd call, check in.'

I smiled. *Is this what* everyone *does now?* 'It's just WhatsApp I think, Mum.' I pulled bread from the bin on the work surface and dropped two slices in to toast. 'I was just looking for whether the girls were about at all.'

'You don't have plans with them?'

I could hear the eager note in her voice and so help me I had to say, 'Oh, I do, I just wasn't sure who was up yet, whether anyone wanted breakfast before the Saturday shopping spree.' It was a lie; a whopping one actually, given that I'd told the girls I wanted a quiet day to myself. They were on standby in case my quiet day turned into a minor meltdown though; Betty's words, not mine. But it didn't feel like too much of a stretch, as possibilities went.

Mum asked all the right questions after that – 'Are you shopping for anything in particular, then?' – and stayed away from all the tricky ones. The spectre of Rowan – the ghosting of boyfriends present – was left on the outskirts, mostly. But when I'd told her that tea and toast were ready my end, she swung around to a more loaded question. 'You're all right, love, aren't you?' she asked, but she said it in a soft voice; I imagined her head tilting to one side. I thought if I listened close enough I might even hear Dad soft-breathing into the mouthpiece, too, as though they were both craning to hear an answer.

I checked the time. We'd been on the phone long enough to tip me into a sociable hour to start calling people to make plans for the day. *Balls to quiet.* 'I think so?' I answered in a way that I thought might be *too* honest. But the prospect of lying, again, about my feelings, again, was … I sighed. 'Everything is a bit much, that's all – you know with Rowan and the engagement and, I don't know, life, generally.' I half-laughed. 'I'm going to have a very kind-to-myself day, though, I promise.'

'Double promise?' Dad asked and I burst out in laughter. I heard what sounded like Mum slapping his arm. 'What? We both live here. She doesn't know I didn't just walk into the room right then,' he added in a voice that he obviously thought was lowered, but not quite enough.

'Well, she bloody does now, doesn't—'

'I double promise both of you, okay?'

'Okay,' they answered in unison.

When I'd pushed them off the phone by offering a third promise, I ate the first half of my toast in dead silence. Then I did the kindest thing I could think to do ...

*

The door was open when I'd got there; she'd texted me on the walk over to tell me it would be. I pushed through slowly, in case I startled her in the middle of something. Not that Fred seemed the sort to be startled by much. And no sooner had the door cracked open, I realised it would have to be a hefty loud intruder to make any noise at all over the sound of her music. Little Mix's 'Woman Like Me' was playing at a nightclub volume and Fred, in a flowing pleated black dress that looked way too fancy for 9 a.m. on a Saturday, was dancing around the open-plan space. When she swept around and saw me standing at the other end of the corridor, her expression was an excited one; she looked genuinely happy I'd arrived, and I tried to remember the last time someone had looked at me like that. *Probably Betty, when I got back from a wine run.* But she still didn't turn the music down. Instead, she rushed the length of the corridor, shut the door – the escape route I'd left ajar behind me – and eased my backpack off with more gentleness than the action seemed to deserve.

'Come and dance,' she instructed, and she grabbed my hand to tug me towards the living area where the music, I soon noted, was even louder.

Fred moved around lyrically; if she'd been speaking, she would have been reciting a love letter to her body. She jutted her hips one minute but then moved in a smooth flow the next; her arms waved around like she was conducting the musicians. And, most impressive of all, there was nothing about her that said worry; nothing like self-consciousness; nothing like she minded, even, that she was being watched. The song soon faded out but it was replaced with Jessie J's 'Sexy Lady', the opening chords for which had Fred gasping in excitement.

'Come!' She pulled my hand again. '*Please* dance with me.'

I laughed. 'What about your neighbours?'

'Ah, my neighbours are cool,' she huffed out; she was shimmying already. 'I put up with their late-night noise and they put up with my early morning dance-a-thons. It's a quid-pro-quo situation. Now ...' She slowed to catch her breath. 'Will you dance with me or is this something you have to be drunk to do?'

'Fred, I ...' I faded when I realised she was being playful; her eyebrow was cocked and she was smirking. 'I never dance this early,' I admitted.

'In which case—' she picked up speed again '—maybe we've worked out why you're sad.' She fumbled with her headband, pulling it free from her mess of hair to unleash curls that fell loosely around her. When her hair settled into place, Fred looked every bit the model; not just a life model, though, but a natural beauty model. The face that belonged on a campaign for joy. 'Come, dance, then you can tell me what's wrong.' She pulled me to her by my hips, and I felt soft against her. Our bodies moved in a way that a male author would describe as seductive or charged or— Eurgh. But there was nothing of that. She moved my body like she were teaching it something, increasing the pace of hip shifts as the music livened around us. We were seconds away from the chorus when Fred flashed me a wide-eyed look and said, 'Wait. If you're going to lose yourself in a dance, I know a better song than this.'

When she moved away my worries flooded back in. I wrapped

my arms across my midriff, as though she hadn't already seen it from a much more vulnerable viewpoint.

'Don't you dare cover that body up.' She was strutting back over to me, clicking along to the opening bars of a song that I didn't recognise. I tried to laugh as I eased my arms away; I ran a hand through my hair, felt in my pocket for my phone, anything to avoid … 'Hey, what's going on?' She stopped in front of me and set a hand either side of my waist.

'I'm feeling … self-conscious.'

'I've seen you naked.' She laughed. 'What's *actually* going on?'

I pushed out a long breath. But I didn't want to look at her. 'Rowan slept with one of his friend's girlfriends.'

It was the first time I'd seen her look truly taken aback. 'What a prince.' No sooner had she said it than she pulled me into a hug. 'We don't have to dance; we don't have to talk. Walk me through what you need, okay?'

I relaxed into the hug. By then, the chorus to the song had kicked in and I found that – despite wanting to cry only seconds ago – I belched out a surprise laugh. The song was, I realised, 'She Drives Me Crazy' by the Fine Young Cannibals. And I remembered it from dancing around the living room at home, with Mum and Dad.

'The song suddenly doesn't feel quite as appropriate as it did,' she spoke into my neck.

I started to shift myself in time with the music and eased Fred away by her waist. She was already smiling, and she matched her movements to my own. I kept hold of her hand and made an archway of our arms for her to shimmy underneath; she spun out the other side at such a speed that her dress kicked up around her. We broke away from each other, then, to do our own thing around the space. I let my hair fall wild and my face go pink and my breath go haggard. I sang to the chorus and made 'Ooh' noises in all the right places. Fred looked thrilled as she clicked and danced and made 'Ooh' noises in between my own. By the time the track was coming to a fade we were both panting like we'd done a back-to-back Zumba session with a cruel instructor. But I thought our satisfaction was likely off the scale.

The next track was another one I didn't recognise. Fred was dancing into the kitchen where the speaker was housed, so she could turn the volume down to something that allowed a conversation. She pulled the fridge open.

'Orange juice, apple juice, milkshake …' She paused to check her watch. 'Probably a tad early for wine but I'm not a hundred per cent opposed to it.' She poked her head around the door. 'What'll it be?'

'Orange juice, please.' I was desperate for something cold. I loitered while Fred poured drinks and noticed, then, that half of the artwork I'd seen during my previous visits had changed. But Fred's self-portrait still hung pride of place.

'Still checking me out?' She came to stand alongside me and handed me a drink.

I smiled and admitted, 'Always.'

There was a comfortable and strange silence while we both stared at the outline of Fred's body. Then she sighed; a hearty sigh that made my stomach turn, because I sensed something was coming. 'Edi, you need more joy in your life.'

Although it hadn't been what I was expecting. 'I'm sorry?'

'Stuff like that.' She gestured to the living area where we'd been dancing, as though our silhouettes still occupied the space. 'Waltzing around the living room to songs that make you make noises; wearing Saturday night dresses first thing in the morning because why save your best for other people? You know …' She turned to face me. 'Joy!'

I wasn't sure whether I'd ever had an epiphany before but … 'Christ, I think you're right.'

Chapter 38

I bought new make-up. A foundation with moisturising action and a mascara that promised to give your eyelashes ten times their normal volume; although it occurred to me, as I was putting it on, how alarming that might look if that were the actual result. Still, I kept a steady hand while I painted on layer after layer – face cream, foundation, eyeliner, eye shadow – and I took deep breaths periodically, pulling in the smell of beef casserole that was stewing in the kitchen. The place had been alive with more smells and noises throughout the day. I knew that some of it had been to keep me busy; I hadn't needed to make an apple pie from scratch, for instance. I hadn't been quite nervous enough to churn my own butter, though, or make a main meal that required anything more than peeling and chopping vegetables while dancing – or at the very least jigging – to the best and worst of mine and Rowan's teenage years. I had a specific playlist for it; tracks that we'd listened to on the car radio when we'd been parked up somewhere for the privacy of it. When Jennifer Paige's 'Crush' came on, though, I'd thought of Fred, sliced the carrot too harshly and caught my index finger in the process – and that put an end to the dance part of the preparations.

For something wholesome, I swapped to the playlist I shared

with the girls. A Spotify set-up where all of us could add but none of us could take away and I laughed aloud, then, and asked the room, 'But isn't that my whole life with those girls?'

It occurred to me that thinking about them for too long might have caused some cosmic thread to start tugging, because, in the minutes after, I got a missed call from both Faith and Betty. I hadn't spoken to either of them – any of them – about my plans for the night. I hadn't needed to, really. I could have told them I was about to suggest a series of threesomes with farm animals and they would have nodded along to my face. They'd have me checked over by a head doctor behind my back, of course, but to my face they would have given me nothing but support. I knew the truth would be the same again of this – whatever 'this' ended up being.

'Jesus, have I even decided?' My reflection didn't have the answer either, though, so she only stared back at me while I brushed on an additional layer of compact powder. When I arrived at a point of not being able to look myself in the eye any longer, I turned my attention to clothes.

Blame Jones' acoustic spin on 'You're All I Need To Get By' came on in the background and I had the clearest image: Betty sloshing about, beer bottle in hand; Faith with her arm around Lily's waist; Cora and Molly slow-dancing together but howling with laughter at the same time. I had the photograph somewhere; a hard copy from when we'd gone retro and taken a disposable camera on a night out with us. It would have been the perfect distractor task to go and search it out, spend ten minutes – if not longer – staring through the image to the finer details in the background, trying to piece together a memory of exactly where we were when it was taken.

But when I checked the wall clock, I realised I didn't have time for distractions. Company would be arriving in the next fifteen minutes, and I was still wearing a Hawaiian-print bath towel and a frown. I picked up pace to the music and moved at a deliberate speed along all the clothes I'd adopted from Fred's wardrobe. I even blinked hard while my fingers flicked *that* denim dress out of the way, one she'd gifted me with a condition – 'You can *only* ever wear this without tights, and without leggings. Deal?' – and she'd sealed it with a kiss on the cheek when I agreed.

In the end I went for a loose-fitting jumpsuit; navy blue and a ten out of ten for comfort. It moved well with me while I bopped to the music, trying still to get my energies up and ready. Prepped to play at being a good hostess, I pulled out restaurant-calibre dishes from the cupboard I only normally cracked open when my parents were visiting; which *must* have meant I was ready for a special occasion. I put dishes into the oven to heat through, alongside bake-from-the-bag bread rolls. Then, in time with the oven door clanging closed, the front door chimed a tune.

I imagined Lily coaching me through a big belly breath while I walked the stretch of the hallway. I exhaled, grabbed the door and yanked it open as though the three things were connected to the same movement. Otherwise, it would have taken me as long to open the door as it had done to choose an outfit.

'Wow.' Rowan had a bottle of white wine in one hand and flowers in the other. But he was wearing a shirt that hadn't been ironed and I felt guilty for having noticed. Given that this was the first time we'd seen each other since *that* night, though, I was only glad that he was brandishing a creased shirt and a bottle of wine, rather than a chapter and verse from the Old Testament and a threat to tell Mum and Dad. 'Edi, you look …' He petered out, leaned in and kissed me – on the cheek. 'You look amazing.'

'Thank you, you scrub up pretty well yourself.' I stepped aside, then, and nodded him along the hallway. 'Come on, don't stand on ceremony for me.' It had only been days since we'd seen each other but somehow it felt longer. I wondered whether he actually looked different, or whether I only thought he did now I was seeing him in a different light. *Have you lost weight?* I thought as I walked close behind him. *Have you swapped …* 'You smell different.'

He sniffed the sleeve of his jacket. 'Do I?' I saw his eyes stretch and then narrow, and I wondered what he'd just realised. 'Weird.' He hurried to take the garment off and dropped it over the back of his chair. 'Probably Ian or Monty.'

I murmured in agreement and then turned around to check the oven. It had only been minutes and I knew the bread wouldn't be done. But I didn't want him to see my face. 'I've thrown together a beef casserole, maybe a stew, definitely something with beef.' I laughed as I closed the oven door. 'Wine?' Rowan had put the bottle on the table and the chill of it was starting to drip off.

'Beer?'

'Of course.' I grabbed a bottle from the fridge and, when I put the drink down for him, I pulled the bottle of wine back for me. It was a screw top, and the Lily in me wanted to undo the lid and chug half down in one go. But instead, I turned around to grab a glass. 'Are you hungry?'

'Aren't I always?'

'Okay, well there's definitely enough to feed at least six people in that pot.'

He laughed. 'Which sounds about right for you, for making dinner for two.'

It felt familiar; this old knowledge of each other. My expression softened as the wine sloshed into the glass. 'I have issues with measurements, what can I say?' I turned with the drink in my hand, then, and Rowan nodded towards it.

'I can see that.'

'What?' I looked down. 'It's a large glass of wine.'

He pushed the flowers towards me. 'Don't forget those.'

'Thank you. They're really lovely, Rowan, thank you.' And just like that we went back to the forged politeness of people who needed to talk about something, but weren't yet ready to.

215

I dropped the flowers into a pint glass and filled it with water. My politeness only stretched so far before my nerves took over.

Unprompted, then, while I was still facing away, Rowan started to tell me what had been happening in his life. There was so much information packed in that it felt like the updates stretched beyond the few days we hadn't spoken for; I realised, then, how little we must have talked even when we'd actually been talking.

'Work is good but pretty mental. They've pulled in a new piece of land further out …'

I busied myself with finishing dinner preparations, as he continued, 'But I've said I don't want to be the ground guy on this one …' There wasn't exactly much to do, though I made a show of pretending there was for the sake of not sitting opposite him. *Which is a* great *sign, Edi, as you well know …* I grabbed cutlery, then even more dishes to have ready for the apple pie, assuming we got that far.

'Do you need a hand?'

'Are we going to talk about the other night?' I belched the words out like involuntary gas and my hand flew to my mouth with an apt embarrassment. Everything in me wanted to apologise – as though to say, *Whoops, sorry, don't know where that came from* – but I swallowed the words back down, and followed them with a large swill of wine. Rowan still hadn't answered by the time I set my glass down, though. 'We don't have to, I just—'

'You think we should.'

'I'm surprised you don't want to, Row, if I'm honest.' A timer dinged in the background and I wondered how inappropriate it would be to turn around and check the casserole. *Are we even having dinner now?* He rubbed at the back of his neck and looked behind me to where the noise had come from. 'It's just the plates having warmed through, that's all. It's nothing that can't wait.'

'I mean, I *am* hungry.'

Something truly uncomfortable passed between us in the seconds after that. We locked eyes and it felt like he was

216

challenging me – but to what? Whatever it was, I didn't rise to it. I only shrugged and, with a murmur of agreement, I turned around and started to scoop one, two, three ladles of casserole onto the warmed plates from the oven. I dropped four bread rolls into a bowl, too, and carried those first – with my wine – to the table; when a room is on fire, only grab the most important things, and I definitely had mine. I flashed him a tight smile before I turned back to get the dinners.

While there was no danger of further eye contact I said, 'I just think there's probably some questi—'

'So you're gay, bi, whatever. Is that where this is going?'

The question landed on me in the seconds that I turned round to face him, with a heavy plate of food balanced in each hand. When I saw his expression, though, both plates slipped, shattered and scattered across the floor, taking cubed vegetables and chunked meat along with them. He looked at me with an expression that I thought must be fury. *Am I being dramatic in thinking that?* The air started to crackle around me. *But no, it's fury – and something like disappointment.* I felt my eyes prick with the promise of tears as I swallowed.

'Rowan, I think we should break up ...'

Chapter 39

There weren't many people I could stand to speak to in the days afterwards. I'd screened calls from Fred, Monty and my parents. Fred didn't know; Monty definitely did; my parents shouldn't have done. Although it crossed my mind that Rowan may have tumbled into the role of bitter ex-boyfriend and outed me to everyone we knew – as being both newly single and maybe, possibly, just a bit gay – and I couldn't decide whether it would be a blessing or curse if he had. But when neither Mum nor Dad went as far to leave a message or send a text, I decided it must have been a safe call rather than one with a motive. The only phone call I made on the night itself was to Faith – 'I did it, I finished things' – and she took everything from there. Within minutes the rest of the girls knew and the group chat was alive with offers of company (Molly and Cora), gin (Lily) and a night out (also Lily). Betty was disconcertingly quiet on the matter until she arrived two days later, as planned, with the rest of the girls in tow. She stepped forward and threw her arms around me the second I opened the door to them.

'You didn't text,' I spoke into her shoulder. She pushed me away, and held me at arm's length.

'I couldn't type anything that didn't make it sound like I was happy.'

Faith slapped Betty's upper arm. 'What did we literally just finish talking about?'

Betty pulled away and reached into the bag Lily was holding, as though Faith hadn't spoken at all. 'We brought treats,' Betty said, ferreting about in the bag still. 'And I brought this.' She turned to face me with a bottle of Prosecco in each hand.

'Are we celebrating?' I asked.

Molly said, 'No,' at the same time as Betty said, 'Yes.' The pair of them locked eyes, and as though sensing something in Molly's expression Betty thought better of it. 'I mean, no,' she corrected herself although she sounded uncertain. 'We're commiserating.' She looked around the group for support – or confirmation – but nothing came. 'Right?'

Cora reached over to squeeze Betty's shoulder. 'Good effort.'

'Look, whatever we're doing, can we not do it standing in the hallway?' Lily asked.

I stepped aside. 'Ladies.' I tapped Betty gently on the backside. 'And you.'

She gave a low squeal. 'That's the most sex I've had all month.'

'You bloody liar,' Molly shouted back from the front of the line.

There was a chorus of laughter as we filed into the living room. Molly tapped the space on the sofa next to her and I squeezed in between her and Faith. While those two fussed over me, Lily and Betty disappeared into the kitchen.

'Do you want to talk about it, or totally avoid it?' Molly asked when I was settled. Not for the first time, I came to think of Molly as the Queen of Break-ups in our group. She was always the one getting her heart broken, as far back as I could remember, and I felt a swell of love and gratitude and—

'You know you're such a good friend, Moll, right?' I blurted out.

She pulled me towards her. 'Of course I know, babe.'

'Drinks, everybody, drinks.' Betty wandered in with a tray of wine glasses, pint glasses and mugs balanced on a tray. 'Everybody grab a beverage.'

'And a snack.' Lily followed her in. 'Get some linings on those stomachs.'

'You're like the mama bear of the group right now.' Faith took a drink.

'You shut your tart mouth,' Lily answered. 'I'm not, nor will I ever—'

'Please don't,' Cora cut her off; we both swapped a quick glance, the memory of her failed (or passed?) pregnancy test still fresh between us. 'One thing at a time. Right now, we're smashing the patriarchy through calling off an engagement. Let's celebrate not having children another day.'

'I will literally agree to anything that means we can clink quicker. I am parched.' Betty's drink was already near touching her bottom lip. 'To Edi, for an act of self-love bigger than anything she's ever done before in her glorious life.'

Lily knocked her glass against mine. 'But an act that's nothing short of what she deserves.'

It took me another hour to relay the events of it all; how surprised he'd been and how hurt. When I'd started speaking to Rowan, everything had tumbled out in such a natural and ordered way that I wondered how long I'd been sitting with the feelings. He didn't ask about Fred directly but I divulged – how we met, how we dated – and he only occasionally shook his head, as though in stunned disbelief. It crossed my mind more than once that perhaps he would have reacted the same no matter the person. After her, I moved on to the structural problems of the relationship.

'What problems, Edi?' he'd snapped, and I'd presented them in a level and orderly fashion. I may as well have whipped out a PowerPoint presentation; at least then I would have had some-where to look other than at Rowan who, by that time, was looking at me like I was talking out of my arse. He was so surprised at my viewpoint of it all – how he'd taken to the break so easily; how his jealousy only flared when I took to the break, too – that my confidence soon started to wobble, right around the time Rowan got confident enough to start talking. In the hours after he'd gone, taking with him half a box of stuff that he'd gathered in a temper, I thought back over what I'd said and wondered what was true, and what was only true to me.

'Don't let him do that,' Cora butted in when I took a pause.

'Do what?'

Lily answered, 'Let him convince you that issues aren't issues.'

'If they're issues to one of you then they're issues to both.' Betty threw three salted pretzels into her mouth and spoke around bites. 'Men do that sometimes. What's it called?' She clicked her fingers, sipped her drink. 'Whatever it's called. They make you think that problems aren't problems because *they* don't see them as problems.'

'Women do it as well,' Lily jumped in and Cora shot her a sharp look. 'I'm just saying.'

'Well, save it.' Betty winked at me. 'One world crisis at a time.'

'Is gaslighting a world problem?' Faith looked up from her phone to ask, and Betty clicked her fingers again.

'Gaslighting. That's the fucker.'

'Eloquent as ever.' I raised my eyebrow at Betty and she shrugged. 'Gaslighting is a bold accusation and, frankly, I pay a counsellor for that level of introspection. But whatever we're calling it, whatever he was trying to do, it didn't work, did it?' There was a murmur of agreement around the circle. 'He made me think things weren't as bad as they seemed – that's all I mean. But I'm grown up enough to know that the person who doesn't want things to end can often dish out a menu of reasons why they shouldn't,' I said this last part directly to Betty, lest she jump in with a PowerPoint presentation of her own.

There was a pregnant pause until Molly jumped in to take the baton. 'Edi, do *you* feel like you did the right thing?'

I rubbed at my forehead. 'When he left, even through all the worries and the doubts and … I don't know, even through the confusion of it all. I think, more than anything, I just felt ...' I petered out, but Molly finished the sentence for me.

'Relieved.'

'Beautiful Edith Parcell.' Betty crossed the room and kissed me on the crown of my head. She crouched in front of me, then, to bring herself level with my face. 'It's my unprofessional and totally lopsided opinion that you did the right thing.'

'Seconded.'

'Thirded.'

Faith burped. 'I'm so sorry, but that wasn't staying in. Fourthed.' She looked around the group. 'Is that what I mean?'

Lily reached over and took Faith's glass away. 'I'm cutting you off.'

'Do you need someone to go over to Rowan's at some point?' Cora topped up my glass as she spoke. 'To collect your things, I mean.'

'No.' I shook my head. 'I don't want for us to be that couple.'

'That couple?' she asked.

'You know, the couple that can't be in a room together.'

Faith nodded, and then narrowed her eyes. 'How much exactly does he know about Fred?'

'Does she know about all of the women he's slept with?' Lily asked and there was a shared rumble of agreement. 'It's none of his goddamn business who Edi has slept with, since or during their relationship. Especially given that he's the one—'

'Easy, snappy.' I stopped her. 'He is the one, but I agreed to it.'

'Babe, you're allowed to moan about him.'

'I know, but ...' I shrugged and downed what was left of my drink. 'I will. I one hundred per cent will. And I'll tell you all about how he cheated and how I hated him and loved him and how I – I don't know, things in betweensed him.' I held my empty glass in the air and waited for someone to take the hint; Cora was the first to grab a bottle. 'But, right now, I don't want to moan, or hate each other, or point-score or – anything, really.

I want us both to be as unscathed as possible. And I want to get drunk with my best friends.' I leaned into Cora for a cuddle and she obliged, with one arm tucked around me and her free hand firmly clutching a full glass of fizz.

Faith reached over and squeezed my hand. 'You're allowed not to hate him.'

'I'm sorry, back up, he *cheated* on you?' Betty's voice was a fraction higher than it had been. Lily motioned to her – a swift hand across the neck – and Betty held her hands up in defeat. 'Not the point, okay, we'll come to that. But whatever, the *real* point is, you're allowed not to hate him, we're allowed to hate him, yada yada.' Then she hurried to add, 'We don't! But, if we wanted to, we could. I'm just saying that much.'

I snort-laughed. I didn't know which one of them had shot her a warning look that time, but it was clear that someone had from the speed of her add-on.

'Maybe—' Molly moved closer '—in the same way you want him to be okay, we just want that for you. Some of us express that in different ways.' She threw a look at Betty then Lily, before turning back to me. 'But it's all any of us want, Edi, for you to be okay.'

And in a way that I'd never believed it before when Rowan had said it, I believed Molly – I believed all of them.

Chapter 40

Mum opened the door and pulled me into a hug. The smell of something freshly baked tumbled out from behind her and I thought, *She must know*. I'd ignored their calls for a couple of days but, when the weekend rolled around, I'd decided I couldn't put a stopper in the fallout much longer. Mum had answered on the third ring and asked if I could give her an hour to get herself sorted – or rather, get something in the oven. I walked along the hallway behind her, all the while wandering closer to the source of the smell. In the kitchen, there were three plates of cookies on the table. She held a chair out for me, nodded towards them and said, 'Tuck in.' But I couldn't bring myself to. On the journey over I'd started to nurse a ball of nerves somewhere in the bottom of my stomach, nearing my pelvis, and the thought of dropping food on its head only made the nerves flare further.

'Tea?' She turned her back on me then, and I took the opportunity for a deep breath. 'Your father has become bloody obsessed with this gardening project he's got on the go.' She clunked about as she spoke: flicked the kettle on; found the matching mugs. I knew her actions by heart. 'He's been outside for a good part of the morning. Even the smell didn't bring him in. I daresay he's out there with a sodding ruler.' There was a loud thump then as she slammed a cupboard closed and I laughed. I was here to tell my parents about my ruined engagement; meanwhile, their biggest problem looked to be that they had separate hobbies for once. 'It's not that I mind,' she said, then, as though noting my laugh. 'Anyway, I'll get him.' She banged on the window and whispered – although, I realised, she was probably mouthing it to him – 'Get in.'

Seconds later the back door opened. 'Edi, love—'

'Shoes,' Mum snapped.

He rolled his eyes and made a show of wiping his feet. 'May I enter?' He bowed, in a theatrical gesture. 'Oh, keeper of the cookies.'

'Sit down, you silly sod.' Mum put a cup of tea in front of an empty seat for Dad, then another in front of me. 'Edi hasn't come over to hear about your plants so don't even start.'

'Edith, I'm shocked.' He sat down and winked at me. 'You mean to say you don't want to spend your afternoon hearing about the growth of a tomato plant?'

'You're pushing it, sunshine.' Mum kissed him on the head and then took the seat next to him. 'You haven't had a biscuit.' Taking it as a cue, Dad leaned forward and grabbed a cookie from the centre plate. Mum tutted. 'I was talking to Edi.'

'Either way ...' He was already chewing. 'I also hadn't had a biscuit.' He made appreciative noises and I wondered whether they were genuine, or whether they were styled to soften Mum. 'Oat and raisin? Am I getting hints of cinnamon?'

I laughed, leaned forward and took a cookie from the first plate. I made a show of sniffing the outer edge and matched Dad's noises. 'Am I getting ... Is that a hint of dark chocolate? Chilli, even?'

'Shut up, the pair of you.' Mum reached for the one plate that no one had sampled. 'Edi, yours is dark chocolate and you ...' She nudged Dad. 'You know bloody well I'd always make your favourite.'

The cookie, at least, gave me an excuse not to talk. But it didn't slow Dad down. 'No Rowan again this time?' He leaned forward for another biscuit. 'He doesn't know what he's missing.'

Mum didn't flinch at the mention of Rowan's name. She must have guessed that something was wrong, I decided then, but not guessed at what. Of course, how could she have? Rowan and I were childhood sweethearts. Looking at my parents for the last twenty-something years had always felt, to me, like looking into our future. And maybe I still was: the sight of them laughing and joking, with cookie crumbs flecking out from their widening smiles. But it just wouldn't be with Rowan. Not for the first time in the days post-break-up, I felt such a swell of sadness that I had to straighten my back up against my chair; for fear that otherwise I'd double over.

It didn't mean I'd made the wrong decision, though, I realised that too; only that I was sad at the decision I'd had to make. 'Which is allowed,' Molly had reminded me (when I called her at one in the morning to ask whether I'd ruined my relationship and life in one dramatic swoop). The girls had taken it in turns to fall asleep on the phone with me; they'd worked alternate shifts to answer my middle-of-the-night phone calls, too. My parents may have a decent relationship, I thought, but did they have a fall-asleep-on-the-phone, call-me-when-you-panic kind of relationship? *Probably.* I sucked in a big breath. But they didn't have *five* of them, did they?

'Rowan and I broke up.'

Dad's cookie fell from his hand and landed on the table with a soft thud. 'What did he do?'

Mum slapped him lightly on the arm. 'Put your testosterone away.' She reached across the table and held her hand palm up for me to hold. 'Are you okay?'

I squeezed. 'I'm sad.' Another breath. 'But I know that's allowed.'

'Of course, sweetheart, of course it's allowed. Do you want to talk about it?' She must have clocked Dad open his mouth because

226

she rushed to add, 'You don't have to, because it's actually none of our business, really.' She looked at me while she said it, but I got the distinct feeling she was talking to Dad. 'But we're here for whatever you need.'

'Of course,' Dad chimed in. 'Of course.'

During one of many phone calls with Lily, Betty, Cora … I'd asked them what they thought I should tell my parents. They said, in the way they always said it, that I should share what I was comfortable with and nothing more. I drew the line at admitting to an exploration of latent sexual preferences then, but I did opt for a partial truth. I didn't tell them about Fred, although I did admit to seeing someone else; meanwhile, Rowan saw more than a few someones. 'But that was part of the agreement,' I rushed to add before Dad could explode with rage. 'It was part of the agreement and it was, absolutely, what we both signed up for.'

'I'm so surprised, Edith, that you'd agree to something like that.' He dropped back hard in his chair and I felt a wave of disappointment hit me from across the table.

'Why?' Mum asked. But when I looked up to answer I realised she wasn't talking to me.

'What do you mean?'

'I mean, why are you surprised she'd do it? Wouldn't you have done?'

'Of course not!'

'Oh, don't take that tone with me. I'm wife enough and woman enough to know there are times when you've thought of other women, just like I've thought of other men. Neither of us have acted on it.' She took a deliberate pause there and waited for Dad to nod in agreement. I couldn't help but smile. 'But not everyone falls in love, gets married and rides off into the sunset. Christ, they didn't half manage it when we were kids, never mind managing it with how hard life is now.'

Dad looked to put some real thought into what she'd said before he answered. 'I see.'

'This other chap.' Mum turned back to me. 'The one you've been seeing?' I couldn't bring myself to correct her; one explosive at a time seemed about enough. I only nodded. 'Are you leaving Rowan for him?'

'I'm not, no.' Although I had been ready and waiting for the question. Fred was amazing; there was no other or better way of explaining her. But I wasn't leaving one long and winding relationship to tumble into another. 'I think, after being with Rowan for so long, it might be nice just to be me for a while. You know?' I looked at Dad who obviously didn't know at all. But when I looked at Mum, I saw it.

'I do.' She turned to get a look at Dad. 'Why don't you make yourself useful and put the kettle on?'

'That, I can do.' He stood and took my cup, then Mum's, and shuffled out of sight.

'One thing, sweetheart, so we know where we are. Did he finish things, or did you … I mean, was it an agreement you came to?'

I hated her assumption that Rowan must have been the one to call the whole thing off. But that was a battle for another time. 'I finished things. It was all too easy for him, Mum, to start seeing other women, and that's actually okay.' I heard Dad make a disapproving noise behind me. 'It really is okay. But he should have time to do that properly, shouldn't he? It's clear that some of this comes from his parents and, I don't know, stuff they have and haven't done for each other over the years. But maybe if Rowan finds himself now, he won't turn into his dad later.'

'Not all men turn into their fathers, you know?' Dad set a mug on the table in front of me.

'I do know that, Dad, that's why … I think he really needs this time. He needs to work out a way to avoid turning into his parents. And I'd quite like to find someone who, one day, will help me turn into mine.' I leaned over and gave Mum's hand another squeeze. She dabbed around the underneath of her left eye and I wondered whether tears were afoot.

'Well.' Dad sipped his tea. 'It sounds like you've thought this through, Edi. Bottom line.' He paused and sipped again. 'I – we – will only ever want you to be happy. I'll put that out there, in case we haven't been clear on it all your life. You're your own person, always have been. You know how to use that head of yours.' I worried that tears were on the way for him, too, then.

'Plus, this is all better to decide now than when you're married.'

Dad snorted and winked at me. 'Or during the ceremony, eh?'

'I now pronounce you …' Mum used a pompous, stuffy voice. 'Husband and—'

'Wait.' Dad used a deliberately girlish tone. 'Can I have a minute, just a quick sec?'

They fell over each other in laughter then, and the swell of nerves I was nursing on arrival started to soften. It felt more like relief again; more like cookie dough, with extra love.

Chapter 41

Rowan and I still hadn't spoken. But the girls and I were in near-constant communication. There were three separate occasions when I'd even been moved to mute the group chat; something I'd never done before and would never admit to having done if any of them asked. The days stretched out, though, and while everything felt brittle around the edges, everything somehow felt a bit more normal as well. Rowan and I had spent so little time together in the weeks before the break-up talk, not seeing him for a full week after didn't feel that strange. What did feel strange, though, was the need to avoid Fred. She'd been texting intermittently, too, but not to check up on me, or to check in with me. Worse, she was texting to share her excitement.

The gallery space for her upcoming show was piecing together before her eyes, and she was thrilled. Deservedly so, too, because, from the pictures she'd sent, the place looked beautiful. The walls, instead of the typical gallery white, were blocked black instead. Fred explained that they wouldn't let her paint them, so she'd roped artist friends in to help her construct screens that would lean against the walls themselves. *Here's hoping no one is pissed enough to fall into one xx*, she said, then sent another message immediately afterwards: *Balls. I hope I haven't just jinxed it.*

Whenever she asked how things were – *What's going on your end? xx* – I did my best to skirt around the bright pink elephant in the room – *Fine! Nothing quite as exciting here xx*. She never pushed for more, although she did text once – late at night, and I wondered whether a glass (or two) of wine had been the prelude – *Edi, I know we don't know-know each other. But I hope you know we can talk. xx night xx*. I'd brushed it off with a polite thank you and said I'd catch her soon. Instead of sleeping after, though, I spent a full hour staring at the ceiling, thinking about how strange it was to hear 'I know we don't know each other' from someone I'd slept with upwards of twenty times.

'You know it's weird that you've kept track, right?' Faith answered when I relayed the same worries to her. 'I know each of those twenty-plus times has probably been genuinely mind-blowing but still, it's weird. Don't be a boy.'

I laughed. 'Boys keep tallies?' No sooner had I said it and the stab of a memory hit …

'No, no you're right.' She sounded pensive, then. 'Boys keep tallies of the number of women they've slept with, not the number of times they've slept with them.'

'Bollocks.'

'I didn't realise you were with Lily.'

Faith laughed. 'What gave it away?'

'I'm just saying it's bollocks and Edi can count whatever she wants. And that women can—'

'Beautiful Lily,' I interrupted her, 'I know whatever one can do the other can do, but, before we get into a chorus about it, could we deal with the reason I actually called?'

'Yes, beautiful Lily, can we?' Faith parroted. 'Edi, what's your worry? That you're not being straight with her?'

Lily snorted and then apologised. 'Sorry, caught me off guard.'

'But I'm not being straight with her, am I?'

'You're right. In my experience with women, they hate to know the people they're sleeping with aren't sleeping with other people. Worse still, they *hate-hate* it when the people they're sleeping with aren't in a relationship with someone else, that's a real kick in the proverbial.' Faith's tone was deadpan. 'In case my tone didn't give it away—'

'Oh, it gave it away,' I said.

'Are you worried she'll want a relationship now?' Lily asked.

'I think so?' I guessed. 'I think that's a worry. But I'm also worried that she'll think I'll want a relationship, and then she'll freak out.'

'Which you don't?' she clarified.

'No. No, I don't think ... I mean, I just had one. A big one. And Fred is amazing but ...' I half-laughed; it was more like letting out a puff of air. 'Everyone is in the beginning, aren't they? I think I just want time to enjoy being ... Edi.'

'Okay, so if you don't want a relationship, and you tell her that you don't want a relationship ...' Faith chimed in again. 'What is there for anyone to freak out about?'

'But ...' I paused. There was a thump in my forehead knocking at regular intervals.

'Babe, but nothing. Fred isn't Rowan.'

A long silence followed her announcement. The thump in my temple stopped being a thump and became a constant pain, so I took myself to the kitchen and rifled through drawers until I found paracetamol. 'Give me a second,' I said, but I was already setting the phone down. I picked Faith (and Lily) up again when I'd thrown two tablets down my throat.

'Are you okay?' Lily asked.

'I don't know.' I'd called for gentle reassurance, or so I thought. But as I leaned back against the fridge and took a deep belly breath, I started to wonder whether that's what I needed from them. *Or do I just want you to tell me what to do ...* 'I'm used to having to make decisions for two people,' I admitted, and *that* was the problem. I didn't have to decide what Fred wanted or needed from me; I only had to decide what I was ready to give.

'Which I imagine is super hard in itself,' Lily answered, and her voice was soft. 'Harder still, though, babe, when the other person you're making decisions for is the person who's *actually* making the decisions, do you know what I mean?'

I took a second to untangle the sentence. 'I think so?'

'Lovely, she means Rowan didn't really give you a choice on things.' Faith's tone was harder than Lily's. 'She's trying to find a nice way of saying that making decisions for two people is hard, but what you're actually used to doing is making decisions for Rowan, disguised like they're decisions for you, even though they're not.'

'Fucking hell, Faith.' There was a kerfuffle where I imagined Lily backhanding Faith's arm, leg, arse; whatever was closest. 'But yes, that's what I mean.'

I nearly laughed. 'Okay, so … So, what do I do?'

I imagined them again, then, swapping a worried glance before Faith asked, 'What do you want to do, babe?'

I sighed. *How am I meant to know* that …

*

I unmuted the group chat that evening.

Edi: *Ladies, assemble*
Edi: *Flowers or chocolates?*
Molly: *what's the occasion?*
Betty: *Chocolates*
Lily: *Chocolates*
Faith: *Flowers*
Faith: *Pah! Kidding. Gimme chocolates*
Cora: *what Molly said*
Molly: *I was literally just checking whether the message even sent*
Molly: *@Edi. Occasion?*
Faith: *Date night?*

Betty: *Non-date night? *wink**
Lily: *Gallery opening*
Edi: *We have a winner!!!*
Lily: *Do I win whatever you don't send?*
Edi: *Seems fair*
Betty: *wait. What do the rest of us get?*
Edi: *a hug*
Lily: *send her both*
Edi: *I'll send you chocs anyway*
Lily: *love you beaut*
Betty: *wait WHAT!*
Faith: *this is where sarcasm gets you*
Molly: *well I'm nice what does that get me?*
Edi: *Moll, you can have flowers*
Betty: *WHAT!*

Chapter 42

It took thirteen unanswered calls in two days but eventually Rowan agreed to see me – or rather, agreed to give me back my possessions. The perk of never having lived together, I discovered, was that we didn't have to dismantle a washing machine straight down the middle or argue over exactly who it was that insisted on the larger television screen when it came to footing the bill. The sad part of me wondered whether this – this niggle of knowing that maybe he and I would arrive here – was why we'd never closed the gap between our homes. *Marriage, though, that would have been fine …* I thought as I folded another of his shirts into a neat square and set it on top of the third box I'd packed. I dropped the box on the back seat of my car and tried to focus on the relieved part instead: relief that there were only three boxes of his things; relief that he said he only had one box and a carrier bag to give back to me; relief that soon, this would all just be …

I sighed and slammed the car door closed. 'Over.'

Rowan didn't help me with the heavy lifting when I arrived outside of his building and unloaded the back of the car. Maybe he hadn't seen me. But he was fast enough to open the front door before I'd even had time to ring the bell. He stacked one box on top of another and squatted to pick them up, then he flashed a thin smile.

'Kettle's on.' He turned and walked into the flat, so I grabbed the last box and followed.

So we'll be talking, then. I made a show of looking around. 'The boys aren't here?'

'They said they'd give us some space. Didn't want to get caught up in …' He waved away the end of the sentence, but then added, 'Whatever.' He pulled milk from the fridge and cups from the cupboard, and I noticed that while he made a drink in 'his mug' – a pitch-black ceramic that grew the Batman logo when hot water collided with it – he wasn't making a drink in the one I'd always used. He handed me the drink awkwardly, with the handle angled between us. 'I packed your mug.'

Shots fired. I nodded and accepted the tea. My mug – or rather, what used to be my mug – was a white ceramic with a photo-booth picture of me kissing Rowan's cheek on the side. And I suddenly felt the need to brace for impact. *What else will be in those boxes?* I sipped my drink, even though it was too hot. 'Should we sit?' I didn't wait for an answer, only took myself to the armchair in the corner of the room and set my cup on the floor, a safe distance from my feet.

'Edi, we really don't need to make a thing about this.'

I frowned. 'Don't we?'

'We're done, aren't we? You're gay now and we're done. That's that.'

'Don't be a dick about it, Rowan.' The words came out of my mouth, but I felt a strong sense of Lily, Betty, Cora. 'This doesn't have to be the world's worst or first break-up. And I'm not *gay*, I'm … Do you know what, actually, it's none of your business what I am at the moment, and you'd be doing yourself a favour if you remembered who wanted—'

'Christ, are you actually about to blame the break on me, *again*?'

It knocked me. *Have I blamed you too much?* I wondered, but I tried to shake the thought away before I could buy it. 'Remind you that the break that was your idea, you mean? I don't remember being in a rush to suggest you sleep with other women.'

He snorted. 'No, but weirdly enough it didn't take *you* long to.'

'Well, maybe you should have thought through the possibility that someone else in the world might want to have sex with me apart from you.' I spoke plainly, didn't raise my voice or rush. But I wanted the truth out there, neatly wrapped with a bow for him to pull apart with his friends over beers – or with a counsellor when he *finally* worked through his issues with his parents. 'It didn't even occur to you, did it,' I added, when he let the silence stretch out, 'that someone else might want me?'

He shook his head. 'Who *are* you these days?'

'Edi, still. Who are you?'

'You don't think you've changed, at all, in the last few months?'

My stomach rumbled with nerves, but I swallowed hard and pulled in a breath. 'How is this about me all of a sudden?'

'You're the one who finished things!' He was shouting now. '*I* thought we were happy.'

'Then why did we need to sleep with other people?'

His shoulders dropped. 'You wanted that as well, Edi, don't make out you didn't.'

But I didn't; did I? I couldn't work out whether it was a question for Rowan or myself. Still, if I'd been in the right relationship I would have been able to ask the question aloud, voice the concerns, share the—

'Are you saying you didn't?' he rushed in when I didn't answer.

Lily and Betty were the only friends who knew I was coming for this visit. I'd needed their moral support – 'Don't you *dare* let him make this a *you* problem' – and worldly wisdom – 'Closure is overrated, anyway!' – and I tried to hang on to every piece of advice – 'Remember, babes, this is *your* chance to clear the air as well as his' – and every offer of help – 'I haven't slapped an ex-boyfriend in … I don't even know how long' – and then I pulled in a belly breath.

'No, Rowan. I don't think I wanted it at all. I think *I* was happy and I think I thought you were, too, even in the early weeks of it all. But no, I didn't want to see you out with other girls. I didn't want to know you were lying about where you were and who you were with and …' He parted his lips as though to interrupt me but I held an index finger up to pause him. 'You can't ask questions you're not ready for the answers to.' He recognised the phrase and closed his mouth slowly. 'No, when I agreed to get married and spend the rest of our lives together, it didn't cross my mind once that you wouldn't be enough for me. Or that I wouldn't – you know, that I wouldn't be – for you.'

He looked winded, so I let him have quiet in the seconds after. There was a box at the far end of the living room with a Tesco's Bag for Life next to it and I suspected they were my worldly belongings; my adult life and then some. I hadn't wanted to sleep with other people. But I'd arrived at a point where it was okay that he – we – had. He needed something he wasn't getting and maybe he didn't go the right way about it but … I sighed. But it was okay. I opened my mouth to say that, though, and Rowan beat me to the punch.

'I'm sorry.'

'You are?'

He nodded, sniffed. 'I don't know why I suggested it.'

'Because maybe things weren't as okay as you think they were?'

'But they were fine,' he protested. Like an angry child, he dropped his fists against his knees and repeated himself. 'Everything was fine.'

I crossed the room and sat next to him. Unprompted, he grabbed my hand and I squeezed his.

'Rowan, don't you want more than fine?' He looked up at me and pulled his forehead together, as though I'd given him a tricky spelling to sound out. I kissed the side of his forehead, then, like Molly, Cora, Lily had kissed mine so many times. 'If you're going to be with someone for the rest of your life, don't you want something a bit better than fine?'

'Our parents have done fine on—'

'God,' I interrupted, 'don't get me started on my parents or yours.'

He laughed. 'Yours have done okay.'

'They have. And I do honestly think they're more than fine, now. But they probably haven't always been.' He opened his mouth to interrupt me again, but I pressed on. 'And I know we could have powered through and made it to the other side of whatever this is. Then, somewhere on the other side, we would have been fine. But how many women did you sleep with on this – whatever we're calling it?'

'Edi, what does that have to do wi—'

'Give me an estimate,' I cut him off. 'The nearest hundred.' I tried to sound light-hearted but from his drooped expression it was clear that he was struggling. 'You don't know, do you?'

He sniffed again and shook his head this time. 'Christ, I'm just sorry.'

'My God, do you think Betty knows how many men she's slept with?'

'I'm not Betty.' He sounded offended by the comparison.

'No.' I squeezed his hand again. 'But you *are* kind of one of my best friends.'

'Even now?'

The girls had taken it in turns to coach me through how this conversation could go – or even, should go. They'd told me in fifty different ways why Rowan and I didn't need to be friends and they'd given a hundred and one examples of former couples who weren't. But when someone has been in your life forever, can you really cut them out? 'Yes,' Lily had said, and Cora and Faith had nodded.

But Betty, surprisingly, had been swayed. 'I get it,' she weighed in, 'I couldn't cut any of you out.'

239

When it was phrased that way, Molly had agreed, too. 'I'm a big believer in keeping ex-boyfriends around,' she'd said.

Cora tapped her hand. 'And that's an issue for another day.' We'd shared a laugh, then, and shared some history and shared an understanding that yes, sometimes people mess up …

'Even now,' I answered him.

But you can't hold it against them forever.

'What happens now then?' He looked wounded and my heart hurt. Most of my adult life had been spent fixing whatever it was that turned his face sad. Now, though, things needed to be different.

'Now, I'm going to take my stuff and I'm going to call the girls and I'm not going to lie, Rowan, I might get a little drunk.' He half-laughed. 'And you're going to move your boxes into the bedroom, and ignore them for maybe two months, but in the interim you'll call the boys, and you'll get a little drunk, too.'

'When will I see you?'

I shrugged. 'I don't know.'

'But if things can still be fine th—'

I pressed my finger against his lips to shush him. 'Fine looks a little different now.'

He kissed my finger, then moved it away. 'Look, maybe this is what we need, you know? Like, maybe in the future, distant future even, maybe when we're grown-ups, we'll drift back to each other and we'll end up the kind of fine that our pa— no, sorry, *your* parents are.' He laughed.

'We are grown-ups,' I said softly, as though maybe he hadn't noticed, but he smiled.

'I see.' He stared at our fingers, that were just about still clutching, and he was quiet for what felt like an especially long time. 'In which case …' He caught my attention with a squeeze and then he gifted my hand back. 'Someone should tell Monty, because that kid …'

I laughed. 'He's not so bad.'

Rowan stood. 'Try living with him.'

I took it as my cue to leave and I stood too, but I felt the weight of the break-up in my belly. I'd been strong and clear and Lily-minded. But I reminded myself that familiar comforts were allowed, too. 'If I hug you,' I said, but didn't look at him, 'I'm hugging you as a friend. Is that entirely clear beca—'

He pulled me to him and squashed the rest of my sentence. 'Edi Parcell, best friend of mine.' He sounded as though he was talking through half-laughs, but I could feel the judder of tears in his chest. 'Bloody love you.'

I squeezed back and pressed my reply into his shirt. 'Bloody love you.'

Chapter 43

Fred opened the door with wet hair and a lazy smile. She leaned forward, kissed my cheek and took away the bunch of sunflowers that I'd held in front of my chest like protective gear for the entire walk to her apartment. This was all an extension of mine and Rowan's break-up, one that I'd drafted and redrafted with the help of the girls – 'Don't be a dude about it, do you know what I mean?' – although they hadn't been altogether helpful when it came to breaking up with a woman – 'See, when a man leaves me ...' – so in the end I'd called Fred, on a whim, and asked if I could drop round.

'I'm about to jump in the shower,' she'd said, 'so give me twenty minutes?'

I'd used that time to write bullet points in the Notes app on my phone and buy flowers.

'Flowers twice in as many weeks. What's the occasion?' She walked along the hallway, leaving me to close the door.

'You are.'

'Cute.' When she turned around to look at me, the colours all connected. 'These match!'

There was a collage of burnt oranges and bright yellows in Fred's hallway. I hadn't remembered much about the décor of the apartment – on account of my head usually being in a spin when I left, or arrived – but the latest flower portraits to bloom in the hall and the self-portrait in the living room had stuck.

'It's sweet that you noticed that. Drink?' She was already walking to the kitchen. 'I've got wine in the fridge if you'd like something with a kick, or coffee in the pot if you'd like something with … Hm, well, I suppose I only have things with a kick. Alcoholic or non-alcoholic, though, I can do.' She started to rifle through drawers until she found a pair of scissors. One flower after the next she hacked away at the stems, and every romantic comedy in the world had taught me that when a woman was wielding a sharp object you probably shouldn't break up with her. I stood on the other side of the kitchen counter and watched her; not from fear or worry, but with deep admiration – mixed with something like gratitude. Her head was angled towards the flowers still, but she looked up and caught me staring. 'What?'

'I didn't say anything,' I snapped.

'No but you're staring.' She dropped the flowers into a vase and turned to fill it with water. 'If you think it's too early for wine then you can have coffee. Ah shit, or tea. I know it's more your thing.'

I laughed. 'You'll have wine even if I think it's too early?'

'Ha! But you see …' She turned in a dramatic swirl and flicked her hair out of the way. 'I'm an artist, dahling. Plus, your decisions don't impact on mine so …' She winked. 'What'll it be?'

'One gallery show and it goes to her head.'

'Hey, you haven't seen the space.' She opened the fridge and pulled the wine out.

'I'd like to, still. If that's okay?' I hadn't even broken things off yet and I was already playing the part of the guilty one; skulking around like Fred mightn't want me in her life anymore. And worse still, she looked like she sensed it. She was pouring wine already, so she only glanced up at me briefly, but I could see she was suspicious.

'Shush, Edi, why wouldn't it be okay?'

There had been a flurry of images delivered to my WhatsApp every day. Fred had sent me possibilities for this half of the space, other possibilities for the remaining half. She wanted a walk-through experience, she'd explained, starting with the girl and ending with the woman, tracked through portraiture. The captions she sent me with each picture became lengthier as the day went on and she became more consumed by her plans. But I hadn't minded. I couldn't remember the last time I'd seen someone with Fred's passion for – well, anything. I sighed, then, and realised that was one of the things I'd miss the most.

'Hey,' she called my attention. 'What's going on?'

'Rowan and I broke up.' I blurted the announcement out at such a speed that she didn't have time to hide her shock at it. 'I'm fine,' I hurried to add. 'Like, genuinely fine. We've talked. Well, to start with we argued a bit but then we talked. I don't really think he wanted to … I mean, when did he ever *really* want to, which I suppose was half the trouble and …' I shook my head. 'You don't need chapter and verse about it.'

She pushed a wine glass towards me and came around to my side of the counter. 'If it'll help—' she pulled me into a hug and spoke into my neck '—then I want to hear it.'

The heat of her breath sent something through me, and I had to remind myself why I was there.

I sipped my drink. 'I told him that I didn't think we were a good fit anymore, but that didn't mean we couldn't still be friends, that we wouldn't be in each other's lives.' I felt a laugh bubble up. 'Christ, I'm like a break-up cliché made up of Molly's exes.'

Fred laughed, too. 'I imagine you were probably more sincere than Molly's exes with it all, if I know you. Come on.' She nodded towards the sofa. 'Sit. You can walk me through it.'

'Fred, I don't know that—'

'So, don't walk me through it.' She landed on the couch with a thud. 'But you've been dodging offers of seeing me for two weeks straight and I'd wager that breaking up with Rowan probably

244

isn't the reason for it.' She tapped the empty seat next to her. 'So, walk me through whatever it is that you called round here to walk me through.'

'Jesus, you're—'

'Abrasive?' She shrugged. 'I've been told.'

When I dropped onto the sofa, I couldn't help but still make eyes at the portrait on the wall opposite. It was every bit Fred, from the waist to the hips to the – I sighed again – everything. Even though I could feel her eyes on me, I decided I'd talk to the portrait instead. Explain to the portrait how amazing she was, and beautiful and kind-hearted and generous, especially in bed, even though that shouldn't matter but my time with her had taught me that a connection in bed *definitely* mattered, even if only a little bit, but yes, it definitely did.

She laughed. 'Okay, so, where is this going?' she asked when I came up for air.

'I think …' I pulled in a shaky breath. 'I think we should stop seeing each other, romantically, I mean.'

She sipped, then, and said, 'Okay.'

'It isn't you—'

Fred leaned forward from her side of the sofa and kissed me square on the mouth to catch the platitude. 'I know.'

'You know it isn't you?'

'Well, I can take a good guess that it isn't me.' She smiled and squeezed my knee on her way back to her own side of the sofa. 'You can finish the line if you want? I just thought I'd save you.'

'You are genuinely one of the most amazing women I've met in my life, and this has been amazing. It *is* amazing, still, like, nothing has actually happened.'

'Apart from the breakdown of the most significant romantic relationship in your life.'

I laughed. 'Yes, apart from that. Because of that, because of that breakdown …' I rubbed at my forehead. *Christ, stop saying breakdown …* 'Fred, I think I just need to be on my own for a while. Rowan, he didn't do anything wrong, not really.' I slapped my hand to my forehead. 'That's a lie, actually, isn't it? Because he *did* do things wrong and he definitely handled things *all* wrong. But Christ, if that isn't just Rowan all over, and I see that now. And, do you know what, I could have probably handled some stuff better in my time, too, it's just – just that, I think, before I get into a new relationship with anyone, I – I'm basically turning into a Hallmark movie as I say this, but I think for a while I need to be in a relationship with me.'

When she leaned forward this time, she kissed my temple. 'Good for you, Edi.'

My head jerked around. 'That's it?'

She hurried to swallow her sip. 'I mean, we're in my apartment, I'm hardly going to wreck the place.' We shared a laugh, then, and she held her glass out towards me. 'Give me a clink, you gorgeous woman, we're celebrating a new relationship.'

'How are you like this?' I knocked my glass against hers.

'Years of practice. And *a lot* of self-help podcasts.'

'Can I have the names of them?'

'I'll start a list.'

I hesitated and waited for her to take another sip before I asked, 'Can I still come to the gallery opening this week?'

She choked on her mouthful. 'Why the hell wouldn't you?'

'I don't know, I …' I spotted her raised eyebrow over the rim of her glass. 'I didn't know whether you'd want me there, after …' I waved at the empty space between us. 'This.'

'Edi, shush. I want you there. Your name's on the list for the opening.'

'Can I add a name?'

'Bold, do you want to bring a date?' She tapped my knee; her tone was playful.

'Actually, I was hoping to bring five …'

Chapter 44

The walls were black and the ceiling was alive with fairy lights. There were spectators gathered around portraits and, even though it wasn't my place, my pride was fluttering inside my chest like an excited swallow. Each canvas boasted a bold display of woman – either a small child reaching up for a hand that wasn't there, or a thin line drawing of a curvature that I recognised as belonging to the artist – and it was clear, from the clever construction of makeshift wall structures, how you were meant to move around the space, too. There was so much excitement, though, fizzing over the tops of wine glasses and bubbling from clusters of conversations into the air, anyone could be forgiven for not following the designated route. Fred had created something beautiful; something, I guessed, a lot bigger than the portraits alone.

'Wow.' Faith came to a stop alongside me. 'This is an experience.'

'Yep, that's Fred all right.'

Betty nudged me. 'Hey, keep it clean.'

'I didn't mean it like that!'

Molly and Cora were already huddled around a watercolour of a foetus.

'How long do you think it will take for them to understand it?' Lily asked.

'Well,' came a familiar voice, 'it can't take them any longer than it's taken the average man in here. Never mind the tits and arse at the end, I think it's the idea of femininity as abstract that really has critics stumped.' Fred looped her arm through mine. 'Hey, beautiful.'

'Fred, this is—'

'Faith.'

Fred laughed and took the hand that was offered to her.

'Amazing,' I finished, 'I was going to say this is amazing.'

'Thanks, Edi, it's … I don't know.' She rubbed her forehead and laughed. 'You know when you want something so much, and you work so hard, and then it happens and, well shit, you can't quite believe it's happened, can you? But now all of these people are here and they're …' She laughed and gestured around the room. 'They're looking at my life, but also your life and women's lives.'

Faith pointed to a canvas on the far side of the room. 'Hey, I think I know that woman.'

Fred laughed. 'I'm sorry, I'm getting a little deep and feeling here, aren't I?'

'Hey,' I chimed in, 'don't apologise for feeling good about this.'

'If anything, we actively encourage *more* self-praise as part of this friendship group.' Lily held out her hand, then, and said, 'Lily. This hot mess is Betty.'

'Pleased to meet you,' Betty added, then went one step further and pulled Fred into a hug. 'This is a mighty fine display of female you've got yourself here.'

Fred was laughing when she pulled away. 'Can I put that on a flyer?'

'I'll be offended if you don't.' Betty looked around to where the others were standing. 'Left to right, you're looking at the arses of Molly and Cora. They're beautiful humans but they're literally juuust learning what it's like to openly talk about having a vagina.'

'That's unfair,' Lily leapt in. 'Cora's quite good at it.'

'Which essentially means that this place will be a maze of experience for them,' Faith added.

'I find that my body is usually a maze of experience for other women.' When I looked around at Fred I saw she was already looking at me as she spoke, and I flushed. 'Unfortunately, though, there are elbows I need to brush with. It's been so lovely to meet you three.' She hugged them all one after the other. 'And please tell Molly and Cora that I've got some diagrams they might find helpful.'

Lily and Betty laughed, meanwhile Faith said, 'I wouldn't mind taking a look at those.'

I tapped her arm. 'Like you need them.'

'You're all welcome to stick around, of course. I don't know whether you have plans?'

'I do,' I answered. 'I'm about to take five women out for dinner.'

'And drinks,' Betty added. 'You should come and meet us later, though, if you're free?'

'Yeah, how does it all work, post-opening?' Lily asked.

Fred looked around the space and rubbed her forehead again. I'd never seen her so red-cheeked – apart from immediately after a climax, but that hardly counted. 'I honestly don't know. I – I *might* be around later, I don't know.'

'No pressure,' Faith said. 'Give Edi a text.'

'I'll do that.'

'And in the meantime go and be a fucking superstar,' Betty instructed and Lily, who had looped arms with her, nodded in support. 'You're a machine.'

Far from Fred leaving, instead the women all swapped senti-ments of support, which took such a long time that eventually someone came to steer Fred away. She apologised – to them, and to us – and we apologised for hogging the starlet. All the while Molly and Cora were *still* trying to work out which way was up on an oil portrait of a vulva. 'Christ, I'm just going to show them,' Faith said, before disappearing, leaving me, Lily and Betty to push our way through to the exit. I took another glance behind us to where Fred was fencing questions and, I guessed, charming the arse off anyone who dared to talk to her. *She really is something …* And then I forced myself to look away.

'Where's the table booked for?' Lily asked when we'd battled our way to the pavement.

'Black and White.'

'Ooh.' Betty nudged me. 'Trying to impress us, are you?'

'Rumbled. I'm trying to get you into bed.'

'You only need to ask.' Faith came to a stop behind us. 'Politely. I have some standards.'

'Can I order pudding?' Molly shouted over Faith.

Cora nudged her. 'You haven't even eaten yet.'

'I'm more in a sweet place, do you know? How sometimes you enjoy more food than others?'

'I don't know, right now I enjoy *all* food. As you can tell.' Cora pinched at her waist.

Three of us opened our mouths to answer but Betty was first to the punch. 'You shut your filthy mouth, woman.'

'You're trash-talking our friend there,' I added. 'And there'll be none of that.'

'Are we getting a taxi?'

'You lazy sod, think of the steps.'

'So, tell me more about Fred. Is she …'

One conversation bled into another and somehow, someone decided we would walk to the restaurant. Our chatter came with undertones of heels on concrete, stifled laughter and loud cursing. By the time we arrived at the door, we were twenty minutes late for the reservation.

Faith huffed. 'Molly, you just *had* to stop and take a picture of the bloody sunset.'

'Well, it was beautiful!'

'It really was,' Lily agreed. 'You know what else is beautiful?'

'Food,' Betty answered and Lily clicked her fingers.

'Right you are.'

I was fumbling with my phone to avoid the judgemental stares of the front of house – a patient man who had promised us a table if we could only wait in an orderly fashion, outside. When my mobile pinged with an alert – Instagram – I felt grateful for a legitimate excuse to keep looking away.

'Oh my gosh, Edi.' Molly's outburst caught me unawares and I flinched. She was craning over my shoulder. 'Do you have your phone set up to alert you when I post?'

'Do I?' I thumbed into the app. 'Christ, when did I …'

But the question died out when the screen unfolded to show Molly's picture:

No filter needed with my girls @edipeedi @gottahavfaith @bettywhuuut @corablimeyharold @lilyinthesun #girlsnightout #fridaynighttreats #ridingoffintothesunset

Acknowledgements

This is the first romantic comedy I've ever written – and it started as a wild experiment to see whether I could write one at all. I'll forever be grateful to Dushi Horti, a HQ editor at the time I submitted the work, for seeing something worth working with here. Dushi carried the book through to acceptance and then carried it further into a big and bold structural edit, and there are so many moments in this story that wouldn't exist without her guidance (some of my favourite moments, in fact). I'm grateful to HQ as a whole for their continued work on the novel to bring it into your hands now, lovely readers, because these people work tirelessly to bring stories into the world and I think that makes them kind of superheroes. A huge thank you to sensitivity reader Philippa Willitts too.

It would remiss of me not to thank my own friends, who in one way or another have informed some of the characters in this book. Harriet – my brilliant and bold big sister – alongside Daria, Claire, Katie, Talis and the token male, Dan Burton, who reminds me so often what it means to be gentle in the world. But no acknowledgements would be complete without Beth; my Lily-Betty-Cora-Molly-Faith rolled into one. Beth, thank you for the belly breaths and the reminders; the rants and the reality checks. Where I'd be without the lot of you, I truly dread to think.

Finally, whether you're a new reader or a reader who has hopped over from my crime writing, I'd like to thank you. This book is unlike anything I've ever written and, because of that, it means more than I can possibly say that it's made it this far in the world. Reader, I hope you've loved my band of loud feminist friends, and I hope you have your own to hold you steady.

www.ingramcontent.com/pod-product-compliance
Ingram Content Group UK Ltd.
Pitfield, Milton Keynes, MK11 3LW, UK
UKHW022257180325
456436UK00003B/130